THE LADY'S TRIUMPH

SHELLEY ADINA
R.E. SCOTT

Moonshell
Books

© 2022 Shelley Adina Bates and Regina Lundgren

License Note

This eBook is licensed for your personal enjoyment only. It may not be resold or given away to other people unless it is part of a lending program. If you're reading this book and did not purchase it, or it was not purchased for lending, please delete it from your device and purchase your own copy. Thank you for respecting the authors' work and livelihood.

This is a work of fiction. Names, characters, places, and incidents are a product of the authors' imaginations. Locales and public names are sometimes used for atmospheric purposes. Any resemblance to actual people, living or dead, or to businesses, companies, events, institutions, or locales is completely coincidental.

Cover design by Tugboat Design. Images used by permission.

The Lady's Triumph / Shelley Adina and R.E. Scott—1st ed.

R091222

❀ Created with Vellum

PRAISE

"Adina and Scott launch their Regent's Devices series with a witty and whimsical flight of fancy in a subgenre they call *Prinnypunk* (Regency-era steampunk); it plays out as a delightfully fun mash-up of Jane Austen and Jules Verne, right down to the hint of sweet romance and the array of ingenious inventions."

— BOOKLIST ON *THE EMPEROR'S AERONAUT*

"I recommend this series for readers who enjoy adventure, subterfuge, and a realistic plot line that will hold their attention and never insult their intelligence. Steampunk, historical fiction, and the wits of two amazing authors blend seamlessly to give readers an adventure that will long linger in their minds."

— HUNTRESS REVIEWS ON *THE PRINCE'S PILOT*

"As with the previous titles in this series, these two authors blend together so well that I am unable to tell where one ends and the other continues. The story (or rather, the entire series) is fun to read. As I neared the ending, I slowed my reading pace. I wanted to make the story last as long as possible... and the ending left me thoroughly satisfied. Brava!"

— HUNTRESS REVIEWS ON *THE LADY'S TRIUMPH*

To all the women and girls in STEM—
your contributions matter!

FIND MORE DARING ADVENTURE
TO LOVE

Sign up for Shelley Adina's mailing list and begin the adventure with "The Abduction of Lord Will."

Sign up for Regina Scott's mailing list and learn what happened in France while Celeste was in England.

Don't miss out!

~

IN THIS SERIES

The Emperor's Aeronaut
The Prince's Pilot
The Lady's Triumph

THE LADY'S TRIUMPH

CHAPTER 1

TRURO, CORNWALL

Early November 1819

*I*f you ask me, she's pining."

No one had asked Thomas Trevithick, owner of the now even more famous Trevithick Steam Works in Truro, Cornwall. Certainly no one would have asked him to state his opinion in such a loud voice, which carried over the lovely sound of pistons pumping and hammers on copper. Yet Celeste Blanchard could not argue with him. Ever since she and her friends had returned from France and presented their air ship as a *fait accompli* to the Prince Regent, it was as if her dear friend Loveday Penhale had wilted, like a silk balloon leaking lifting gas.

Celeste understood. To have invented something so marvelous as *Lark Deux*, their second air ship, sailed it through the skies from enemy territory to land upon the Prince's very doorstep, and then been sent home, with no further word, for nearly two months! And to have searched in vain for the person who had stolen their plans and provided them to Napoleon's underlings. Who wouldn't feel a bit despondent?

The entire countryside had welcomed them back, but now whispers were beginning to circulate in manor house and public house alike. If they had truly won the Prince's prize, as His Royal Highness had promised, why hadn't it been delivered? Emory Thorndyke and Captain Arthur Trevelyan's word aside, had Celeste and Loveday even met the Prince? Or were they merely two foolish young ladies who thought themselves better than they should be?

Celeste lifted her blue wool skirts and sidled in next to Loveday at the workbench to bump her shoulder. "We have no reason to pine. We have achieved that which none other can claim."

Loveday sent her a wan smile. "Indeed we have. Though it would be nice to have that achievement acknowledged in some concrete way." She bowed her blond head once more over the two sheets of metal she had been evaluating for weight and material properties, but her shoulders under her chambray work dress were slumped.

The doorway of the steam works opened to admit two older men. Celeste recognized the taller as Mr Thorndyke, Emory's father.

"There he is, just as I promised!" Mr Thorndyke declared with a nod into the shop.

Their friend set down the hammer he had been using and straightened from his own workbench a few feet away. He, at least, showed no ill effects of the wait. He had simply gone to work on his next invention, a boiler of appropriate size and weight to power a carriage. In that, he hoped to go the great Richard Trevithick one further.

The light through the isinglass windows caught on his sandy hair as he turned toward the doorway. "Father? What brings you here?"

Mr Thorndyke had not been supportive of engineering and tinkering, until Emory had invented the steam pump that was even now emptying Cornish tin and copper mines of the seawater that had plagued them for years. The lifting gas emitted by underground thermal springs had once sickened men and put others out of work. But now, folded into the pumping process, the gas was stored in barrels and would make him and several other gentlemen of the neighborhood rich should air ships become as commonplace as she and Loveday hoped, crossing oceans and continents like so many migrating birds.

Some day.

In answer to Emory's question, his father looked to the shorter man at his side.

Dressed in velvet breeches and a fine wool coat with lace at his cuffs, the fellow minced his way across the floor of the steam works as if he thought the metal filings and sawdust scattered about might leap up and attack him. He came to a halt in front of Emory, grey head high and shallow chest puffed with his own importance. From the satchel at his side, he selected an envelope.

"Emory Thorndyke," he announced in a voice surprisingly deep for one so slight, "His Royal Highness thanks you for your service."

Every tool hung suspended. Even the pistons hissed to a stop. Celeste glanced at Loveday and saw her eyes widen.

Emory accepted the envelope, turning it in his large hands

as if he could determine its provenance and reasoning through the vellum.

"Well, go on, boy," his father urged, stepping closer. "Read it."

Grip visibly tightening, Emory broke the red wax seal.

Their visitor didn't wait for him to read it. He turned to Thomas, evidently rightly thinking he must be the master in charge. "Am I correct in assuming I might find Mr Rudolph Clement here as well?"

The air rang with the sound of a hammer abruptly dropped on the slate floor.

Thomas's gaze followed the racket to one of their youngest engineers. Swallowing, Rudy ventured forward, his face turning red. "Aye, sir," he said, bobbing his head. "I'm Rudy Clement."

The messenger produced another envelope. "His Royal Highness thanks you for your service, sir."

First Emory, now Rudy? Could there be something in that satchel for Loveday and Celeste, or had they truly been forgotten?

Frowning, Rudy broke the thick seal with trembling fingers. He read with maddening care the words contained therein. Then his head jerked up, and his gaze veered toward Loveday and Celeste. "Miss Penhale, Miss Aventure—His Royal Highness thanks me for my help with the air ship."

"As well he should," Loveday said magnanimously. "Without your help pulling that skin of silk out of the harbor last summer, there would have been no prototype."

Celeste smiled, but she was, in truth, more interested in what the Prince had written to Emory, particularly as the king's messenger did not appear inclined to offer her or Loveday an envelope.

"What does your letter say, Monsieur Thorndyke?" she asked.

Emory raised his gaze to hers, the sea-green depths swimming with possibilities... and shock. "He offers me a—a—" His voice failed. "A *knighthood*. For my pump."

His father whooped and clapped the messenger on the shoulder, nearly oversetting him. "Did you hear that? My son is to be knighted," he shouted to all and sundry. "Sir Emory Thorndyke of Truro, praise all the saints!"

"Sir Emory Thorndyke of London," Emory corrected him, his gaze on Celeste. "It seems I have been invited to join the Prince's Own Engineers at St James's Palace."

He was leaving? The floor seemed to open between them, widening a gap she had tried so hard to close.

But of course he must go. He had earned this. His pump not only cleared the mines of seawater and gas, but the lifting gas was vital to winning the war with Napoleon.

The messenger righted himself and tugged down his waistcoat before turning to her and Loveday, eyes narrowing. "Did I understand correctly? You are Miss Loveday Penhale and Miss Celeste Aventure?"

After six months of using a false name, Celeste was just beginning to accustom herself to it. She nodded, even as Loveday said, "We are."

Once more he dipped into his satchel to offer them a pair of envelopes thicker even than the one he had handed Emory. "You are also commended for your service to the Crown. His Royal Highness hereby awards you the Prince's prize and commands that you travel forthwith to London, to claim it and to take your places among the Prince's Own Engineers."

~

LOVEDAY FOUND the stool at her workbench by luck and memory alone and sank onto it. She didn't know where her legs were. Or her feet. The rest of the steam works and everyone in it had faded to a fog and a murmur. Her entire being was concentrated on this miracle in her hands. This dream. This lovely vellum with her name inscribed upon the front in a hand so fine it might have been written by an angel.

Her hands shook as she broke the wax seal.

Be it known to all that in consideration of and in gratitude for her contributions to the safety of the Kingdom, its Sovereigns, and their grateful Subjects, Loveday Maria Penhale of Hale House in the Duchy of Cornwall, jointly with Celeste Aventure of the same, are the recipients of the sum of five hundred gold guineas heretofore known as the Prince's prize, with the recognition and appurtenances thereunto.

Be it further known that said Loveday Maria Penhale is granted forthwith a seat among those known as the Prince's Own Engineers. She is commanded to appear at St James's Palace on the first day of December in the year of Our Lord 1819 to take her place and join His Royal Highness, George Augustus Frederick of the United Kingdom of Great Britain and Ireland and of the British Dominions beyond the Seas, Prince Regent, in augmenting the body of knowledge and instruments of war in this Nation's fight against the tyranny of the usurper Napoleon Bonaparte.

By my hand and seal this second day of November, 1819.

The Prince Regent's elegant *George P*, with its graceful loops on the *g*'s, and his personal seal in red wax, ended the letter.

Loveday came to herself with a gasp when her lungs demanded air. Beside her, on her own stool, Celeste lifted her head, her face as pale as the stiff folds of the letter in her own shaking hands.

"Can it really be true?" Loveday whispered.

"We are among the Prince's Own." Celeste's musical voice had become a croak. "We, so far away and unknown."

"Not so unknown," Emory said, his own letter with its seal and ribbon dangling from fingers that must be as numb as Loveday's own. "Not since you landed *Lark Deux* upon the Prince's front lawn at Portsmouth. No one will ever forget that moment, His Royal Highness least of all."

"May I be the first to offer you congratulations and all good wishes, Miss Penhale," Rudy said shyly. "Tez honored I am to know ye. My mum will be beside herself to see this letter of mine, signed by the Prince himself, and it's all because of you and Miss Aventure."

"Blanchard," she thought she heard Celeste whisper, though it did not carry past her own ear. *"Blanchard."*

Only a very few knew that Celeste still lived under an alias, lest someone discover that her mother had been Napoleon's Chief Air Minister and therefore one of England's sworn enemies. The fact that Celeste herself had worn that title for a few short weeks was known to even fewer in England—Loveday herself, Emory, and Arthur Trevelyan. And that secret should never pass their lips to put their friend's life at risk. Even with this new and stunning recognition of her efforts, how galling it must be to enjoy her newfound fame while being obliged to sail under false colors!

Belatedly, she realized the royal messenger was straightening his back again. Was there still more in that satchel of his?

"I offer my humble congratulations to all of you," he said, clicking his heels as he bowed. "I must be off to perform yet one more commission."

One more? Loveday's eyes met Celeste's as certainty filled her. "Arthur!" For who else could it be? "He will be a member of the Prince's Own, too! Oh, how thrilling for them all at Gwynn Place."

"Where is the logic in that?" Emory asked, obviously puzzled at the speed of their conclusions. "Our friend is not an engineer. He is a soldier."

"The messenger's commission could be to Lord St Aubyn," his father said with, to Loveday's mind, utterly unreasonable prudence. "To do with the aeronautical outpost they're planning on St Michael's Mount, perhaps."

Loveday bit back a highly unladylike *bosh!* as the sound of the royal messenger's carriage departing the yard came through the doors. Both were perfectly possible, but did they have to stick a pin in her hopes that all four of those who had endured the fear and hardships of France might be similarly rewarded?

"We must go home at once." She laid an urgent hand on Celeste's arm. "I am bursting to tell Papa and Mama. And I cannot wait to see Gwen's face when she sees the Prince's own hand on this letter to me, her hobbledehoy of a sister."

"To think that His Royal Highness has written to us personally," Celeste agreed, though she must still be in shock, for her voice sounded a little flat even yet. "And perhaps we will hear news from Gwynn Place before long."

There would be no more work done at the Trevithick Steam Works today. Thomas clapped Emory on the back and invited him, his father, and Rudy Clement to the local public house to celebrate. Poor Emory tried to demur, but he was no match for Thomas—to say nothing of Mr Thorndyke, who carried everyone before him.

"The news of Emory's elevation to the knighthood will be all over the county by dinnertime," Loveday predicted with a smile as she and Celeste climbed into the cane whiskey. With a glance at the lowering November sky, she lost no time in shaking the reins over Rhea's back and setting off on the familiar road home.

"And then watch every young lady of marriageable age for twenty miles set her cap for him," Celeste said, tying the blue ribbons of her bonnet as they bowled along the streets of Truro. Her hair, which had been nothing but a cap of dark curls when she'd been washed ashore on Hale Head this past summer, was long enough now that it barely fit within the bonnet, with a few curls escaping to frame her face. "He will lose sight of the little French girl he once called friend in the crowd clamoring for introduction at every ball and assembly."

"What a poor opinion you have of him," Loveday exclaimed as Rhea made the turn onto the road that cut across country toward the sea. "Little French girl! Rather, the only woman to fly the Channel from east to west—twice—and outwit Napoleon at his own game." She snorted. "Little French girl. *Pffft!*"

This outburst brought a smile to Celeste's lips at last. "I am glad to see you in better spirits now than when we drove into town," she said. "I did not want to intrude by inquiring what was wrong. I thought you might tell me on your own."

Loveday shook her head. "Just a case of the blue devils. The waiting. The not knowing if the Prince meant to stand by his word. You know how he is… he gets caught up in some new mechanical project and loses track of all else. We saw it, even during our brief sojourn in Portsmouth."

"Not this," Celeste said with confidence. "Our air ship design is too important to victory. He would no more forget the ones who had built it than he would forget his own—" She stopped.

"Bereavement?"

"Not the comparison I had hoped to make," Celeste confessed. "I was going to say *family*, but then I remembered."

A father who was mad more often than not. A mother who loved the man he had been yet was obliged to be separated from him, presiding over the court. A daughter who had died. A wife who lived apart in her silly palace in Brighton with another man.

"You are quite right. I am sure the Prince would rather think about us and our flight than any of his personal troubles," Loveday assured her. "And I am thankful for it. Even the fact that you must put up the umbrella now, or risk both of us being soaked to the skin, cannot dampen my soaring spirits."

"Our dreams have come true," Celeste said, as she opened the umbrella just in time. The wind was rising, and the first heavy drops spattered the road. "Though I wish the proof of them had been addressed to the right person."

"I felt your distress," Loveday said. "But it is not safe for you to be known just yet."

"I know." Celeste moved closer so that the umbrella would

shelter them both. Their bonnet ribbons snapped in the wind, and Loveday clucked to Rhea to pick up her pace. "When we prove ourselves among the Prince's Own Engineers, I swear that any success I enjoy will be in my own name. Blanchard will no longer signify an enemy of the English Crown, but someone to be celebrated for her service to it."

"Until you give up that celebrated name for that of a certain handsome knight," Loveday said slyly.

A wave of color rose in Celeste's face. "If we have learned anything since that day I washed up on the beach, Loveday, it is that you and I must never tempt fate."

With a rueful nod of acknowledgment of this truth, Loveday focused her attention on getting them home before the fringes of the storm passed overhead and the part that meant business overtook them.

The Prince's Own Engineers! She had seen the words with her own eyes, and she still could hardly believe them. Perhaps now Mama would resign herself to what Papa already knew— that Loveday was destined for the workshop, not the ball-room. Although, my goodness—there must be any number of ballrooms in London. Imagine—she and Celeste might be invited to York House! Or Spencer House, or Apsley.

The thought of these vast, glittering ballrooms would be terrifying were it not for her friends' company. Why, Celeste and Emory, she and Arthur would—

Arthur. Did he have an envelope addressed to him in the royal messenger's satchel, as they hoped? Or was he at this moment planning nothing more than giving gentle exercise to his leg after all its exertions in France? Had the carriage from London bowled along this very road, or had it taken the other route for St Michael's Mount?

Suddenly, without the possibility of Arthur's welcoming smile and steady, intelligent eyes to be found in the company, the bright visions of York House dimmed, leaving its gilded expanses empty and hollow. They had suffered so much together. Surely they were not to be separated in their moment of triumph? Surely fate, which they had tempted too many times and yet come out unscathed, would not choose today to insist upon a reckoning?

Gwynn Place

"A gentleman from London wishes to speak to you, Captain." Mrs Polgarth, the housekeeper, stepped into the drawing room, her eyes as wide as though she had seen an apparition in the front hall.

Arthur Trevelyan looked up in surprise from the Truro newspaper. His parents laid down their books, and his sisters Cecily and Jenifer paused, their embroidery needles suspended over the fine fabric in their hoops. Outside, a catspaw of wind flung raindrops against the window, harbingers of the storm that had been boiling for some time out in the Channel.

"For me?" Surely it was not a messenger from the Walsingham Office. Representatives of His Majesty's fledgling intelligence service tended not to go about announcing themselves. A letter would come disguised in a more banal wrapping, such as a book from a subscription library.

"Well, show him in," his father said, "now that our curiosity is piqued."

In a moment, the apparition himself appeared with a bow, making the entire family stare in much the same way as Mrs

Polgarth. The breeches—the lace! Was this what they were wearing in London these days?

"Which of you gentlemen have I the pleasure of addressing as Captain Arthur Trevelyan?"

Arthur schooled his face into dignity and rose with only the slightest wince as he put his weight upon his bad leg. "I am he, sir."

The man reached into his satchel and produced a lidded box of shaped leather, long and flat and closed with a brass buckle. "For you, sir, with His Royal Highness's compliments. If it please you, I shall read aloud the topmost document. When you have apprehended all, I shall be pleased to answer any questions."

The Prince Regent. Not the Walsingham Office, then.

Mystified, Arthur took the box from him and set it on the table. Cecily whisked her workbasket out of the way but did not stir from her chair, which gave her a good view of the mysterious delivery. He did not sport with his sisters, for his own curiosity burned like a flame.

The buckle was undone and the lid flung back to reveal several documents written in an elaborate and flawless hand on vellum. He picked up the topmost, hoping it would explain the rest, and handed it to the messenger. That personage flung back his shoulders, unfolded it, and in a voice that might be more appropriate for the town square, began to read.

George Augustus Frederick, by the Grace of God of the United Kingdom of Great Britain and Ireland and of the British Dominions beyond the Seas, Prince Regent, to all Archbishops, Dukes, Marquesses, Earls, Viscounts, Bishops, Barons, Baronets, Knights,

Justices, Provosts, Ministers, and all other Our Faithful Subjects, greeting.

Know ye that We have made and created and by these Our Letters Patent do make and create Our right trusty and well beloved servant, Arthur Gerran Trevelyan, Captain of the 32nd (Cornwall) Regiment of Foot, Viscount St. Ives—

Jenifer and Cecily shrieked, leaped up, and seized each other to jump up and down like a pair of lunatics.

"What?" Papa said as his book fell off his knee to the floor. "What did it say? I can't hear in all this racket!"

Mrs Polgarth and both the upstairs and downstairs maids, who were clustered in the doorway, promptly clapped their hands over their mouths.

The messenger waited until order was restored.

—and to the same, Our right trusty and well beloved servant, Arthur Gerran Trevelyan, have given and granted the Viscountcy in recognition of his bravery and actions above and beyond the call of duty behind enemy lines in despite of the usurper Napoleon. And by this our present Charter We do give, grant, and confirm the name, style, title, dignity and honour of the same Viscountcy, and Him Our said right trusty and well beloved servant, Arthur Gerran Trevelyan as has been accustomed We do ennoble and invest with the said Viscountcy by girding Him with a sword, and by putting a coronet on His head, that he may preside there and may direct and defend those parts to hold to him and his heirs Viscounts of the United Kingdom of Great Britain and Ireland for ever.

"Bless me," his mother said, fumbling for her husband's

hand. "There must be some mistake. Our Arthur? Can it be true?"

Wherefore We will and strictly command for Us, our heirs and successors, that Our said right trusty and well beloved Arthur Gerran Trevelyan may have the name, style, title, dignity, and honor of the Viscountcy of St Ives aforesaid unto him and his heirs male of his body lawfully begotten, by his name, style and title of Viscount St Ives in the Duchy of Cornwall in the United Kingdom of Great Britain and Ireland as is above mentioned.

In witness whereof We have caused these Our Letters to be made Patent. Witness Ourself at Westminster the first day of November in the eighth year of our Regency and the fifth-ninth year of the Reign of Our right Royal Father, George the Third.

Arthur stared at the royal messenger, stricken utterly speechless.

Perhaps the man was used to such a reaction, for he set the letter aside and carefully unfolded a document so beautifully inked and colored, and bearing a seal of such gilded splendor that the first inklings of what was happening to him finally began to sink into Arthur's comprehension.

"These, my lord, are your Letters Patent creating the viscountcy. You are ennobled and hereafter to be styled Viscount St Ives, as the proclamation has said, with lands and a small manor outside the town of St Ives, the deeds pertaining to which are here, in this box."

"I—I am a viscount?" This could not really be happening. Things like this didn't happen to ordinary soldiers invalided out of the army.

"Indeed, your lordship. Perhaps it will seem more real to

you when I read your Writ of Summons to Parliament. For following your investiture, you must take up your seat without delay."

"My... seat?"

"Yes, my lord. Allow me."

Another official-looking square of vellum was shaken out, and once more the messenger straightened with the consciousness of whom he represented.

George Augustus Frederick, by the Grace of God of the United Kingdom of Great Britain and Ireland and of the British Dominions beyond the Seas, Prince Regent, to our right trusty and well beloved servant, Arthur Gerran Trevelyan, Viscount St Ives, in the Duchy of Cornwall, greeting.

Whereas by the advice and assent of Our Council for certain arduous and urgent affairs concerning Us, the State, and defense of Our Kingdom and the Church from the usurper Napoleon, styled Emperor, and his airborne armada, we have ordered a certain Parliament to be holden at Our City of Westminster on the fifteenth day of November next ensuing and there to treat and have conference with the Prelates, Great Men, and Peers of Our Realm.

We command you upon the faith and allegiance by which you are bound to Us that the weightiness of the said affairs and imminent perils considered (waiving all excuses), you be at the said day and place personally present with Us and with the said Prelates, Great Men, and Peers to treat and give your counsel upon the affairs aforesaid. And this, as you regard Us and Our honour and the safety and defense of the said Kingdom and Church and dispatch of the said affairs, in no wise do you omit.

Witness Ourself at Westminster the first day of November in

*the eighth year of our Regency and the fifth-ninth year of the Reign
of Our right Royal Father, George the Third.*

Well, that, at any rate, was straightforward and not quite
so flowery as to render its information unintelligible.

"I am to go up to London," he repeated. The messenger
inclined his head. "Be… invested. Take up my seat in the
House of Lords on the fifteenth. And thereafter, to advise His
Royal Highness on how we may defeat Napoleon's air ships."

"Yes, my lord. You have apprehended it perfectly."

Oh, would he stop calling him that! But Arthur supposed
he had better become accustomed to it. For there could be no
declining or even arguing with the gold leaf and elegant
calligraphy of the Letters Patent. Or with Prinny, who had
inflicted this life-changing event upon him without so much
as a by-your-leave or a whisper of warning.

What would Loveday say when she heard? Would their
comradeship, the warmth of feeling that might become something more in time, be entirely doused by the weight of this
news?

How long was a man expected to stay in London once he
had taken his seat in the House, pray tell? Good heavens,
people stayed there for months—from Easter to August. How
on earth could he inspect his new property and understand
his responsibilities—to say nothing of helping his father
oversee the Gwynn Place farms and the planting—if he were
cooped up in London from planting to harvest?

The months of being obliged to live so far away seemed to
stretch into impossibility. And what of the aeronauts on the
point of arriving for training—aeronauts who must be
billeted and entertained and wouldn't they be just the sort of

men to suit a woman like Loveday? Providing, of course, she did not decide to become an aeronaut herself and join their number.

Oh, this was a disaster. What had possessed the Prince to take away his life and foist upon him a—

"A viscount!" his mother warbled, on the point of tears. "Oh Arthur, I am so proud I can hardly breathe. May I see?"

He reined in his galloping emotions with an effort of will. "Of course, Mama."

She fell into his arms and sobbed with joy, and it was only after some minutes and the application of two handkerchiefs that she could take in the documents, though she refused to touch them lest she spoil them.

"Please tell me we do not have to call you *my lord*," Cecily said, hunting for a dry spot on her own handkerchief and completely missing the shocked expression on the royal messenger's face.

"Certainly not," Arthur said, appalled.

"Only in public," Papa told her. He beamed at Arthur. "His lordship, by Saint Piran's holy robe! Well, well, don't look as though you've had a dunking in the sea, my boy. Cheer up— we'll have no trouble finding a wife for you now, will we?"

CHAPTER 2

Truro

"Are you mad?"

Emory kept a pleasant smile on his face as he sliced into the mutton their cook had served for a very late and very celebratory dinner. "I like to think not, sir. Indeed, I have been giving this matter considerable thought since the King's agent was here today. I may have developed the pump that is helping Wheal Thorne and other mines here in Corn-wall, but I can claim no credit for the air ship. I can only think that the Prince is offering me a place among his engineers because he mistakenly thinks otherwise. The ones he wants are Loveday Penhale and Celeste Aventure. While I must accept the knighthood or risk offending half the county, I must decline the other."

Even if the thought of sending Celeste off to the metropolis alone hollowed his chest. He would not be the only one to appreciate her ingenuity, her daring. What chance would a country inventor, even one recently knighted, have against the glittering aristocracy she'd meet there?

Unfortunately, his father's face was turning a shade of red usually reserved for the gauges of steam engines about to burst. His sisters, all seated around the dining table with them, began to look acutely uncomfortable as well. Georgiana, the youngest, was pleating her linen napkin into precise folds, her dark curls trembling. Thomasina, his middle sister, had stabbed her fork into her mutton with a strength he would not have known her slender frame possessed. And Henrietta, his older sister, had that stern look on her face that never boded anyone any good.

"I'm sure whatever those two concocted is no match for your skills," his father argued. He leveled his fork in Emory's direction. "This could be the making of you. You'll not reject it on some whim."

"It is no whim, Father," Emory said, applying himself to the mutton and pudding on his plate. "I could not live up to the honor and integrity you instilled in me if I accepted this offer."

His father dropped his fork with a clatter, and Georgie flinched.

"If you won't think of yourself, think of your sisters," their father huffed. "You become a knight and an advisor to the Prince, and their status is elevated as well. We might even be able to find husbands for them at last!"

Georgie sucked in a breath, and Tommie squirmed in her chair.

Henri raised her chin. "We are not unhappy in our situation, Father."

Tommie glanced between Henri and their father. "But I'm

sure any of us would be delighted to wed, should the right gentleman show interest."

"They're more likely to show interest if they think this family is going somewhere," their father said in a tone that brooked no contradiction. "Use that brain of yours to some purpose, boy. How else am I to marry off your sisters? Or am I to keep up their maintenance forever?"

Henri rose from her seat at the foot of the table. "Certainly not. Why, I'm sure you'd prefer to order your own meals, see to the running of the household, mend your own clothes, and tend the kitchen garden. Perhaps Georgie, Tommie, and I should step aside and allow you to do so immediately."

She picked up her plate and stalked from the room. Tommie rose and followed, leaving her plate behind. Georgie snatched a pudding off her plate before doing the same.

Their father shook the grey curls only nominally bound into a black ribbon at his nape. "Women. No gratitude at all."

No recognition at all, more like. Emory hadn't realized such a thing might be applied to a woman until he'd watched Loveday and Celeste triumph over every adversity. It was grossly unfair for him to be welcomed into the Prince's Own riding on their coattails—or trains, as the case might be.

"I thought you insisted that I was to take over the running of Wheal Thorne," he told his father, bracing himself for the tirade any mention of the future of their family mine usually raised.

His father waved a hand. "Henri is competent enough for the nonce. And you won't stay in London forever. The sooner you invent something to end this war, the sooner you'll be coming home. Time enough then to find a local lass to wed, someone befitting the name of Lady Thorndyke." He smiled broadly before lifting a forkful of mutton in a toast to that happy individual.

Lady Thorndyke. He could think of only one person he wanted to bear that name. They would be thrown much together in London if he went as his father desired. Working side by side, even. Could he hope to win her hand there, if he could not at home?

Hale House

"No, maidey, we'll hear no more of it."

Loveday's entire family had been chivvied into the drawing room, where she and Celeste had shared the news of the Prince's prize and their wonderful, miraculous summons to London. The letters from the Prince had been passed from hand to hand, the exclamations growing louder and more disbelieving, until they had reached her father.

At which point he might as well have pulled the rug out from under her and tumbled her to the floor. The very breath seemed to have been knocked right out of her.

"No daughter of mine—or guest, either—will be going alone to the other end of the country, no matter how great the honor." He folded the Prince's letter and handed it to her with an air of finality.

"Papa!" This couldn't be happening. All their dreams were about to come true—and now this? What objections could he possibly have? "The Prince Regent himself has asked us to come. You cannot mean we should refuse a royal request."

"I can and I do. The Prince does not have a daughter of marriageable age—"

"Mr Penhale!" Mama remonstrated. "His daughter has only been dead these two years. Have some compassion."

Papa reddened, for he himself had worn a black ribbon on his sleeve for poor Princess Charlotte and her little boy. "Be that as it may, my mind is made up."

"Sir, may I enquire as to your reasons?" Celeste ventured.

Loveday admired her courage, if not her wisdom. Papa was not used to explaining himself to the ladies of his household. Mind you, she would have asked had not Celeste done so first. This was no time to be missish and demure. Their dreams—their very lives—were at stake.

"You need reasons, do you?" he demanded. "Are you so ignorant of your positions in society that you would leave all and surround yourselves with strangers—male strangers, at that—of whom we know nothing? Where would you live? *How* would you live when you are not gallivanting about St. James's drawing the wrong kind of attention from all these engineers and who knows who else?"

Loveday gasped at the injustice of these charges. "Papa! We would be doing no such thing. We have been summoned to do vital work for England, not to *gallivant*."

"Em— Sir Emory Thorndyke would be at St James's with us, sir," Celeste said. "When we are not engaged in our duties for the Prince, he of course would be our escort and our protector."

Oh, clever Celeste!

The prospect of Sir Emory Thorndyke, who now outranked him, appeared to give her father pause. But not for long. "And where are you to be housed, pray? For it is certain that my purse does not extend to establishing households in

Mayfair. It is barely adequate for this one, to say nothing of three girls to dower."

"That will not be the case for long, Papa," Loveday said in a burst of inspiration. "Our work is on air ships. The sooner we help make the Prince's fleet airworthy, the sooner they will require lifting gas, and the sooner those barrels in your warehouse in St Mawes will make you and Mr Trevelyan and Mr Thorndyke rich."

He narrowed his gaze at her. "But before that happy day, maidey, you have nowhere to live in London, and we have no acquaintance there who could be prevailed upon to take you in."

Oh, how could he allow something so inconsequential to scuttle so great an opportunity!

"It seems a fairly common practice to take rooms in an *hôtel*, sir, if one has no acquaintance with whom to make one's home," Celeste said.

"We will have claimed the prize money shortly after our arrival," Loveday added with a massive effort not to shriek like a fishwife. "Our accommodations and expenses until the day of victory over Napoleon need not come out of your purse."

For a brief, shining moment she thought this infallible logic might sway him. And it might have, too, had not Mama lifted her chin and waded into the fray.

"Lodgings," she sniffed, as though thousands of people did not take lodgings every Season. At least, so the papers seemed to indicate. "You may be able to afford a dozen suites of rooms in buildings all over Town, my dears, but it will signify nothing if you do not have a suitable chaperone with whom to live."

Loveday and Celeste stared at her, slack-jawed.

Mama gave a nod as though this clinched the matter. "I certainly cannot go, for what of Rosalind and Gwen?"

"Oh!" Gwen cried. "Oh, let us go, all of us, do! Please say we may go to London with you, Loveday. I am sure we will be no trouble at all."

"Indeed, Gwen and I will share the smallest of rooms without complaint," Ros said eagerly. "At least, I will."

"Absolutely not!" Papa roared. "No daughters of mine are sharing any sort of rooms in London!"

But Loveday noticed he had not crushed the lodgings idea altogether. She pounced. "Mama, I agree with you completely. Ros and Gwen are much better off here, where they may be increasingly known to our social circle."

"What social circle?" Gwen wailed, to be hushed by their mother.

"That leaves us with only two matters to be managed," Loveday went on, doing her utmost to control the storm of her emotions and sound calm and reasonable. "Sir Emory's presence as a friend and escort at St James's solves any difficulty in the workroom or laboratory. We might take modest but suitable rooms not far away, so that we would have no need of horses or a carriage."

"I should think not," Papa snapped.

"So all that remains would be to find a respectable widow or spinster of some years who is willing to serve as chaperone for a limited time. I cannot see our spending much more than a twelvemonth there. Napoleon's plans are too pressing, and the need for the air ships too acute."

"A twelvemonth!" Papa, who had resumed his chair, leaped to his feet and began to pace before the fire.

Never a good sign.

"I cannot spare you for a week, never mind a twelve-month," he said. "The fact remains that while this appointment to the Prince's Own is a great honor, it is one you must enjoy for its significance, not its substance. I forbid you to go to London to take it up, and that is my final word upon the subject."

And with that, he strode from the room. A moment later, they heard the side door close with vehemence.

"Oh, dear," Gwen sighed. "He will not be persuaded now. He has gone to the horses."

Their father's refuge in times of trial.

"And it was such a good plan, too," Rosalind said mournfully. "Until you brought up the chaperone, Mama."

"The most important part," Mama informed her middle daughter down the length of her nose. "If you think my concerns for propriety are unreasonable here, it is nothing to what is expected in London. There, a young lady may never be alone except in her own bedchamber. She must always be accompanied, lest anyone whisper that she is fast or indiscreet, and her chances of matrimony vanish in the shifting winds of public opinion."

Her chances of matrimony had never been great to begin with, Loveday thought rebelliously as she curtsied and pulled Celeste from the room. And if she were in London, three hundred miles from Arthur Trevelyan, they were lower even than that. So from a purely practical point of view, her behavior with or without a chaperone would be unremarkable one way or the other.

But, she thought, closer to tears than she had ever been, her parents could not be accused of being purely practical.

She and Celeste were to be thwarted by convention, and there was not a blessed thing either of them could do about it.

THE NEXT DAY looked as dreary as Celeste felt. The rain had not departed, the November skies were perpetually blustery, and the temperature had dropped even farther. She hugged closer the paisley shawl Gwen had loaned her. If they were ever able to collect the Prince's prize, perhaps she could convince Loveday to replace all the lovely dresses they had been forced to leave behind in Paris, since they were not to spend the money on an establishment together.

Yet, how could they claim the prize if they must remain in Cornwall? It could not be that they would be denied this opportunity. That they would be forced to give up the reward of having done what no other could do.

She was a woman grown, living in this house out of friendship, not duty. Why could she not go alone and claim her half of the Prince's prize?

Mais non. She refused to leave Loveday behind. She had never had such a friend, so attuned in thought, so willing to act. So clever she might discover a way to beat Napoleon once and for all!

"We must find answers to their concerns," she told her friend as they headed for the stillroom, where Mrs Penhale had told them to meet her to plan activities between now and Christmas. Christmas! Never had she thought when she'd left France and her mother in May that she would be spending Christmas in England, an orphan!

"As soon as we are finished," Loveday said before they entered the room, "we will repair to the workshop and list our options. There must be a solution to this impasse short of kidnapping my entire family and conveying them to London, will-he nill-he."

Celeste nodded, the steel in her friend's voice raising her hopes. But once they had joined Mrs Penhale, they had only sat discussing evergreen boughs and Christmas geese for a few moments before there came a knock at the front door.

Celeste met Loveday's look. A chance to escape early, perhaps?

A moment later, Morwen, the Penhale maid, bobbed a curtsey in the doorway. "Beggin' your pardon, madam, but Mr Thorndyke is here."

Emory? Celeste couldn't help the leap in her spirits.

Mrs Penhale's brow puckered as she appeared to debate the propriety of entertaining a visitor in such a space as her stillroom, then she raised her head. "Show him back, Morwen. I'd very much like to congratulate him on his elevation."

The maid returned with Emory. His hair was wild, as if he had ridden all the way from Truro without a hat, and his face was flushed.

Celeste surged to her feet. "Emory! What has happened? Are you ill?"

"*Sir Emory.*" Mrs Penhale curtseyed, with a look at Celeste as if to remind her that etiquette must be followed, even in cases of most dire emergency. "How kind of you to call. Our heartiest felicitations on your elevation, sir."

"Thank you, Mrs Penhale, Loveday, Celeste," Emory said with a nod all around. "And congratulations are in order for Loveday and Celeste as well. It is amazing to think of the three of us among the Prince's Own."

Loveday's smile snuffed out even as her mother said, "I'm sure you will be a credit to Cornwall, but I fear Loveday and Celeste must stay here."

Now his smile faded as well. "They won't be going to London?" His gaze veered to Celeste as if seeking confirmation.

"No," Loveday said. "Father has forbidden it."

The finality of it squeezed the air from Celeste's lungs, as if she had dared to rise far too high.

"Why?" Emory asked. "This is a great honor, and their skills are sorely needed."

Mrs Penhale sniffed. "Be that as it may, there are insurmountable problems. And it isn't as if they had another reason to be in London."

Celeste stared at her, an utterly audacious idea forming. An idea that only the most reckless, forward woman in the world would entertain. But young ladies who did as they were told did not fly air ships across the Channel—twice—nor outwit emperors at their own game.

She took a step closer to Emory. "But we must go, Madame Penhale. I am certain this is why my dear Emory has come to speak with us today. He and I are betrothed. We must not be separated."

Emory froze. "Betrothed!"

Celeste took his arm and gave it a squeeze, willing him to play along. "*Oui, mon cher*. I know we promised to say nothing for a time because of your father's concerns about my worthiness, but with your so wonderful elevation and appointment, I do not see how that is possible any longer. We must go to London, and we must go together."

He gazed down at her, a storm raging in his eyes. Had she so shocked him? Would he call her out for a liar?

As if the thing were done, he snapped a nod. Tucking her arm closer and folding his hand over hers, he met Mrs Penhale's astonished gaze. "Yes, Celeste and I are betrothed. I would not dream of leaving her behind. Nor would I expect her to go without Loveday beside her. So you see, dear lady, something must be done."

"So it would seem," Mrs Penhale said faintly. "I must speak to Mr Penhale at once. Pray excuse me." She hurried from the room.

Loveday turned to Celeste. "You're certain about this?"

"The very question I'd like to ask," Emory said, releasing her.

Heat was already rising in her cheeks, and she wished desperately she might fan her face with Mrs Penhale's still-room book. "I do apologize for the surprise. But I fear we must try, if it will make them see the necessity."

"Not every betrothed couple is inseparable," Emory said. "There are far too many war-time engagements to prove the point. But very likely Mrs Penhale will take the matter more seriously."

"And, as soon as we are secure within the Prince's Own, you may call off the engagement and end expectations," Celeste assured him.

A smile hovered about his mouth. "I'm not sure how it's done in France, but in England, a gentleman may never cry off."

"Oh, no!" Celeste pressed her fingers to her lips. "Then I will do so! Never would I wish to entrap you."

Something crossed his face, like a balloon blotting out the

sun. "I have done nothing I would not wish to do. We will leave it at that for now and hope your daring ploy will be enough to sway Loveday's parents."

"They will say we still require a chaperone," Loveday said, picking up the book as if she had heard Celeste's thoughts and fanning herself with it. The scent of bay leaf and thyme from the dried bunches hanging from the rafters wafted past Celeste's nose. "What of Henrietta, Emory? She might be considered old enough—though she would not thank us for saying so."

"Needed at home and at the mine, especially with my leaving," Emory said. "Your mother cannot go?"

Loveday shook her head. "She has Gwen and Ros to consider, and Papa immediately scotched the merest suggestion of all three going up with me. Could we convince Mrs Trevelyan, do you think?"

"She is in the same position with Cecily and Jenifer," Celeste reminded her.

"There must be someone!"

Celeste threw up her hands. "I am no help. The only other lady with whom I am well acquainted in England is Madame Racine."

Loveday's smile blossomed. "Perfect. She is well known in the parish. Mama and Papa both respect her, and she is a frequent caller here. I am certain they will approve. Now, we have only to convince her."

CHAPTER 3

Gwynn Place

There had been something about the urgency of the note from Mrs Trevelyan inviting the Penhale family to dinner that evening that had made Mama insist they go, despite the short notice and over Papa's protests. He had still not recovered from the news of Celeste and Emory's engagement and was very much irritated by the fact that he had not been applied to for permission to court her, since he considered himself her guardian. Even worse—he still would not budge from his edict, and there had been no time to apply to Madam Racine for chaperonage.

Mama had no such concerns, for she was positively giddy in the carriage.

"Something is afoot, my dears," she said. "After all the excitement of yesterday and today, I cannot but believe it must be so."

"The royal messenger did say he had one more commission to carry out," Loveday offered. "Some thought it might be for Lord St Aubyn, but I am convinced it was for Captain Trevelyan. Now we only remain to be informed of its nature."

Her reputation as a prophet was made, in her own family, at least. But even she could not have suspected the magnitude of the news Mr Trevelyan announced so proudly once dinner was served and generous glasses of fine French Sancerre poured.

A viscount! Arthur had been created a viscount! A man of property, and prospects, and future wealth. The realizations struck Loveday like blows, one after another. He had just been removed as infinitely far out of her reach as any star was removed from the moon. Indeed, the news she and Celeste had been so uplifted by paled into insignificance next to this!

"I must go up to London without delay," Arthur said with all the gravity his father had been unable to muster in his pride in his son. "First, for my investiture, and second, to take my seat in the Lords. The Prince Regent, it seems, requires both funding and a plan to defeat Napoleon once and for all. I expect he will get the former, and I may participate in debate upon the latter."

"A viscount," Rosalind breathed. "How very thrilling! You are the first one I have ever met, Captain—er—your lordship."

"He has assured us we do not need to call him that among the family," Cecily assured her.

"But we are not his family," Mama said. Then Loveday thought she heard her murmur into her glass, "Not yet."

Mama had best bid a fond farewell to *that* dream.

"My daughter and Celeste have also had good news," Papa said. "You were aware they had won the Prince's prize, but they were informed also that they have been offered places among the Prince's Own Engineers."

A sip of Arthur's wine went down the wrong way, and he took refuge in his handkerchief until he had himself under control.

"Have you indeed?" Mr Trevelyan laid down his knife and fork. "Oh, very well done, ladies! I knew you would make Cornwall proud."

"Along with Sir Emory Thorndyke, my fiancé," Celeste said. "As I am sure you have heard."

"Fiancé!" Jenifer and Cecily exclaimed together.

"The Prince's Own?" Mrs Trevelyan repeated.

Mama hastened to say, "It is a very great honor, but quite impossible, I fear. Imagine His Royal Highness asking two young ladies of good family to abandon everything, travel to London, live on their own goodness knows where, and work among a lot of strangers!" She shook her head. "Even with Celeste's betrothal, I'm simply not sure how it can be done. Mr Penhale has forbidden it, of course."

Arthur's gaze was like a sudden wind, causing Loveday to lift her head and reveal all the misery in her face this blithe statement could possibly provoke. He rammed the handkerchief into a pocket. "Forbidden it?" he repeated and turned to her father. "But my dear sir, why should you do that?"

Papa swallowed his beef with an audible sound. "It is settled. Better we should speak of your prospects, sir. When is the extraordinary session of Parliament called?"

"The fifteenth. But this matter cannot be settled, surely. Loveday and Celeste must go. It is of the utmost importance to the nation that they do!"

If Loveday had had the courage, she might have kissed him for that.

"We have discussed it at length, Cap—my lord," she stammered instead. "The sticking point centers on two things. Papa has forbidden our going up alone, as is quite natural. But if we can secure lodgings, and a respectable chaperone, then all might be different."

"Miss Penhale, have the goodness to call me Captain, as usual. Until I am invested, I can escape being called *my lord* when I am among friends. But somewhere to live? There, it is within my power to assist you. I will be going up to Town very soon—within a day or two. With your parents' permission, I will endeavor to find you a respectable house, preferably furnished and with a staff. Would that be suitable?"

The entire table erupted in opinion, contradiction, and general uproar.

When Loveday could be heard, she said, "But surely Viscount St Ives will wish to find his own house while he attends Parliament?"

Arthur waved this away as unimportant. "Emory and I can hire lodgings and be perfectly content, I assure you."

"This is beneath your consequence now, sir," Papa said severely. "No indeed, I cannot permit it."

"Being of service to my friends could never be beneath my consequence," Arthur said. "Emory and I will be perfectly comfortable in some respectable rooms close by. He must be able to escort Loveday and, er, his fiancée back and forth to St James's. We shall find something within an easy distance, of that I am sure."

Another storm of protest, but Viscount St Ives—for so he was now, investiture notwithstanding—would not be moved. Loveday and Celeste would go to London, and it was only a matter of finding a chaperone that now delayed the business.

"For the sooner we go, the sooner we all may begin our

duties in service to this country," he said so firmly that Papa and Mama had no choice but to yield.

Loveday reached for Celeste's hand. Her squeeze was returned with such force that her fingers were white when they were released.

"I cannot believe it," Celeste breathed under cover of a toast. "I will not be convinced they will let us go until we see the river Thames with our own eyes."

"We owe him more than we can ever repay," Loveday murmured, and her heart squeezed inside her chest.

Bad enough that every young lady in the whole of the Duchy would be setting her cap for Arthur now. But in London? Why, even the daughters of dukes and earls would vie to be seen on his arm, or dancing with him in the glittering halls of the rich and powerful.

She had given him only the barest hint of her feelings, despite the kisses of months ago that still haunted her dreams. For in truth, she had been unaware of the depth of them herself until this moment.

The moment when she realized that her drive to accomplish great things might mean that she would lose the greatest thing of all.

The love of a good and worthy man.

"LOVEDAY, MAY I HAVE A WORD?" In the flurry of his father ordering the Penhale carriage and all the ladies finding pelisses and gloves, Arthur put a hand under Loveday's elbow and tugged her gently into the passage that led off the entry hall to the back of the house.

"Certainly," she said when he released her arm. "But first, may I offer you my heartfelt congratulations and good wishes on this unprecedented and most well-deserved honor?"

In the light from the sconce above them, he had the barest glimpse of the dimple at the corner of her mouth as it came and went. It was like a tiny gift. "Thank you. Your good wishes mean much to me."

"When Prinny said that more honors would be forthcoming, I hadn't an inkling he meant such an astonishing thing. Had you?"

"Certainly not. But enough of that—tell me, is it true? About Emory and Celeste? When did this happen? He has not breathed a word, and I only saw him this afternoon. He came to tell me his news, and I had perforce to tell him mine."

"No wonder he looked as though he had been out in a storm," Loveday said with a laugh. "He must have come to us immediately afterward, but before he could reveal your secret, he was plunged into his own."

"About which you are going to tell me, and quickly, before your mother realizes I am closeted in this corridor with you without a chaperone."

"Do not repeat that odious word to me." She stepped a little closer to speak in a low voice. "The engagement is all a ruse. Papa was adamant that we should not go to London, and so Celeste announced in front of my mother that they were engaged and not only must she go with him, but they should include me!"

Arthur leaned a shoulder on the wall, feeling rather as though he needed something to hold him up. "And Emory went along with it?"

"He did. Mama, you see, has had hopes of him for Celeste

ever since the summer, so she is convinced they have played right into her hands. The tide turned in that moment, and your offer to find a house for us has clinched it. Now all we must do is convince Madame Racine to act as chaperone, and we may depart as soon as we can pack our trunks."

"Good heavens." But why should he be surprised, after their recent adventures together? "Your parents should know by now that when you are determined on a thing, they must give way or be bowled over."

She gazed at him a moment, her eyes shadowed. "You do not blame Celeste? You do not think me forward, or indelicate, for falling in with the plan?"

"Certainly not. I for one am relieved at the prospect of having my three comrades-in-arms with me in Town. We shall brave its terrors as well as its delights together."

The tension around her eyes relaxed. "I had dared to imagine the same. In fact, the prospect of being in London at all without your company quite took the shine off its—as you put it—delights."

He hardly dared hope that she meant what he thought she meant. "Are you saying you would have missed me had the Prince not decided to reward and summon me in this way?"

Hot color flooded her cheeks, and her lashes fell. "We—we have come so far—done so much."

He opened his mouth to agree. To say what was in his heart. To find out if her feelings were as tender as his.

And then she added, "It would be a shame to break up the quartet, would it not?" The gaze she turned up to him was open and frank. The gaze of a friend.

He cursed himself for framing them as comrades a moment ago. Could he have been more of a fool?

"I will do everything in my power to see we remain so," he assured her, wrestling his emotions into order. "And now I have just heard your mother calling your name. You go first, and I will follow in a moment."

With a smile, she slipped through the door.

He leaned his head back on the wall and thumped it ever so softly against the plaster. Why had he called her comrade? *Why* had he not spoken?

Because she deserved to hear such a declaration in some more salubrious place, that was why. A ballroom. A rose garden. By a lake with swans, for heaven's sake. Not in a back corridor with the racket of their two families saying their farewells and the servants' hall not ten feet away.

But his hopes were not extinguished. Indeed, he was every bit as pleased as Mrs Penhale about Celeste and Emory's engagement, even if it was a ruse and a shameless means to an end. For Loveday would be hearing those words daily. *Fiancé. Engagement. Wedding.* Surely it would soften her feelings and make her even more amenable to the company of an old friend while she conquered London society and became the guiding light of the Prince's Own?

He would make it his business to be the man upon whose arm she strolled. In whose arms she danced. In whose company she was most comfortable.

He pushed off the wall with a sudden spurt of determination. It was of the utmost importance that he depart for London immediately. There would be time enough for his investiture and Parliament and all that palaver. But the very first order of business was to locate a house and make sure it was fit to receive a lady.

And that it had a garden. Preferably planted with rosebushes.

HAVING DEALT with her husband's last remaining objections in the privacy of their bedchamber, Mrs Penhale set out the very next day with Loveday and Celeste to put the question of being a chaperone to Madame Racine. The little Frenchwoman had a cozy cottage on a hill overlooking both Truro Harbor and the steam works. She listened as they all sat sipping tea in her withdrawing room while Mrs Penhale explained that Loveday and Celeste intended to travel to London and stay for a time, which meant they required a gentlewoman of some age and experience in the world to live with them.

"So, we wondered if perhaps you might be willing to be that gentlewoman," Loveday's mother finished.

"Travel to London?" the émigré said with a wrinkle of her nose. "I fear that is too far for these old bones."

Celeste had often thought the Frenchwoman resembled her own mother—dark hair threaded with silver, grey eyes, fine features, quick movements, and the judicious use of a walking cane. Surely *La Blanchard*, Napoleon's Chief Air Minister, would never have been so timid. She glanced over at Loveday, who straightened on the sofa.

"But we would feel so honored by your presence, madame," Loveday said. "Think of the opportunities to see the great metropolis. The museums, the theatre."

Madame Racine favored her with a kind smile. "As dear

Celeste could tell you, when one has seen L'Opéra in Paris, the London attractions do not seem as grand."

"It is a great deal to ask that you leave your home here," Mrs Penhale commiserated.

The opportunity was slipping through their fingers, like a rope whipping free of its moorings. Celeste edged forward on her seat.

"*S'il vous plaît*, madame, I will be open with you. I am engaged to Sir Emory Thorndyke, and I cannot bear to be parted from him. You will have heard he has been invited to join the Prince's Own Engineers."

"Everyone in Truro has heard," Madame Racine said. "I am sure he will be a credit to his family, and to Cornwall."

"As could we," Loveday protested. "We too have been invited to join the Prince's Own. Think what we could contribute."

"Now, then," Mrs Penhale said firmly. "Madame Racine has considered our request and explained why it cannot be. Let us speak of other things."

Celeste opened her mouth, prepared to beg if she must.

Madame Racine held up a hand. "Let us not be hasty, my good Madame Penhale. You know I hold Mademoiselle Aventure close to my heart. See how unhappy I have made her?"

Celeste closed her mouth. It was not so difficult to put on a sorrowful face. She glanced from lady to lady before dropping her gaze and waiting in silence.

"*Non*, I cannot bear it," Madame Racine said. "And dear Miss Penhale, deprived of the opportunity to make her mark? It is not to be borne. *Voila!* I will accompany you. We will show all of London that the women of Cornwall are to be reckoned with."

Glancing up, Celeste wasn't sure who looked the more shocked, Loveday or her mother.

Loveday recovered first. "Thank you, Madame Racine! We will make you proud, I promise."

Madame Racine smiled, her grey eyes twinkling. "Of that I have no doubt, *chérie*. Of that I have no doubt."

CHAPTER 4

LONDON

A fortnight later

Madame Racine's capitulation had left the Penhales with little further to argue over. Mrs Penhale had attempted to rally by worrying further about suitable lodging, but a letter came from Arthur saying he had found them a house to lease at the very edge of Mayfair—the most fashionable district in London, according to Gwen and Ros. Emory had left ahead of them, and he and Arthur were already situated in a gentlemen's lodging house near St. James's.

Henrietta Thorndyke had made sure to inform Celeste of the fact when the latter came to town to pick up a few tools and supplies from the steam works. Henri had seemed a bit mystified as to why Emory had been so insistent that she speak to Celeste. Celeste and Emory had decided not to share their pretend engagement with his family. It had been all Celeste could do to keep the matter from circulating in the steam works. The fewer lies told, the better.

The last remaining obstacle was a suitable carriage. Madame Racine had an old hooded landau, but it would make for chilly travel in winter, even if the axles would withstand so long a drive over rutted roads. In the end, they settled on traveling post-chaise at a leisurely pace to allow the wagon to keep up. Celeste, Loveday, and Madame Racine arrived in Mayfair late on a Saturday afternoon, with young Kip Sandow from the Penhale stables driving the wagon just behind, Madame Racine's older maid, Honore, bundled up on the bench beside him. All around, tall stone townhouses bumped shoulders as they looked out on iron-fenced squares with trees bare for winter.

"We shall be very happy here, I think," Madam Racine said, alighting on Loveday's arm and gazing up at the four-story narrow townhouse Arthur had found.

Celeste liked it immediately. The black iron fence in front and the black shutters on the windows contrasted with the gleaming white stone in classical propriety. But the jaunty red door proclaimed that those who lived here had a dash of daring as well.

"Lord St Ives said the mews are around the corner," Madam Racine told Kip as the postillion urged the carriage away. "You may unload the supplies there."

"But be sure to bring the sideboard into the house," Loveday called. "I'll come down to show you where to put the rest of it."

Their former stable boy tipped his cap and clucked to the horse, which plodded forward as if just as ready to see the journey done. But, by the grin on Kip's face, it was evident that at least one of the party was delighted beyond all measure to be in the great metropolis.

"Still I do not understand why your *chère maman* would wish to send furniture with us," Madame Racine said, climbing the brick stairs to the door. "I understood the house came fully furnished."

"That is my understanding as well," Loveday assured her, setting her green wool skirts in place on the stoop. "This is a piece with special meaning to me. She was insistent that I should take it."

Because Loveday had modified the articulated chest so that it could contort into the most useful shape using its gears and pulleys. The piece seemed to have a mind of its own, however, and Mrs Penhale was of the opinion that it would only obey Loveday.

She was likely right.

Any number of pieces would have found themselves at home in the elegant little house. That much was apparent as they entered. The entry hall was tiled in squares of black and white marble, with pale green walls and a high ceiling that drew one's eye up the rosewood stairs. With a dining room and study on the ground floor, withdrawing room above, and bedchambers on each of the upper stories and servants' chambers on the top, there was plenty of room.

An elderly woman with a spine so straight it might have been carved from the same marble as the floor dipped a curtsey as they entered, grey skirts pooling. "Welcome to Beswick House. I am Mrs Heath, and I will be serving as cook and housekeeper."

She made the claim as if throwing down the gauntlet. Very likely some tenants preferred to bring their own staff. She was making her place clear.

"Very good, Mrs Heath," Madame Racine said. "And I believe we have a housemaid as well?"

"Maisie comes in during the day, madam, as do I," Mrs Heath assured her. "We leave at seven sharp and return by five. If you notice anything amiss while we are out, leave a note in the kitchen, and I'll see to it first thing."

At least the last was said with some semblance of a smile.

"We will settle in and then have supper," Madame Racine told her. "You have that nearly ready?"

She nodded. "Nice barley soup and fresh rolls, madam, along with spinach in butter sauce and baked biffins for dessert."

Celeste's mouth was watering. She'd always been fond of the pressed apple treat. Madame Racine merely nodded an acknowledgment in dismissal.

"I have not had to climb so many stairs in a while," their chaperone commented as they started up. "I will take the bedroom on the main chamber story. You two may have the ones above it."

Which meant any time they left their room, they would have to pass hers. She had the makings of a very good chaperone.

Celeste could not mind. When she and Loveday had been in France, they had had to sneak around for their own safety. She had every hope that her days of clandestine activities were behind her.

IT TURNED out that Beswick House had been the home of a rather grand family in days past and possessed a large butler's pantry. There being no butler in their own small household, and Mrs Heath having her own comfortable sitting room, Loveday promptly claimed it for herself and Celeste as their new workshop.

The articulated sideboard tumbled itself in from the kitchen garden and frightened poor Maisie into a screech. She leaped back and pressed herself against the wall, rigid with fear as it passed her.

"Get that thing out of here!" Mrs Heath roared, brandishing the knife with which she was chopping parsley, likely to garnish the soup.

"It is quite all right, Mrs Heath," Loveday assured her. It would never do to frighten the cook and housemaid out of the house on their very first full day in residence. "It is only a piece of furniture. It is designed to move easily, you see, so that one does not have such a struggle lifting it."

Neither she nor Maisie looked convinced.

"We shall use it in our workroom. I promise it will not trouble you." To that end, she gave the sideboard an encouraging push and it tumbled through the pantry door to reassemble itself along the only empty wall, the rest being taken up by the door, floor-to-ceiling shelving—lovely—and a window that looked out on the servants' entrance and the steps up to the street—the prospect of daylight lovelier still.

She and Celeste had so little in the way of dresses and gowns that settling in on Saturday had only been the work of an hour. That left them Sunday free to attend services in as grand a church as she'd ever seen and then concentrate on filling the butler's pantry shelves and the compartments of the sideboard with the supplies and tools they had brought with them while Madame Racine saw to arranging the rest of the house to her liking.

"Surely they will allow us to work on things at home," Celeste said. "And we must have more paper for our own drawings as soon as possible. Look, Loveday—this linen drawer is perfect for the purpose, being both wide and shallow."

After devouring a meat pie and little poppyseed cakes for dessert, Loveday would have thought the last few days would have worn her out. But as the clock in the hall on the ground floor chimed one, she was no closer to sleep than she had been at eight this evening, when they had discovered a cabinet in the drawing room to be a Broadwood square pianoforte, and everyone in the household had learned what a poor musician she was.

Thank goodness for Madame Racine, whom Loveday knew to be the opposite, and with a large repertoire to boot.

Since she could not sleep, perhaps she might be more useful in the workshop, organizing and puttering and generally tidying up.

She wrapped a warm paisley shawl over her nightdress and knotted it in the small of her back as the country-women did, then with her candle in one hand and her slippers in the other, she tiptoed down the stairs. They creaked only a little, the sounds such as what any house might make as it settled. When she reached the foyer, she put her slippers on and hurried down the kitchen stairs to the workroom.

"It's only me," she whispered to the sideboard as she entered the room, and she could swear she heard it settle back into place.

Hm. Or perhaps there was more to the soft sounds than that. Perhaps she ought to ask Kip to bring in a mousetrap.

A lamp soon bathed the room in golden light, and a sense of contentment at being co-mistress of their own kingdom filled her. Here were rolls of drawings to be laid flat in the tablecloth drawer. Here were magnifying glasses and brass rings to tuck into the baize-lined silverware drawers, should she ever wish to make another far-scope. In this burlap sack were gears and cogs and clock parts aplenty for those tiny bits of machinery that were so necessary, but which no one ever saw, such as those in the sideboard. She separated them out by size and then found a series of small drawers one above the other, so they would remember the gradations.

She had just realized that she had been standing motionless over several turnscrews and ball-peen hammers, trying to keep her eyes from closing, when she heard a door open and shut.

With a blink, she leaned over to look out into the darkened kitchen. "Hello? Mrs Heath?"

Good heavens, it couldn't be five o'clock, could it? The window of the workroom was still black as pitch, but it was November, and the tall houses made daylight's arrival later than it was over the gentle hills at home.

She held up the lantern and ventured out, trying not to be a ninnyhammer and frighten herself in the shadows of the worktable and the great hutch where the dishes were neatly stacked.

No one was there.

She did, however, discover the back door into the garden to be unlocked. She cracked it open to peer out, but could see nothing in the darkness. Clouds rushed over a waning moon as the wind came up, bringing her the scent of mulch and wet earth, for the garden contained nothing save vegetable beds, a path bordered by ornamental trees, and a few thorny, dormant stalks of rosebushes.

It must have been Kip, up early to bring in coal or some such. She had best not lock the door, so that he might come in again.

She shivered as the frigid wind pressed her nightgown against her legs. Suddenly the prospect of a warm bed seemed very welcome indeed. She closed up the workroom and hurried upstairs, where she cuddled down into bed and was instantly asleep.

EMORY BROUGHT a hack at half past seven on Monday morning to escort them to St James's. Celeste and Loveday hadn't been certain what to expect, so they'd dressed with particular care. Celeste's sky-blue wool with the white lace ruff at the collar might have been one of Gwen's discards, but a few tucks here, added lace to the sleeves there, and *voila!* It was reborn. Loveday's Turkey red wool gown was both daring in its color and stylish in its design.

But Celeste took one look at Emory and shook her head. "This is what you wear to meet again with the Prince?"

Emory spread his hands and looked down at the common navy coat and dark trousers fastened under the instep of his shoes. "Well, it is a workshop, not an assembly room. And none of the Prince's Own has seen His Royal Highness in days."

Loveday sighed.

Madame Racine rode with them this first day, her head high and her watchful gaze moving from Loveday beside her, to Celeste across the coach next to Emory. Celeste made sure to sit just a little closer than she normally would have, to further the ruse that they were engaged. Emory did not seem to mind. Indeed, he had a smile on his face, as if well pleased with himself.

Outside, she caught glimpses of the mighty city. After touring the Continent with her aeronaut parents, she had lived for many years in Paris. Narrow city streets and towering stone buildings were no strangers to her. Even though Loveday had spent the better part of a month in Paris recently, she still gawked out the carriage window as they rolled through Mayfair and across a busy street Emory said was named Piccadilly, of all things. Barely noticeable behind the carriages, wagons, horses, and lorries, workers were busily banging away at the cobblestones.

Madame Racine deigned to glance out the window at last and frowned. "What is it they do?" she asked Emory as they made their way past.

"The Prince is having a grand set of townhouses and a new park built," he explained. "The new street to access them will be Regent Street, and it will need to come in at an angle. I understand this will be Piccadilly Circus when it's completed."

As they started down St James's Street, Celeste spotted an elegant white stone building. Gentlemen in fine coats were entering, and others peered out the bow window at passersby.

"What is that?" she asked.

Emory's face appeared to have stiffened. "White's, a gentleman's club," he said in a voice equally constrained.

"No women allowed," Loveday concluded.

"A waste of time, then," Celeste agreed, and he seemed to relax.

"You will likely find yourselves too busy for many social events," he told them, sounding rather pleased by the fact. "The Prince's Own have committed to work from eight in the morning until six in the evenings Mondays, Tuesdays, Thursdays, and Fridays until the war has been won."

"I can understand having Sundays off for services," Loveday said, tearing her gaze away from the sights. "But why should we not work Wednesdays? Or Saturdays, for that matter?"

Pink climbed in his cheeks, as if he had been caught in some falsehood. "Apparently Saturdays are reserved for preparing for balls and such, and Wednesdays are reserved for preparing to attend Almack's."

"For heaven's sake," Loveday said with a sniff. "Do they not know we are at war?"

But even Celeste had heard of the famous ladies' club in London. "Surely Almack's is closed now. We are not in the Season."

Emory tugged at his gloves. "Apparently many of the patronesses are in London with their husbands for the special session of Parliament. But I wouldn't be concerned. It's doubtful any of us will rise to their notice."

Most likely not. She had a feeling she and Loveday, at least, would enjoy working on Wednesdays.

The carriage drew to a stop before a sturdy red brick building with twin crenelated turrets and two massive black, arched doors. A guard was stationed on either side, gazes wary and rifles ready.

"Welcome to St James's Palace," Emory said before opening the door and hopping out to let Celeste and Loveday down.

"I will return for you at six," Madame Racine promised, "and you will tell me of your triumphs."

Emory shut the door, and the carriage rolled away.

Celeste put a hand to her bonnet and glanced up at the towers. On the highest point, a gold weathervane shifted with the wind. L'Ecole des Aéronautes had had such a vane. Knowing which way the wind was blowing was critical for ascensions.

"I approve," she said.

One of the guards raised a brow before carefully schooling his face.

"Sir Emory Thorndyke of the Prince's Own Engineers," he told the closest guard. "With me are Miss Penhale and Mademoiselle Aventure. They join the unit today."

She thought they might argue, but the guard merely tipped up his chin. "We were informed. You may pass."

"Is it always so guarded?" Loveday asked as they passed through the black doors into a long corridor hung with tapestries.

"His Royal Highness and two of his brothers have residences here," Emory told her. "Even if we weren't at war, I imagine that would require a certain amount of security."

He led them down a series of corridors that began to remind Celeste of Napoleon's palace of the Tuileries. Did every monarch require a labyrinth to feel safe in his home? Finally, they entered a wood-paneled room nearly two stories tall. The upper two-thirds of each wall was covered with armaments in fanciful arrangements, from a medallion of long bows and arrows with a gold shield in the center to rifles in a herringbone pattern and cutlasses crossed like a woven mat.

"Just passing through," Emory told the three red-coated guards seated at the round table by the fire.

They watched every stride across the wide plank floor.

"The guard room," Emory explained, opening the door in the far wall. "And this is the workshop."

Beside her, Loveday drew a long breath in awe.

It was not as large as her mother's workshop in Paris, but it was far more elegant. The high, domed ceiling encouraged lofty thoughts. The bank of recessed, arched windows along one wall let in light to illuminate work even on so grey a day. Between each pair of windows stood a white marble bust of what must be famous creators from history. They seemed to beam down beneficently on the workbenches that ranged in two rows down the center of the room and the tall book-shelves on the opposite wall, filled with the knowledge of the ages.

Five men were already at work, each at their own work-bench. Four heads came up as Emory, Celeste, and Loveday entered. One just as quickly lowered his head in dismissal. Two of the gentlemen came forward to greet them.

One was nearly as wide as he was tall, with thick blond hair that stuck out in odd places, as if he had been tugging at it.

"Are these our ladies?" he asked in a voice that echoed.

"Miss Penhale, Mademoiselle Aventure, allow me to present Mr Augustus Guelph, our resident meteorologist."

Celeste and Loveday curtsied. Mr Guelph waved a meaty hand. "No need to stand upon ceremony here. We are all workers together for the good of our country and the world."

"Was that your weathervane I saw on the tower?" Celeste asked him.

He clapped his hands together with a sound like thunder. "Well done! Yes, it was, and you would be surprised at the difficulties I had convincing them to allow it. But how are we to know when to launch if we cannot tell wind speed and direction?"

"*Certainement,*" Celeste agreed.

"Launch." Loveday seized on the word. "Then we *are* planning a new air ship."

"More than an air ship," the other man assured her. Younger than Mr Guelph by at least ten years, if Celeste was any judge, his black hair was parted in the middle and arranged about his face in curls any young lady might envy. His chocolate-colored eyes were deep set and as adoring as a spaniel's. "Outside, in the Engine Court, you will see the prototype we are building."

"This is Jacob Barnes," Emory supplied in a voice that seemed to have grown chillier. "He specializes in the properties of materials."

Mr Barnes's bow was elaborate and low. "Ladies, a great pleasure."

"I'll introduce you to the others," Emory said, putting a hand to Celeste's back and propelling her past the handsome engineer.

She might have resented his direction, except that she was eager to meet all those the Prince had assembled. Humphry Davy was a chemist who had, according to Emory, invented any number of useful items, including a lamp safe enough for miners to take underground. Small wonder he knew of the fellow. In his forties, Davy had wavy, mahogany-colored hair and a boyish face with a decided twinkle in his eyes.

"I have also had the good fortune of being born in Cornwall," he told them all when Emory finished eulogizing him.

"Then we are well represented indeed," Loveday assured him.

The next man was younger still, perhaps a little older then Mr Barnes, with shiny brown hair cropped short about his ears and tumbling over his forehead, and a prominent chin. He was a mathematician of some note and skilled with clockwork.

"Though I have plans for an analytical engine," Mr Babbage confessed to Loveday, a blush rising in his cheeks. "Capable of reasoning out problems too difficult to calculate by hand."

The final member was the fellow who had so disregarded them when they'd entered and indeed, steadfastly ignored them until Emory was standing right beside him.

"Mr Stephen Cummings," Emory told Loveday and Celeste, "who specializes in electromagnetism."

She might have guessed as much by the number of metal bars and coils strewn about his workbench and a sort of four-sided tank with tubes coming out of it standing nearby. But just as his work was a mess, his brown hair, beard, and mustache were so neatly trimmed she wondered what he paid his valet for such precision.

"A tinkerer and an aeronaut," he drawled with barely a nod to acknowledge them. "How original—but then His Royal Highness is ever an independent thinker."

Celeste gritted her teeth, but Loveday made a show of glancing around.

"Do we expect him today?" she asked.

"We live in hope," Mr Cummings said. He returned to his work without further comment.

Emory drew Celeste and Loveday away, to where two vacant workbenches stood side by side. "I believe these are meant to be yours."

Celeste's heart lifted, as though she were standing in a basket and had been whisked upward toward the fulfillment of her dreams.

CHAPTER 5

*L*oveday ran a practiced eye over the contents of her bench. Its drawers contained many of the same tools they had in the butler's pantry, and hanging from hooks on a gantry that ran the length of the two rows of benches were coils of rope and wire. Sheets of copper and tin, buckets of screws and rivets, and lengths of piping in several diameters left her feeling confident that they would be well supplied with what they needed.

"Let us hope there is no Toussaint attached to the unit to slow our work," she muttered to Celeste.

Mr. Guelph approached bearing a roll of plans, which he spread on Loveday's bench.

"The Prince is aware that you are starting work today," he said, placing bolts on the corners to hold them down. "He has left you an assignment."

Loveday felt a rush of excitement.

"He would be pleased if you would review these drawings, paying particular attention to the communications system."

"An on-board system of communications?" Loveday asked,

puzzled. "Why, the gondola cannot be so large as to need such a thing, surely. Everyone is within speaking distance."

Mr Guelph shook his head and smiled. "Come with me to the window."

He indicated that they should look out into the courtyard, then stood aside.

"*Incroyable*, Loveday, that cannot be *Lark Deux?*"

She stared. "No. It is at least half again as large. She will hold a crew of ten, if my eyes don't deceive me. Goodness, will we be permitted to board her?"

Mr Guelph chuckled. "Board her, and hammer on her, and install devices in her. We are in and out of her all the time. The hull arrived two weeks ago, fresh from the shipyards at Portsmouth, and ever since, we have been building her out at a rapid rate."

"But I still do not see the need for communications within the ship," Loveday said. "At most, one might raise one's voice to be heard all over the deck."

Their guide shook his head. "You mistake me, Miss Penhale—I was not clear. You are to work on a system to communicate *between* ships. In flight."

"Oh, my goodness. Celeste, let us look at the plans at once!"

She could barely keep from breaking into a run as they hurried back to the bench and the set of plans that held such a momentous invention. She turned over the large sheets one at a time, both of them anxious to be the first to spot the call-out for it.

Then Celeste's finger landed on a carefully drawn circle. "Is this it? Surely not."

"It cannot be. Those are simply flags." Loveday peered at

them more closely. "In fact, these are the flags the navy uses. When we were in Portsmouth, remember, we saw the signal officer using them on deck as two ships departed the harbor."

"But of what use is that?" Celeste asked, clearly as confused as she. "Our air ships might be separated by as much as a mile or more. One might see a ship, but without a far-scope, one would never see flags."

Loveday looked up to find Mr Barnes watching them from his bench, which backed on that of Celeste, his eyes dancing with amusement. "You know so much about the navy, do you? I suppose two ladies such as yourselves must draw a great deal of attention when walking along the waterfront."

Loveday frowned at him, completely unable to account for such irrelevance. "Mr Barnes, who was the engineer who proposed flags as a means of communication?"

"I can't remember. It was on our earliest drafts. One of the admirals, probably. They stick their noses in here from time to time, and Mr Guelph has to take them for a drink to get rid of them."

"Well, we won't be using flags. They do not pull their weight. Every ounce can mean the difference between maneuverability and being the target of a cannonbomb, and besides that, in the heat of battle it would take too long to parse out a signal from ship to ship." Loveday found a fresh sheet of paper and ink in the center drawer to begin a list of improvements. "If the Prince wishes communication between ships, then we will dispose of these and come up with something more practical."

"Here half an hour and criticizing already?" came Mr Cummings's voice from the next row.

"That appears to be our assignment," Celeste said with

great clarity of enunciation. Loveday had noticed that her consonants became exceedingly crisp when she was annoyed.

"Never mind him," she told her friend. "We must make a list of possibilities. And to do that, we must board the prototype to see what has been done so far."

"Allow me to escort you," Mr Barnes said instantly, coming around the end of the row.

"It would be better if I did," Emory said, crossing the space between. "Since I may claim acquaintance with the ladies."

"But I have been here longer than a week," Mr Barnes retorted, and as though that clinched it, showed them to a door that led across a corridor and outside.

Loveday would rather have boarded with Emory's guidance, but there was nothing for it. Her skirts snapping in the wind, she held her bonnet with one hand and accepted Mr Barnes's hand up the short temporary staircase. The prototype's hull was held upright by stocks, much as a seagoing vessel would be held upright in the ways at the shipyard. A crane and pulley system had clearly been used to lift in the boiler, which was nearly half again as large as the one in *Lark Deux*.

"They have wasted no time," she said to Celeste. "Look here, at the steam-powered rigging system for the bow sail. And my goodness, the steering vanes are practically sails as well."

"It did not look like that on the drawings."

"We make improvements at speed," Mr Barnes said. "Mr Guelph is often hard pressed to keep up with us and is frequently here at night, recreating the drawings to match."

"The flags, evidently, are a placeholder," Loveday remarked. "I do not see any."

"No point, if you are going to develop something better," Mr Barnes said with a shrug. "I confess I'm glad it wasn't my assignment. Metals and hulls, now, are much more to my taste. Talking ships are a bit beyond me."

Talking ships. What an interesting idea. Or listening ships, at least. Imagine giving a command and having a ship obey one's voice!

Loveday bent to see something in the stern. "Oh, Celeste, look. The navy, too, has replicated our cupboard for the picnic basket."

Celeste laughed. "A hundred years from now, that cupboard will still be in every ship design, and no one will know why. Come, let us have a look at this boiler."

The boiler was sleek and glossy and unspoiled. "Has it not been fired?" Loveday asked Mr Barnes, looking up as she crouched next to the firebox. It held only enough ash for a cooking fire.

"We did a burn-in to test all the piping and their tolerances. It is a fine piece of work, if I do say so myself."

Loveday was quite ready to say so as well. "And the exhaust system?"

He ran a hand along the gunwale. "The original had it running along here, but ours goes straight down to the hull, does a ninety-degree turn to travel along the keel, and releases it out the stern."

She glanced at Celeste, who looked as affronted as she felt.

"The Prince's Own did not feel that the exhaust running through the copper piping would create a source of heat for the crew?" she inquired as politely as she was able. "We have been as high as a thousand feet, and it is cold indeed."

"The higher one rises, the lower the temperature drops,"

Celeste said. "But perhaps the engineers did not know this, having never flown before."

"Oh, we've flown." Mr Barnes did not appear much bothered by her tone. "When we first signed on, we were taken down to Portsmouth and sent up in your little ship. A fine job, ladies, I must say. It was the greatest moment of my life."

Oh, thank you very much for recognizing our little ship, since no one has ever built one before. Loveday bit back the words.

"It was the envy of every man Jack of us," he went on. "No one begrudges you the Prince's prize. Our happy task is merely to improve on what you've done. A bit like gilding the lily, but there it is. The only difference between *Lark Deux* and this girl here—" He patted the gunwale again. "—is size. And number. The Prince wants at least half a dozen by Christmas. The hulls are waiting—we have only to complete this one and the building will begin. Hence the need for the ability to communicate between ships."

Loveday felt slightly less angry and allowed herself to be mollified by Mr Barnes's compliments as they were guided back into the workshop.

"Come, Celeste. Let us exercise some flights of fancy and think of every method possible whereby ships may communicate."

But when her friend pulled up the stool beside her, she seemed distracted. "Loveday, I beg your pardon, but I wish to look at the ship again. Something is bothering me."

"Certainly."

This time, to her relief, it was Emory who walked outdoors with them, though quite unnecessarily, in her opinion.

"Don't tell me you, too, have been told that a lady may

never go about unaccompanied in London," she said, trying not to be cross with him.

"No indeed," he said mildly. "But I heard what Celeste said, and I have enough experience to know that her hunches ought to be listened to."

Celeste gave him a smile that made his cheeks redden—or it might have been the wind. "Thank you for saying that," she said. "I am reconciled somewhat to the loss of our lovely copper piping."

Instead of climbing back into the ship, she walked around to the stern. Sure enough, two pipes protruded from the hull to convey the smoke from the firebox out of the vessel. Celeste regarded them with a frown.

"Loveday, do you remember our flight in May and how it seemed different from the one in August?"

"Certainly," Loveday said. "*Lark Deux* was larger and not made of a cut-up coach."

"We added air propellers, too. But they were controlled by the helm. This is fixed on an Archimedean screw, as part of the exhaust system."

Loveday waited, then gazed at the pipes. "It seems odd, doesn't it?" she said. "All that hot air, making it work harder."

"Smoke, more like," Emory said. "Coal exhaust is mostly unburned particles. Hot, black smoke."

"But it is not powered by the hot air." Celeste seemed to direct her remarks to the stern, but Loveday knew better.

"Cold air is heavier," Emory said. "Lending more thrust."

"But here in the stern, Loveday is right," Celeste said, circling to the other side. "It does seem as though the exhaust system will interfere with the air movement. Particularly if the smoke particles begin to build up on all the metal parts."

Emory studied the assemblies closely. "While I agree it bears further thought, and a discussion with the others, it does mean a redesign. And that is not what the Prince has assigned to you."

Celeste nodded. "We must return to our list of possibilities, I suppose. That is, if Mr Barnes will keep himself to himself long enough to allow us to compose it."

"Do not be too hard on Mr Barnes," Emory said. "He is self-taught, like Loveday. His genius with materials and their uses is as great as yours and Loveday's with flight and mechanics."

"I did not know that," Loveday said, regretting her brusque treatment of him. "I salute him—though that does not make up for the fact that he is a dreadful flirt. Did you hear that remark about the navy and the waterfront?"

"I did. I also heard you trim the man's sails. So no harm done, I hope?"

"*Non,*" Celeste admitted. "We may admire the gentleman's intellect while deploring his manners."

"There he may be forgiven, too," Emory said. "I heard a rumor that he was born on the South Bank, far from all good society. He was taken in by the curate of a church, who saw promise in him and gave him an education." Emory paused.

Celeste eyed him. "There must be more to this story."

"There is. I only hope you will not think me a prattlebox."

"Heavens, if we do not hear things from you, how are we to keep ourselves informed? The scandal sheets?" Loveday laughed. "Out with it, Emory."

He moved closer, though there was no one else in the Engine Court but themselves. "I heard that before he began his rise to greatness, he was a talented thief."

"Goodness." Loveday had not been expecting *that*. "I hope he is reformed?"

"I believe so—he held the curate in much affection and left that life behind. But as I say, this is all rumor and gossip and I hope you and he will forgive me for passing it on."

Returning to the bench for the second time, Loveday could see that Celeste was still thinking—and not about Mr Barnes, either. Sometimes ideas needed to steep, like leaves in a teapot, before the concoction was viable. Look how many weeks of thought and puzzling through possibilities it had taken to redesign the articulated sideboard.

Loveday took up the pen and had the petty satisfaction of writing *Flags* at the top, then crossing it out with such vehemence the pen sputtered. Then she wrote, *Pigeons*.

"They take too long to train," Celeste murmured, pulling up her stool and propping one elbow on the bench as she watched. "And how would one train them to go to a particular ship? Different foods aboard as inducement?"

Loveday smiled. "It would work with the chickens at Hale House."

Celeste took the pen and added, *Mirrors*. "Flashes of light, with so many flashes for each message. One flash—full speed ahead. Two—enemy sighted. *Comme ça*."

"That would preclude sailing in poor weather, or at night."

"True, though one would not wish to do either."

"You did, if I recall. In war, one might likewise have no choice. It is a better possibility than pigeons, I grant you." Loveday tapped her chin. "Arthur and Emory discovered that the automatons in Boney's ships used a low-frequency pulse from the ground to signal the ships and keep them on course. Can we use that somehow?"

"A pity we sent the one pursuing me to perdition," Celeste said. "We might have harvested a device—like Old Job's Pisky that protects the smugglers from *sous-marins*—and examined it."

"Yes, but you were quite busy on that occasion, and unable to stop. On second thought, the system was used for guidance," Loveday mused. "Our purpose is communication between human beings at a distance. Would it even apply?"

"I do not see how."

Regardless, she added *Pulse beacon* to the list.

"If a ship half a mile distant may not hear a sound," Celeste said, "may it use artificial light? Those beacons, you recall, had blue glass."

"Only so that the flight path could be known to the soldiers guiding the unmanned ships. I do not think the lamps had a signal in themselves." Loveday wrote *Signal lights*. "A lighthouse, of course, uses artificial light to communicate. The aeronauts would be familiar with such a thing."

"But now we have the opposite problem. It is only good at night," Celeste pointed out. "Many of my mother's ascensions were made at night for that reason. The small bombs she threw out exploded in cascades of light caused by gunpowder." She sighed. "All the colors—red, yellow, and white, of course. How the crowds would cheer for—"

"That's it!" Loveday exclaimed. "Colors!"

She scribbled *Colored smoke* on the list and circled it.

Celeste made a face. "I was not speaking of smoke."

"Remember what Emory said. The engine emits black smoke. What if a chemical were added to a modification on the exhaust so that the smoke would turn color? It would trail out behind the lead ship."

"Minerals were added to the gunpowder to create the colors." Celeste's eyes had lit up. "But we would give them meaning. Yellow—enemy sighted. Green—turn to starboard. Red—fly to port. White—full ahead. Black—well, black would mean nothing. All is well, I suppose."

Loveday craned her neck toward the bench of Mr Humphrey Davy, the chemist. "He is there. Let us put the idea to him."

When they explained their idea, the chemist's brows rose, then pulled together as he considered it. "At what point would the minerals be added to the exhaust system?"

"Fairly far along," Celeste said. "These are merely powdered minerals, but they do react with heat to produce the colors."

"We would not want chemical reactions occurring too close to the boiler," Loveday agreed. "Can there be a hatch, perhaps, just before the pipe exits the hull? A crew member might stand by with a rack of minerals to spoon them in like sugar into a cake."

Mr Davy appeared to be fighting a smile. "Or a set of tubes with stops that can be pressed to measure them out." He glanced at the other men, all focused on their work. "It is a better idea than flags, at least. We meet weekly to exchange and refine ideas. On Thursday, be prepared to present a drawing, and we will take a vote. If it is unanimous, Mr Barnes will apply himself to it."

Loveday was recovering from their ideas being taken up in committee, as if this were Parliament. "Must every adjustment and change be voted on?"

Mr Davy nodded. "Most of them. From our number, you may conjecture that one engineer may not operate alone.

Each thing he—or she—touches affects the work of another."

"Of course," Celeste murmured. "We will be prepared on Thursday, then."

The words were barely out of her mouth when they heard a commotion by the door, and Mr Guelph came in with a lady on his arm. He caught sight of them and brought over a motherly looking woman in a cinnamon-colored pelisse trimmed in loops and arabesques of black ribbon soutache. Her hair was the color of treacle, and her brown eyes twinkled.

"My dear, may I present the newest members of our company, Miss Loveday Penhale and Miss Celeste Aventure. Ladies, my wife, Lavinia."

They both dipped curtseys and rose to find the lady beaming upon them. "I cannot tell you how delighted I am to find young women contributing their abilities and fine minds to the Prince's Own," she said.

Loveday's skin tingled with such surprise it was almost shock.

"You do not think we ought to have stayed at home and minded our needlework?" she blurted.

Mrs Guelph laughed. "You have been reading the newspapers, I see."

"No indeed, ma'am," Celeste ventured. "We have only just arrived in London. Our business here at St James's was much more pressing."

"Then let me advise you to pay no attention. But let us speak of happier things." She tilted her chin. "I have come to invite you to a ball."

Celeste gasped and clasped her hands. "Oh, madame, you are too kind. But surely you do not mean Loveday and me alone?" She glanced over her shoulder at Emory, who bowed in acknowledgment.

"I extend the invitation to all here, of course," Mrs Guelph assured her. "And those who are married must certainly bring their wives. It is to be held at our house on Saturday evening. My dear husband's aunt, Lady Selwyn, is staying with us and the ball is in her honor—she is a great supporter of her nephew's toils here." She beamed at Mr Guelph. "And she tells me that she is nearly positive His Royal Highness may make an appearance!"

Saturday! But how were they to catch up in their contributions to the work of others here, if they must be subjected to such silliness as a ball? Bad enough they did not work on Wednesdays. As for dear Prinny, when did he ever turn up when he was expected? He was much better at turning up when he was not.

"I do beg your pardon, ma'am," Loveday said a little desperately, "but I do not know if we can attend. We have most urgent work that must be completed—"

"Oh, but you must!" Mrs Guelph said, her eyes widening.

"You haven't been in town a week and already you feel the urgency of our task," Mr Guelph said soothingly. "But it is not so urgent that you may not attend, Miss Penhale."

"But—" She exchanged an agonized look with Celeste, who was perfectly aware of what they had to accomplish. Thursday was only the beginning.

"When I say you must, I am not thinking only of Lady Selwyn," Mrs Guelph told her. "I am thinking of the gentleman I have already invited. Someone known to you. Surely the work you speak of may wait—for you would by no means wish to offend the newly invested Viscount St Ives, would you?"

~

WEDNESDAY, it felt almost odd not to be going to the palace. Very likely Celeste was supposed to sit in the withdrawing room, hoping for a call from her supposed fiancé. Loveday had wanted her to help complete the drawing of the prototype smoke signaling system. Much as she would enjoy that, or Emory's company, she had an utterly different occupation in mind. After months of hand-me-downs, she could hardly wait for new clothes. Loveday ought to be thinking of dancing with Arthur and finding a new gown. Luckily, Madame Racine knew of a French modiste on Bond Street, so they sent for a hack and headed to the most famous shopping area in London.

It felt almost as if they were on a holiday. Like someone on her grand tour, she joined Loveday at the window.

"Jackson's Boxing Emporium," Celeste read aloud from a sign on a building. "Is that where Gentleman Jackson instructs his pupils, do you think?"

"With Angelo's Fencing Academy," Madame Racine acknowledged. "A number of émigrés have learned the art of the foil from the Italian master at arms."

"And there—Edward Orme's shop," Loveday said. She nudged Celeste. "He invented those transparent prints we've been seeing in the magazines."

They were ingenious, made from a resin material that changed the coloring of the print with a flip of the page. Other shops carried perfumes, pastries, and publications. But what struck Celeste was the utter lack of automation. In France, even a farmer's cart might be powered by steam, and *chaises roulantes* roared along country roads at considerable speed carrying their two passengers inside a blur of spokes. Here, there were only carriages, horses, and pedestrians. In France, a lady might bring an automaton to carry her packages. Here, footmen followed her dutifully, arms laden.

"A shame we did not bring back an *automouton* or two from France," she murmured to Loveday as the coachman came around to hand down Madame Racine while a street boy held the horses. "Think what a stir we would make having them carry our purchases on their backs."

Loveday's smile broadened, as if she too were remembering the little fleece-covered clockwork devices that kept Napoleon's palace free of dust and cobwebs.

Celeste's answering smile faded as she stepped onto the pavement. How much farther had the Emperor gone since they'd left? She had fled France in such a way as to make Captain La Croix, one of her mother's seconds, the most likely candidate for Chief Air Minister. He knew the dangers of the approach his former colleague, the villainous Captain Toussaint, had attempted to take, using guidance systems to direct air ships flown by automatons. Would he be more prudent? Or take risks that might improve his standing with the Emperor?

"Here we are," Madame Racine announced as they approached a shop with fabrics draped about the window in bright satin and rich velvet. "Madame Vermeil will know exactly what we need."

A cloud of orange-blossom scent drifted out as they opened the door and stepped inside. Fantastic creations draped dressmaker frames, while bolts of fabric and spools of notions lined the shelves. A tall woman with clothing likely designed to emphasize her swaying hips, Madame Vermeil came forward to clasp Madame Racine's hands. *"Ma chère. Ça fait trop longtemps."*

"Yes, far too long since we have seen each other," Madame Racine answered, kissing her on both cheeks. "But English, please, Annette, so my young friends will not misunderstand."

Annette Vermeil turned her polished smile on Celeste and Loveday. "Welcome, ladies! How might I be of service?"

Loveday looked to Celeste, evidently handing off the management of the task to her, and she raised her chin, relishing it. "We will each need three day dresses of sturdy material, two evening gowns, and two ballgowns, the last four untrimmed, *s'il vous plâit.*"

"Someone has been studying her French," Madame Vermeil said admiringly.

"Mademoiselle Aventure fled France to avoid an unwanted marriage," Madame Racine explained, repeating the story Celeste had put about. "She makes her home in Cornwall now, along with Miss Penhale. They have earned the Prince's prize and are members of the Prince's Own Engineers."

"Ah," Madame Vermeil said, eyes lighting up. "But surely if you are working beside His Royal Highness, you must be gowned in the best."

"As best we can, given our budget," Celeste explained. Five hundred guineas would not reach to the end of the twelve-month if they did not manage their expenses carefully. "I thought if the evening gowns and ballgowns were untrimmed, we might switch the decorations and make it appear we have more than the set."

Madame Vermeil's brows lifted. "How wise. Because you are such good friends of Madame Racine, allow me to offer another service. I have, on occasion, received gowns back from a client who decided my excellent taste did not match her needs at the moment. Perhaps I might make them over for you, so your funds and wardrobe go farther?"

"*Parfait!*" Celeste proclaimed.

An hour later, they exited the shop with parcels of satin ribbon, Swiss lace, and silk flowers to be used as trim. A day dress and a ballgown each had been fitted and were to be delivered before Saturday, with the promise of more gowns ready to be fitted the week following.

"We must celebrate," Madame Racine said as they settled into the carriage Madame Vermeil had hailed for them. "Gunter's, for sweets? Hatchards, for a new book?"

The latter was most tempting to Celeste. Even she had heard of the famous London bookstore, purveyors to the Prince Regent and the Royal Society of Engineers.

"The British Museum?" Loveday suggested.

Celeste's grin must have been evident, for Madame Racine smiled and called up to the coachman.

And so, in short order, they found themselves in the premiere exhibition of British culture, history, and science.

"The ground floor is reserved for the Library of Printed Books," the elderly docent who escorted them explained as he led them up a sweeping set of stone stairs. "Those generally do not amuse the general public."

"Neither of us would turn down the opportunity to peruse the annals of the Royal Society of Engineers," Loveday murmured to Celeste.

Celeste's attention had been caught by the painting on the

ceiling high above them. In muted golds and rose, Phaeton begged Apollo for an opportunity to drive his chariot. Even then, the young had longed for more technology.

And even then, some warned against it, for the same artist had painted the ceiling of the first room at the top of the stairs to show Phaeton falling from glory.

"An odd message for a museum," Celeste said quietly to Loveday with a nod upward.

Even odder were the next few rooms, through which the docent hurried them. "Manuscripts of various ages, donated by our patrons," he droned, steps crisp. "Nothing of interest to young ladies."

Loveday's face settled into a scowl.

But when he began to rush them through the Saloon and all its mineral glory, she planted her feet in front of the nearest case and refused to be budged.

"Wouldn't you prefer to see the gold and gemstones?" he asked, clearly puzzled.

"Iron holds a greater fascination," Loveday said without taking her gaze off the display above a set of drawers. "Can you tell me why they chose to order these by color rather than chemical composition? It makes it terribly difficult to correlate possible industrial use."

His mouth opened and closed, but no words came out.

Celeste smiled prettily at him. "I am certain a man such as yourself must have many more important duties to attend to besides shepherding us through the museum. We will happily rejoin you at the end of the tour."

"Well, not happily," Loveday muttered as he bowed and took himself off. Celeste couldn't tell if that quick step meant he was relieved or annoyed by her dismissal.

"Nicely done," Madame Racine said, watching him go. "Now we may do as we like."

"My plan exactly," Loveday said.

They spent the next little while touring through the minerals, discussing the use of several in coloring smoke. Their chaperone had seemed just as fascinated by the study, following them around and listening, head cocked, to all of Loveday's points and speculations. They also discovered any number of interesting specimens, from bitumen, which could be used for combustion, to diamond, which could be used for cutting.

"And wearing on one's hand," Madame Racine said, waggling her fingers at Celeste. "Perhaps you can interest Monsieur Thorndyke in a tour of this salon."

Or perhaps Emory would find another lady to wear his ring.

The thought snuck in like a cat after mice. She shoved it away and shut the door on it.

When they had seen all forty-two cases, they moved on to the next room, which housed massive specimens of basalt, granite, and limestone. The room beyond held petrifications of ancient plants and animals, and the ones following it contained stuffed creatures from around the world. Out the final door lay a gallery with sculptures of various lineages.

Loveday stopped and turned in a circle. "But where do they put the inventions? Surely a place of such learning must have considered those."

An older gentleman and lady had been strolling among the stone creations, a docent watching from the far wall. Now the well-dressed couple moved back toward Loveday, Celeste, and Madame Racine.

"Mrs Horton and I were wondering the same thing," the gentleman said with a bow of acknowledgment.

"Indeed," his wife said. "I was given to understand we might see the diagram of His Royal Highness's first invention, the gramatophone, or speaking horn, for improving hearing in the aged. They say he envisioned it after spending time with his dear mother and father. Surely the curators would not hide it away."

The docent must have been listening as well as watching, for he hurried forward. "I regret that we have recently had to lock up the rooms containing technological advances for safe-keeping. Only Monday, we discovered a piece missing—the very diagram you mentioned."

"Stolen?" Loveday whispered to Celeste. "The Prince's own invention? How was that possible?"

Mr Horton shook his head. "Some will stop at nothing to gain an advantage in this war," he told the docent.

A chill went through Celeste. She had been afraid of that very thing. Yet how on earth could a device designed to improve hearing help turn the course of the war?

Their shopping and sightseeing of the day before had bolstered Loveday's spirits—and the fact that she and Celeste had a clear and thoughtful drawing to show their fellow engineers did even more. But when she and Celeste were invited forward to present it at the Thursday committee meeting, her knees still shook, and it was all she could do to keep her voice from shaking as well.

Thank goodness for Emory, whose eyes and smile were steady and encouraging.

When they had presented the idea of using the modified exhaust system to produce colored smoke, and their drawing of the small addition that would dispense the minerals into the pipes had made its way around the table, Loveday braced herself for the debate Emory had warned would follow.

"It seems workable," Mr Guelph said at last. "More so than flags, at any rate."

"And visible over a greater distance," Mr Davy said. "I estimate half a mile at least."

Loveday dared to take a breath.

"It's nonsense," Mr Cummings said abruptly.

So shocked were she and Celeste that Loveday questioned her own hearing. "I beg your pardon, sir?"

"I said it was nonsense." He rose and addressed not the two of them standing at the head of the table, but the other engineers. "I do not blame these young ladies for never having been in the heat of battle. But I have. To be brief, there is nothing but smoke and explosions and blood and chaos on the field. If they will permit me—" He bowed to Loveday and Celeste. "I can surmise with a fair amount of accuracy that it will be the same in the sky. When we add unpredictable winds to the melee of explosions, falling rigging, and ships being blown to bits, any smoke beacon would be swept away in an instant and simply add to the poor visibility for any ships coming in behind."

He seated himself, leaving the room silent and Loveday feeling as though he had slapped her. Such a public set-down was certainly the next closest thing.

"Duly noted," Mr Guelph said, as though this were nothing out of the ordinary. "May we have a show of hands for the proposed revision? All in favor?"

Davy, Guelph, and Thorndyke raised their hands.

Barnes, Babbage, and Cummings did not.

Mr Guelph wrote the results neatly in a book bound in oxblood-red leather and held out his hand for their drawing. It went into the book, never to be seen again, though there were drops of perspiration on it and more than a few tears as proof of how hard they had worked.

"Rejected," Mr Guelph said. "Next? Mr Cummings?"

As expressionless as a pair of automatons, Loveday and Celeste took their seats at the very bottom of the table, just below Emory, whose seniority was only a few days greater than theirs.

"Don't mind them," he whispered as Mr Cummings made his way forward. "I know you'll come up with something even better."

I should not dare, Loveday thought. She didn't belong here. She was merely the smallest of minnows in a school of porpoises and whales. She did not even dare take Celeste's hand and squeeze it in mutual misery, in case Mr Cummings saw the movement and they were sunk even lower in his opinion.

She would not cry. She absolutely would not allow him to affect her spirits. Or at least to know he had done so.

It was not until his suggestion for an electromagnetic pulse that would send enemy ships off course was as roundly rejected as their own had been that she began to come to herself. Especially when she and Celeste were able to vote nay with an unladylike degree of satisfaction. He was as stone-faced as ever when he returned to his seat, but something in his explanation of how the system would work had set up a tingling in her mind despite her vote.

She opened her own small notebook and dipped the quill in the ink set between her and Celeste's places, for evidently they did not yet rate an inkstand each.

Pigeons. Electromagnetism. Flight. The chaos of battle.

"Mr Cummings," she said across the table as Mr Davy walked to the front, "would an electromagnetic pulse be disturbed or thrown off by explosions or winds in the heat of an aerial battle?"

He gazed at her with obvious dislike. "No."

"By the interference of other ships?"

"Yes. To repeat myself, solid objects would be its target." His tone indicated she had been a naughty girl for not listening.

"But if the target were removed—or moved under its own steam—the pulse would continue to its destination?"

"Theoretically. To what do these questions tend, Miss Penhale?"

"Oh, just following a train of thought. Thank you, sir." She turned to give Mr Davy her complete attention.

When the meeting concluded with handshakes all round, Celeste joined her at her bench. "You are up to something. I know that look."

For answer, Loveday opened her notebook. There, she had doodled a pigeon in flight, then below it, a small, square body with a hinge so that messages could be slipped inside.

"A flying snuffbox?" Celeste tilted her head as though that would make it more comprehensible.

Loveday's pencil was busy on the drawing. "A steam boiler no larger than a fist. A circulating tail. Articulated wings so that it might change direction when the pulse is interrupted." She looked up at Celeste, saw that her attention had been caught, and went on. "And here, in place of a head, an electro-magnetic device to find its way to its destination. Each ship in the fleet would have a different—a different—" Goodness, what would it be called?

"Target?" Celeste hazarded. "Address?"

"Address. The pigeon would follow the pulse to its corresponding address and deliver the message."

"A flying messenger." Celeste sat rather suddenly on the stool. "Is it possible?"

"The Prince has made it our job to find out."

"But you know what that means."

Loveday looked over her shoulder at the most unpleasant person she had ever met. He was already at work with his magnets and coils and whatever was going on inside that box with the glass sides.

"I know," she said. "But if Arthur can challenge a French behemoth in the thick of battle, then I can march up to Mr Stephen Cummings and ask for help."

"Now?" Celeste looked dismayed.

"I am not a glutton for punishment," she said. "Tomorrow morning will be soon enough. It will take me all of twenty-four hours to screw my courage to the sticking point."

That evening after dinner she and Celeste were in the small parlor to the right of the foyer. Madame Racine sat in an armchair by the fire, paging through *La Belle Assemblée* and alternately sighing with longing and clicking her tongue in distaste. Celeste was laying out trims for a bodice and trying various colors of ribbon with the Swiss lace, while Loveday was happily engaged in doodling a device in her notebook. The mention of the *automoutons* yesterday and Madame Racine's resignation to the steepness of the stairs in the house had combined to give her an idea. On a side view of the staircase, she sketched a device rather like a tea tray with articulated legs. Activated by a pulley system like the weights in a clock, it climbed the stairs using the wrought-iron spindles of the banister. She pictured it taking messages, small items, and even linens up and down, sparing both Madame Racine and Mrs Heath the trouble.

A knock came upon the street door and in a moment their housekeeper appeared to announce they had callers.

"Viscount St Ives and Sir Emory Thorndyke," she said with

considerable relish. Clearly her estimation of the young ladies she served had just gone up several notches.

Loveday and Celeste curtsied as the gentlemen came in. Arthur looked positively elated at finding them at home.

"I know this is hardly the time of day to pay calls, but still, we are glad to find you at home. I'm pleased to see you looking so well," he said to Loveday, once greetings were concluded and Mrs Heath had bustled off to fetch refreshments. "Emory told me of your trials today at the meeting of the engineers."

She made a face and offered him a chair while Celeste cleared away the trims into a toile-covered box. "It was rather a trial by fire. But its end result was that I had an idea, and unfortunately, it is Mr Cummings' help I must request to see if it is viable."

"You're a brave woman," Emory said. "How can I assist?"

"As a friend, your support is invaluable," Celeste said.

"And as an engineer," Loveday added, "I wonder if you might fabricate a prototype before next Thursday."

"Now you have me intrigued," Emory said with a smile. "What am I making that would take precedence over Mr Barnes's bulletproof sheathing for the hull?"

"A flying snuffbox," Celeste told him.

When both gentlemen laughed as though it were a jest, Loveday realized she would need to be more pointed in her explanations. She brought out her notebook with its oxblood-red cover.

Emory noticed at once. "That is supposed to stay in our workshop," he said. "Our notebooks are specially made and considered to contain state secrets."

Madame Racine's eyebrows rose, but she said nothing, her hands folded in her lap.

"I shall never bring it home again, then. But look." She opened the notebook and showed him the drawing of the pigeon. "Can the two of us fabricate this in time for the next meeting Thursday?"

He took the notebook and studied the page. "The container is the size of a snuffbox?" At Loveday's nod, he said, "Yes, of course. The wings will take longest, especially if you want the articulated joints to work."

Loveday looked him in the eye. "I don't want it merely to work. I want it to fly."

He stared at her. "On Thursday. In the workshop."

"The workshop with the twenty-foot ceilings. On a leading rein, if we must, for it will have no guidance system."

A slow nod, his brain clearly picking up speed like the pistons in the Puffing Jenny at the steam works. "And Cummings?"

"He, too, is smarting from today's failures. Both of us have something to prove in order to reinstate ourselves in the eyes of our peers. Once he sees the pigeon fly, I'll wager that his engineer's mind will not be able to resist the challenge of applying his electromagnetic pulse to it—and the Prince will have his communications system."

"What will you wager?" Arthur said, clearly enjoying the sight of two mechanical minds meshing together. "A slice of cake?" he added as Mrs Heath came in with the laden tray.

"A glass of sherry," Emory suggested, noting the presence of a decanter.

"A—a dance at the ball on Saturday," Loveday said in a burst of inspiration. "If Mr Cummings does not agree, you must dance with me, Emory. And if he does—" What would she wager if he did?

"Then I will," Arthur said.

Loveday felt a tingle run through her at the prospect. While Celeste tugged Emory aside to quiz him about steamboat paddles, she pulled her chair closer to Arthur and helped him to a piece of cake.

"I hope you do not feel I have coerced you," she said, wondering if she would ever learn to curb her tongue before it got her into trouble. Surely by the time a person was twenty she ought to have learned that, at least?

"Certainly not. I came here with no other purpose but to secure the first two dances with you. If one of them is to be the reward of a wager, it makes no difference to me. I shall come out the winner in any case."

How very kind and gallant he was!

"Then you shall have them," she promised. "Thank you."

"But Loveday, are you sure that you and Celeste are in the right place?" The laughter faded from his hazel eyes, leaving them concerned. "I cannot feel right about your being exposed to such censure—especially when you have not even been members for a week."

"In engines, they call it the burning-in process," she said wryly. "I shall either burst my seams and be useless, or come out finely tempered and strong."

"My money is on the second."

"I hope you will not be disappointed. But enough of that. I want to hear all about your investiture. What was it like? What have you been doing since? Have you been to Parliament and been shown to your seat?"

Laughing, he told her, and before long Emory and Celeste

had joined them. They were a merry party over the tea and sherry and cake, so that even Mrs Heath beamed as she came to take the tray away.

"But surely you have engagements this evening and cannot afford to while away your time with us?" Loveday asked when an hour had passed and they made no move to go.

Arthur made a face, and Emory grinned. "His lordship here is hiding."

"Hiding?" Loveday exclaimed. "Why, I expect the invitations are coming so thick and fast they make a positive blur at your door. Whyever should you hide?"

"Three reasons," Arthur said. "One, if I accepted even a fraction of them, my leg would probably re-break itself in the ballroom, causing no end of upset. Two, Emory and I were rash enough to accept an invitation to a ball last evening."

"The new viscount caused such a stir among the females present at the crush that he was responsible for no fewer than fourteen attacks of the vapors... at least, so said the papers this morning," Emory confided in a theatrical whisper to Celeste. "These events had, of course, no relation to the heat in the room."

"Oh dear," Loveday said, unsure whether to laugh or cry at the picture of Arthur dancing with other young ladies. Probably titled heiresses. Pretty ones. "And the third reason?"

"I need the company of friends," Arthur said simply. "I miss Cornwall and Gwynn Place. I even miss my sisters. I am very glad that I do not have to miss you both." But his gaze lifted to Loveday alone. "This little house feels like a safe harbor from the whirlwind of society."

For once in her life, Loveday could not think of a word to

say. So she smiled in appreciation, and something about it seemed to satisfy him.

~

THE NEXT MORNING, Madame Racine deemed it acceptable that her charges should walk the three-quarters of a mile to St James's in Emory's company, since he was the fiancé of one of them. "We will call for a hack when the weather is foul, but cooped up in the palace as you are all day, you must have some exercise. On days such as today, I shall use a carriage myself."

"Are you sightseeing without us?" Celeste teased her. "That is hardly fair, madame, when we must devote nearly every day to our duties."

"Certainly not." Madame Racine raised her chin. "I do have friends here, young lady. I am not so ancient that I may not visit them when I am not obliged to accompany you. I doubt that you will be interested in coming with me."

Politely, Celeste murmured that of course she would be interested.

"Nonsense. No young person wishes to hear about another's youth in case there is a sermon involved. No, I will keep such pleasures to myself, my dears. Now, off with you. You must not be late."

It had not occurred to Loveday that the spirited old lady would have friends anywhere but in her own neighborhood. "How silly of me," she confessed to Emory and Celeste as they walked briskly down the street. "She has been in England for twenty-five years—since the Terror. Of course she must have friends scattered all about the country, many of them titled, no doubt."

The walk took the edge off her nerves, which was fortunate, for they found Mr Cummings already in the workroom and the others not yet arrived.

"No time like the present," she whispered to Celeste as she took off her bonnet.

"*Bonne chance,*" Celeste murmured back.

She approached the man's bench with a straight back and a determination to be pleasant. "Good morning, Mr Cummings."

He did not look at her, all his attention upon a screw he was tightening on the box. "Miss Penhale."

"I wonder if I might ask your assistance with another idea we have had for the communications system."

"I am, as you see, busy."

"But it directly involves your specialty, sir. Other than the archives of the Royal Society of Engineers, you are the only authority whom I may conveniently consult."

"Does it have something to do with the questions you asked yesterday at the meeting?"

"It does, in fact." She opened her notebook and slid it under his arm so that he only had to look down.

"A flying snuffbox," he said flatly. "You mock me. Remove that at once. It is in my way."

"It isn't a flying snuffbox," she said, reining in her indignation as she scooped up the book. "It is a dispatch case on articulated wings, powered by steam and guided by an electromagnetic pulse between air ships."

He completed the last turn of the screw and straightened to face her. "If the Prince ever comes to view our progress, I am going to ask that you be removed from this company," he said, his eyes blazing. "How dare you?"

How dared he, more like!

"The Prince is perfectly aware that Celeste and I built the ship upon which his hope of victory rests," she said with consonants as crisp as ever Celeste's could be. "If you will not cooperate with us, sir, or at the very least discuss the idea, it is not *we* who will be leaving in disgrace."

His face reddened and seemed to swell, and she wondered if he might have an apoplectic fit then and there.

Emory and Celeste drifted into her field of vision, ready to intervene at a moment's notice. She felt their support in the way a beleaguered soldier welcomes reinforcements. But this was her battle, and until she was vanquished, she would not leave the field.

Mr Cummings appeared to control himself with a great effort. "So you are reduced to threats, are you?"

"I was threatened in the first instance," she pointed out simply. "Now, will you please get off your high horse and consider my proposal for just one moment?" She went on even as he took a breath, probably to shout at her. "Yesterday, you said that if the pulse, or signal, were interrupted by a large object, like another air ship, it would still be able to locate its destination once the object removed itself. Celeste and I believe that if a unique target for the pulse were located aboard each air ship, a dispatch box—let us call it a pigeon, for short, because it carries messages—would be able to fly to specific destinations regardless of obstructions. During a battle, for instance. Are we correct in our theorizing, sir?"

He let out the breath in a gust of impatience, but he was listening. That was something.

"You have no training," he got out.

"Only extensive reading of engineering treatises and monographs, as well as histories of physics and mechanics," she said.

"How are you able to theorize in this way?"

Had she caused that much offense? She decided to answer as though he were not being sarcastic. "Needs must where the —er, Old Scratch drives," she said, daring to relax her pugnacious stance. "The Prince desires a communications system. We must provide him one. To be brief—if Celeste and I can build a prototype body, can you put the brain in it and send it to a target?"

She had the distinct feeling he was no longer looking at her, but at some air battle in his mind, and pigeons darting between ships, carrying orders.

"It is not in my remit," he said.

"Perhaps not," she agreed. "The source of the pulse and the target need only be small. And only the target might be built into the ship outside. As an experiment, it is limited in both scope and time."

"And time is what we do not have."

"I agree," she said. "Which is why I will have a working prototype by Thursday. If you can build brain and target, we may demonstrate it at the meeting."

His color began to return to normal. "I cannot promise success."

"I would think you brash if you did."

"But if this works—" His eyes at last met hers, and while there was doubt in them, there was a tiny spark of dawning excitement, too.

"Exactly," she said. "Thank you, sir." She dipped him a curtsey and returned to her bench.

Emory and Celeste met her there, at which point she noticed all the others had arrived and were studiously working, heads down in case objects began to fly.

Emory said in a normal tone, as though nothing had just happened, "I am going to need some sheets of copper, a hammer, some brazing, and a pair of metal shears."

"And I the narrowest gauge piping we can find," Celeste said. "Let us get to work."

CHAPTER 7

"O ur first London ball," Celeste said to Loveday as the hired carriage pulled up in front of the Guelph townhouse Saturday evening. "Who would have imagined?"

Loveday wasn't the only one staring out the window this time. Augustus and Lavinia Guelph had one of the larger houses on the square, set off from the street by a curving carriage drive where dozens of vehicles were taking turns stopping so their passengers could alight. Once more, Celeste could only marvel at the lack of automation. This country needed Emory's steam carriage sooner rather than later.

The other advances were not evident at first when they climbed the colonnaded steps and entered the wide, marble-tiled entry hall. But one of the matrons jerked away from the paneled wall as the footman helped her off with her evening cloak. "That was hot!"

"Steam heating," Loveday murmured to Celeste with a nod to a metal grate fitted into the paneling. "He must have a boiler on the kitchen level."

Celeste felt the warm air coming out of the grate as the

footmen removed their cloaks as well. *"Superbe!"* she told Loveday as they followed the other guests down the corridor. "Perhaps we could interest the owner of our house in installing such."

"Doubtful," Madame Racine said, nose up, as if the air smelled of the coal that had warmed it. "The expense would be too great. Monsieur Guelph's design is nothing more than a curiosity."

"For now," Loveday whispered to Celeste as they approached their host and hostess at the end of the corridor.

"Miss Penhale, Miss Aventure," Mrs Guelph said with a glowing smile. "How lovely that you could join us."

"Allow me to present our chaperone, Madame Racine," Loveday said.

The lady inclined her head. "Thank you for inviting us, Madame Guelph. Your home is lovely."

"Thank you," she said. "Augustus, say your welcome to our guests."

Mr Guelph looked surprised to see yet more people in line. "Yes, welcome, welcome. The more the merrier, I always say. Lady Selwyn, allow me to introduce our newest engineers among the Prince's Own."

Lady Selwyn was of a height with Celeste, her grey curls piled high and her dark eyes snapping with interest and intelligence. They curtsied, and then Mrs Guelph smiled fondly before redirecting her gaze to Loveday and Celeste. "If you tire of dancing, there is a card room just up the stairs. I find those more mathematically inclined favor it. And Augustus has set up one of his smaller telescopes on the uppermost floor. I believe he's pointed it toward Mr. Herschel's new planet."

"Georgium Sidus," Mr Guelph said as proudly as if he'd been the one to locate the planet. "Named after our illustrious king."

"For now," Mrs Guelph said fondly. "Very likely they'll change it to something Roman or Greek. Someone has suggested Uranus, I understand."

"We are hoping for a lady's name this time," Lady Selwyn said. "Artemis or Hera, perhaps."

"That would be only fitting," Loveday agreed.

They moved on to make way for the rest of the guests.

"He is an astronomer, then," Madame Racine mused as they entered the large salon Mrs Guelph was using for her ballroom. Sofas patterned in green and gold had been positioned along walls draped in brilliant yellow silk, while the massive crystal chandeliers above cast glittering light down on the guests.

"Meteorologist," Loveday supplied as they moved deeper into the room, the silk skirts of the dresses that had been delivered that afternoon swishing against parquet. "He is charged with determining the best times to launch air ships across the Channel."

Her dark brows rose. "How impressive. But I thought such men were all in Greenwich, with the navy."

"Emory says he is on loan," Celeste answered, glancing around. After standing in throngs to watch her mother and father ascend, she had no fear of crowds, yet she could not deny the longing inside her for a glimpse of the one face that had become dear to her. Surely, as her supposed betrothed, Emory would be expected to dance attendance upon her. Or at least to dance.

Perhaps she should have cried off by now. She had

promised to do as much when she and Loveday were established among the Prince's Own. But that standing felt rather shaky at the moment, and Emory had not mentioned any inconvenience. Best to let sleeping dogs lie, as the English liked to say.

At least their colleagues were well represented tonight. She spotted Mr Cummings by the refreshment table, studying the punch so fixedly he might have been considering it as a possible replacement for water in a steam engine. Mr Babbage and a sweet-looking lady who must be his wife were already lining up for the first country dance. Mr Davy and a woman who was likely his wife were in discussions with another knot of gentlemen—and she was not enjoying herself, if the bored look on her face was any indication.

And Jacob Barnes was bearing down on them, smile already potent.

"Miss Penhale, Miss Aventure, a pleasure," he said, offering a bow. "You did not tell me you had a sister in town as well."

Madame Racine tittered as she offered him her hand. "I see I must watch you carefully, sir, or you will sweep away my charges with your honeyed words."

"Ah, if only it were that easy," he lamented, bowing over her hand. "But with so many gentlemen in attendance, I must do what I can to be memorable."

There certainly were a large number of gentlemen in attendance. Surely the English attempted to balance the numbers, as they did in France. Yet Mrs Guelph had invited easily twice as many men as women. Or were the ladies waiting to make an entrance?

Celeste glanced to the door to find the last few guests trickling in, Emory among them. Suddenly, the pink satin ribbon felt too tight under her bosom, her gloves too loose on her arms. She fussed, heart starting to beat faster, as he ambled up to them.

It seemed she and Loveday were not the only ones to seek new fashion in London, for his black evening coat was tailored to his lanky frame, and the color of his satin-striped waistcoat matched his eyes.

"Celeste, Loveday," he greeted. "Madame Racine. Barnes."

"Sir Emory," their colleague acknowledged. "Come to steal a march on me?"

Emory held out his arm to Celeste. "Come to ask my fiancée to dance."

He slumped. "Ah, yes. I suppose I tried to forget for a moment." He rallied and turned to Loveday. "But then, what partner can compare to England's flower fair?"

"I believe I am also engaged for this dance, Mr Barnes," Loveday said as Arthur pushed his way through the press to their sides. He too wore what appeared to be the requisite evening black, though his waistcoat was a creamy white with an intricate weave.

Not to be outdone, Mr Barnes turned smoothly to Madame Racine. "Take pity on me, dear lady."

Madame Racine raised her chin. "I do not dance, but you are welcome to sit beside me on the chance that one of these ladies might oblige you for the next set."

He graciously offered her his arm, and they moved toward the seats along the wall.

"One advantage of our engagement," Emory said as he took his place across from Celeste in the line for the country dance, "is that I may dance with you as often as I like."

Celeste fluttered her lashes at him. "While I am inclined to allow other gentlemen a dance or two, in all fairness."

He did not look amused.

She decided not to tease him further. As they finished the first set, she linked her arm with his and led him toward the doorway.

"You want to play cards?" he asked, surprise tinging his voice.

"Non, pas du tout," Celeste promised him. "I want to see this planet named George."

Like a good chaperone, Madame Racine intercepted them before they could leave the salon. "You are not dancing?" she asked, glancing between the two of them.

"I was hoping to look at the stars through the telescope," Celeste explained. "Sir Emory was accompanying me."

She thought Madame Racine might argue, but their chaperone merely nodded. "Then you are in good company. I am not feeling well. Surely other ladies will watch over you. I will ask our hostess for a place to lie down a moment."

Celeste glanced closer. The older lady did look flushed, and perspiration marred her forehead at the edges of her purple turban.

"Chère madame, are you certain you wish to be alone?" Celeste asked. "Perhaps we should leave."

"And deprive you of the chance to see the stars? *Non!"* She shook her head. "I need only a few moments to collect myself. I will find you when I have rested. So, behave."

"Of course," Celeste promised with a smile.

She and Emory headed up the stairs, where a footman pointed them to the second flight into the top floor of the house. Several couples were waiting for a chance to look through the eyepiece of the long brass telescope trained out the window.

Oblivious to the frigid air crawling in, Mr Guelph was keeping an eye on his treasure. He wiped down the eyepiece with a cloth after each guest and adjusted this dial and that level.

"Ah, Miss Aventure, Sir Emory," he said as they stepped forward for their turn. "I thought you'd make your way up here sooner or later. Couldn't wait to catch a peek, eh?"

"A decided attraction, sir," Emory said. He stepped aside to let Celeste go first.

She bent to the eyepiece. In the night sky, stars popped into view, gleaming yellow and blue and red like gemstones scattered on velvet. And there, that faint bluish haze, that was the planet?

"Amazing," she said, straightening. "But you must speak with Loveday. She has made a device that can see even farther."

Their host's brows rose. "Indeed. You can be sure I'll discuss it with her at the first opportunity. In fact—" He glanced around. The other couples had left.

"Keep an eye on it for me, will you?"

Emory didn't have a moment to agree before Mr Guelph barreled out.

"You will want to look," Celeste told Emory in the quiet that followed.

"Why?" Emory asked. "The most beautiful sight of the night is standing right in front of me." He bent closer. Celeste raised her chin and closed her eyes, shivering in anticipation.

"Now, that's a statement I might have to steal."

Emory straightened, and Celeste could have wished Jacob

Barnes to perdition. Leaning against the doorjamb, he grinned at them both, then sighed theatrically. "Ah, young love. Truly a marvel."

It would be a marvel, if it were only true.

"So I am the spoils of war, then?" Arthur took Loveday's gloved hand and turned her as they met in the middle of the two lines of country dancers. "This second dance, if I recall, indicates you have won the wager with Mr Cummings."

"Indeed I have," she told him. "And it was not easy. He has agreed to create both source and target for a prototype."

He peered at her as they cast off and came together farther down the set. "Your skin appears to be intact. And your hair is unsinged—unless that new way of doing it conceals burned ends."

She laughed, and one or two eyebrows rose among the chaperones seated along the wall. "Indeed not. I never think for more than two minutes about my hair, but Celeste is rather more attentive about these things. Do you like it?" Instead of her customary Psyche knot, Celeste had drawn it higher to the crown and created loops of smaller braids. Around Loveday's face, tendrils curled, softening the effect.

"I do," he said simply. "You look lovely, and the gown suits you."

A blush suffused her face, and she was thankful to turn away and cast off into the next figure. When the dance ended, he said, "It is a pity I cannot ask you for a third. There are enough tongues wagging as it is—I dare not subject you to idle talk."

She did not want to see him ask someone else out on the floor, either. Of course she had no claim on him—not she, the tinkerer next door. But as a comrade-in-arms, perhaps she might have a very slender one.

"Arthur, did you notice the heating system Mr Guelph has had installed in the house?"

"I did, after nearly singeing my sleeve. I suppose it interests you, does it?"

"It does indeed. Could I prevail upon you to escort me downstairs so that I may see the boiler?"

Now it was his turn to chuckle. "Only if you explain to Mrs Guelph why we frightened her staff half to death by our unexpected appearance."

They strolled off the ballroom floor and wasted no time in locating the stairs down to the kitchen. Instead of bursting in on the staff, who must be frantic trying to keep up with supplying food upstairs, Arthur stopped a footman and asked him to take them to the boiler.

When he had complied and gone, Loveday took it in.

"Imagine dedicating an entire room to such a thing. But they must, I suppose, with the size of the wheel, to say nothing of the pistons." She stood on tiptoe to read the gauges. "It is operating perfectly. Look, even the pressure is maintaining a constant level. Enviable."

"Thank you, miss," said a voice behind them. They turned to see a man nearer sixty than not, with white hair and a broad smile, and wearing evening attire. "If I am not mistaken, you are Miss Penhale?"

"Goodness," she said in surprise. "I am indeed. How did you know?"

"I read the newspapers, miss, and Mr Guelph has spoken

well of you. Described you to a turn, he did. Besides, what other young lady in a ballgown would be down here?"

"Only one other," Arthur said with a smile. "Miss Aventure is upstairs with the telescope."

The ruddy face creased upward with good humor. "I am John Malvern."

"Arthur Trevelyan." Arthur offered his hand, and the poor man hesitated, clearly recognizing the name.

"Your lordship." He took the proffered hand and shook it. "Now, may I ask what you are doing in my boiler room besides examining the gauges?"

"We came to see how it operated," Loveday said. "I assume those pipes up there along the ceiling take the heated air all over the house?"

"They do, miss. All except the fourth floor. But we discovered after our first winter that the servants' rooms were warmer because of the general warmth of the entire building."

"Does it not cost a fortune?" Arthur asked.

"We have dispensed with fires in each room, sir, and redirected all our coal here," Mr Malvern said. "Fires are not needed, except when I must repair something and perforce cool the system down. But that has only happened twice. We built her well to start with—modeled after a steamboat's boiler, don't you know."

"Are you an engineer, sir?" Loveday asked. For clearly he must be.

"Aye, I was a friend of Mr Guelph's father, rest his soul. I was upstairs avoiding the widows when the footman told me Betsy had visitors." Again that twinkling smile.

"Who maintains, er, Betsy, sir?" Then Loveday added, "The footmen?"

"Close," he said. "Since the maids do not have to lay fires or sweep hearths, I have trained them to keep an eye on these gauges and feed the monster when she needs it."

"Have you indeed, sir," Loveday exclaimed. "You might make an engineer out of one of them yet."

"I hope so. We need more women like you, miss, if you don't mind my saying so. And now I will take myself back upstairs. If you have any other questions, you will find me in the cardroom."

"Thank you, sir," Arthur said. When he had gone, he turned to Loveday. "We should go, too, before we are discovered."

"I think we are sufficiently chaperoned by the staff," she said dryly. "There is no door to this room. And besides—"

I thought you would not come, said a hollow voice, seemingly suspended in the air.

Both Loveday and Arthur froze, peering into the dark corners of the room, then Loveday went around behind the boiler. There was no one there. Not even a mouse. The slate floor, from what she could see, was spotless.

We must be quick. What do you have for me? Another voice, nearly indistinguishable from the first.

Loveday stared at Arthur, then looked up to where a pipe vanished into the ceiling. What room was positioned there? Goodness, surely they were not about to eavesdrop on an assignation?

She darted out the door, Arthur close on her heels. When they were up the stairs and once more in the corridor leading to the ballroom, she paused to catch her breath.

"What a strange phenomenon," Arthur said. "It is almost as

though the pipe conducted the voices. I am glad we did not stay longer."

"I shudder to think what we might have been subjected to," Loveday agreed. "And now I ought to locate Madame Racine. She told me she was not well, and by now will have recovered, or will wish to go home. Either way, I should like to reassure myself that she is looked after."

"Of course you do." He took her hand and bowed over it. "We will see you before Thursday, I hope? I confess I would like a demonstration of your flying snuffbox. At least, that is what Emory calls it."

She must not enjoy the strength of his hand too much. Yet, when he released it she felt the loss. "We will be working long hours. Yet Wednesdays are sacred to society's demands. Perhaps we might see you and Emory for dinner?"

"I would like that above all things." His smile was brief. "And now I suppose I must return to the ballroom and do my duty."

"Your injury seems to be healing well. I did not notice so much as a hitch, even in the turns."

"I am good for perhaps two after this, but no more. Perhaps I will emulate the estimable Mr Malvern and hide in the cardroom." He bowed, then straightened his shoulders and returned to the dancing.

Loveday turned away feeling rather satisfied that she hadn't had to suggest the cardroom and thus look like a dog in the manger. Really, she must point her mind to more productive things than Arthur's dance partners. Such as how the pipe downstairs had conducted sound as well as heat. Why, it was rather like the gramatophone the Prince had invented. And if the boiler was situated approximately there… she saw the pattern of pipes in her mind... then it would follow that the one she sought would surface approximately here...

Oh dear—the assignation.

The door to her destination was closed, and Loveday did not dare disturb the occupants if—if—well, she would just step away. Curiosity was all very well, but some questions did not need to be answered.

But it was high time that she located Madame Racine. She found Mrs Guelph in the refreshment room, pressing cake and ices upon Lady Selwyn.

"There you are, dear," she said. "Is the viscount with you? Are you enjoying the dancing?"

"Very much. And no, he has returned to the ballroom. Excuse me, Lady Selwyn, but... Mrs Guelph, how is Madame Racine?"

The lady paused in her arrangement of petits fours upon a plate. "Madame Racine? Is something amiss?"

"Yes, she said she was going to find you and ask if she might lie down. She was feeling unwell. Can you direct me to her?"

"My goodness, I feel terribly remiss if that is the case." The smile had fallen from Mrs Guelph's generous mouth. "I have not spoken to her since you all arrived. Oh dear, the poor lady. Well, come with me. I know exactly where I would go if I needed a moment's respite. Pardon me, your ladyship. I will return in a moment."

In the morning room, they found a cluster of gentlemen arguing about horses, and in what was clearly Mr Guelph's study they found the couple's eldest daughter, reading. After chivvying her chick back into the ballroom and locating a partner for her, she was Loveday's once again.

"One more place before we go upstairs. Though I doubt dear madame would venture up. The stairs are rather steep." She headed straight for the door that Loveday had not the courage to open.

"Mrs Guelph, I do not think—"

The lady breezed through. Loveday hung back in case an exclamation of embarrassment were to come. When none did, she ventured into the room.

It was a library, smelling of leather and beeswax and the bouquet of flowers on the reading table. Discreetly let into the wainscoting was a grate, signifying that Loveday's mental picture of the pipe's destination had been accurate. A sofa faced a hearth filled with a cleverly cut paper fan three feet high, and upon the sofa cushions lay Madame Racine.

"Here is our quarry," Mrs Guelph said in a low tone, pleased at her ability to run a guest to earth.

"Mmph—*Quoi? Que est-ce c'est?*" Madame Racine stirred and sat up. "Loveday, child? I'm so sorry—did I miss the Prince?"

"No, madame. He has not made an appearance." She had been fairly certain he would not. "We were worried about you. Are you feeling better?"

"Yes. Yes, I am. Are you ready to go?"

Loveday had no desire to return to the dancing, but Celeste and Emory could not still be looking at the telescope. She must steel herself to go back into the ballroom. She would not look at the other dancers, lest she see some young Lady Snootyboots dancing with Arthur. "I will find Celeste."

"If you must go so soon," Mrs Guelph said, "allow me to send for a carriage."

She bustled out, and Loveday perched on one of the chairs. "Have you been here the whole time, madame?"

Her chaperone gave her an odd look. "We came together, child."

She shook her head. "No, I meant in here. In the library."

"What an odd question. I was in the retiring room for some time, cooling my face with a cloth. Does that satisfy you?"

Loveday realized she had overstepped. "I beg your pardon, madame. Celeste and I will see you in a few minutes."

As she reluctantly made her way into the crush in the ballroom, she realized that one of the voices sounding so hollowly in the pipe might have been Madame Racine's. It had been slightly accented, though the other had not.

But that could not be. They had awakened her out of a sleep deep enough to leave her confused upon opening her eyes. There had only been ten minutes between Arthur's leaving and Mrs Guelph locating her.

How very strange. No, Loveday must have mistaken the layout of the pipes after all. She had better keep her wits about her, lest their demonstration on Thursday show errors even greater.

CELESTE HUMMED to herself as she spread marmalade on her toast. A lovely evening, and once they had returned from church later this morning, a sure-to-be-prosperous day. How very satisfying.

Madame Racine had ordered a tray in her room, but Loveday had *The Times* spread open beside her on the table, one hand idly stirring sugar into her tea. "You seem in a good mood," she commented.

Celeste smiled. "And why should I not? We were much in demand last night."

"Even if you are thought to be betrothed," Loveday reminded her.

The falseness of it nearly made breakfast unpalatable. But no, she would not think of that now.

"And you are thought to be edging in that direction," Celeste countered. "Two dances, my, my."

Loveday made a face, but in the cool morning light Celeste could see the spots of color burning on her cheekbones. "There are moments I wonder if the feelings between Arthur and me are as fictitious as your engagement. I do not know how he managed to extricate himself from the morass of expectations in that room."

Celeste set down her toast. "Arthur admires you. It is obvious. And I think you admire him. Your families would be, how do you say, beyond the moon if you were to make a match."

"Over the moon, yes. So I've been told." Her frown gathered as she scanned down the page.

Perhaps they both needed to think of something else.

"What do you see of interest?" Celeste asked, retrieving her toast and taking a bite. Ah, but Mrs Heath was talented with preserves. It was as if Celeste had sipped a succulent orange.

"Surprisingly little," Loveday said, then her frown grew. "But wait—what's this?" She bent over the tiny print. "Princess Caroline and her retinue may be relocating inland from Brighton."

"*Quelle horreur,*" Celeste drawled before taking another

bite. The Princess of Wales clearly did not concern herself with the opinions of lesser beings about her *affaire de coeur* with her Italian count. Not even the opinions of her royal husband.

"It is not her relocation, but the reason that should concern us," Loveday said. She lifted her gaze to meet Celeste's. "French air ships have been spotted off the coast."

Celeste nearly spit her mouthful across the table. She swallowed hastily. "Then La Croix must have grown bolder."

"Or Napoleon more determined," Loveday said, lowering the paper. "We may be thankful they have not attempted to land as yet."

"And we may be hopeful that the Prince's Own will discover something to stop them," Celeste added.

Quickly. For time was clearly running out.

Emory was the first to arrive Monday morning at the St James's workshop. He hung up his greatcoat on the rack by the door, then went straight to Celeste's workbench. Anyone else glancing at her sketches of possible uniforms for aeronauts would have found them fanciful, but he saw the function under the form. Goggles to protect the eyes from wind. A belt with loops for tools. A shorter wool jacket with pockets for compass and Loveday's far-scope. All very practical.

But the greater space on the bench was taken up with the piping in the process of being run into his tiny steam engine for the pigeon. The firebox was so small it would not last long, but he supposed it would not have to cover much more than a mile before it was restoked.

The thought of the flying snuffbox made him smile as he arranged the spray of hellebore carefully, so the dew from their dusky red blossoms wouldn't stain her plans. It had cost him his last pence for the week to purchase the winter roses from the flower seller this morning, but the cost would be worth it if they brought a smile to her lips.

Lips he might have tasted last night if it hadn't been for Jacob Barnes's interference.

He wiped the scowl from his face. This false engagement gave him every excuse to show Celeste how he felt about her. He would not waste it with might-have-beens, but focus instead on what might yet be.

"Sir Emory," Cummings acknowledged, stopping to remove his own greatcoat.

"Cummings," Emory said with a nod as he headed toward his workbench.

The older man came to join him. "Very good work on that new piston design. I had not thought to set the valves in that arrangement."

"Always something new to try," Emory said.

Cummings stood for a moment, head cocked, as if he could not decide what to say further. Then he straightened. "Forgive my impertinence, but it is clear you are a man going somewhere. The Prince obviously has the utmost confidence in you to offer you this post. I have no doubt someday there will be a baronetcy, perhaps even a title associated with your work."

How his father would preen. "That is for His Royal Highness to decide. Knowing my work makes a difference in the lives of others is sufficient reward for me."

Cummings shook his head. "And humble as well. You must know you could do better than Miss Aventure."

Emory stiffened, his chin pulling in as he straightened with affront.

Cummings immediately held up his hand. "No, hear me

out. I speak only from concern for your future. I can see the attraction in those dark curls and sweet smiles. I will allow that Miss Penhale has some original ideas, but it is equally clear that our young French colleague is here because of her connection to you. Yet, instead of showing gratitude, already she appears to be switching her allegiance to Barnes. In short, she seeks to advance herself through whatever means necessary."

Emory's hands fisted at his sides, and it was all he could do not to seize Cummings by his precisely tied cravat and shove him out the nearest window. "I will not have this conversation with you. If you had any understanding of her character, her intellect, her accomplishments, you would be warning her that *she* was the one who could do better than to marry a jumped-up country tinkerer like me. Attend to your work, sirrah, and leave me to mine."

Cummings inclined his head and made a show of strolling to his own workbench.

Emory drew in a breath and forced his fingers to relax. He had work to do, on the bulletproof hull, on the tiny boiler, and on his future with Celeste. He would not allow Cummings's bile to dim his hopes.

By Tuesday morning the prototype pigeon was almost ready to fly. To Loveday, it was a thing of beauty, though someone like Madame Racine might be forgiven for mistaking it for a species of beetle. Well, to her mind, there was a reason that scarabs had lasted so long in the ancient imagination. Rather than flapping its wings like an actual pigeon, Emory had built its wings to be shorter and more powerful, so that they made a buzzing sound with their rapid movement. The dispatch compartment was below, and spanning the two parts at the stern was a tiny boiler with the innovation contributed by Celeste.

"I was inspired by the steamboat paddles," she confided to Loveday as she incorporated it into the stern of the little device. "They turn, but instead of pushing through water, they push through the air."

"If this works," Loveday murmured, "we may suggest it at the rear of the ship outside. Such a thing could almost replace the forward sails. We ought to pose the question to our mathematician, Mr Babbage."

There was one piece left. With a glance at Celeste and a tilt of her head, she indicated they were ready for Mr Cummings's contribution. Carefully, Loveday carried the pigeon, which was about the length of her forearm, over to his workbench.

"We are ready for the brain, sir," she said with a smile.

"That presupposes it is likewise ready," he said.

Loveday's stomach turned over. "We had agreed the prototype would be working by Thursday," she said. "Do you need more time?"

He actually huffed a laugh. "Do not be so literal. I meant your presupposition was correct." He reached into a metal crate next to the bench and drew out a—well, Loveday hardly knew what she was looking at. He seemed rather pleased at her astonished silence. "This is the brain. The target I have affixed under the bench, here."

"But Mr Cummings, this is far too large for the purpose." She felt almost ill. "You have seen the proportions of the prototype as we worked on it. Why, if you affixed this to the pigeon, it would dive into the sea upon launch from sheer weight."

"It would not, if the wings were strong enough."

"Such wings would also mean more weight," Loveday said. "We do not build an albatross, sir, but a pigeon, with a rapid wingbeat and greater maneuverability during an air battle."

"You underestimate it," he said stiffly. "Here, tie the thing on and let us see if it will at least move in the right direction."

Unwillingly, Loveday allowed him to tie the apparatus on top of their lovely sleek device, completely ruining its aerodynamic outline. Emory ignited the boiler. Cummings tinkered with the guidance pulse. Finally, they walked to one end of the room and with a flourish of his hand, Cummings indicated Loveday should launch it.

How very generous of him!

When the wings' pitch and speed indicated it was at full steam—a gauge, they must remember a gauge on the next iteration—she tossed it in the air. Celeste muffled a shriek of excitement as it lifted, hesitated, then seemed to wobble in the direction of the target. Three feet, four... and then it turned belly-up and nose-dived to the floor, landing with a crash on poor Mr Davy's workbench.

"Oh no!" Before the still-beating wings could chew up his papers, Loveday dashed over and seized it. "You see? I told you it was too heavy!"

"Indeed," came a thoughtful voice from behind them. "And how exactly would you improve it?"

With a gasp, Loveday whirled, the pigeon still struggling to free itself from her grip.

The Prince had, at last, arrived. Dressed in a simple coat of blue superfine, with a white shirt and simply tied cravat, he beamed at them all, his blue eyes twinkling behind his spectacles.

Everyone in the room bowed low, and Celeste curtsied to the floor.

The blessed engine was still burning! With a yelp, Loveday dropped it and the impact, at last, stilled the device.

Finally she was able to curtsey, too, and pick up the poor pigeon at the same time. "Your Royal Highness."

"Well met, my own engineers," he said pleasantly. "I apologize for not coming before now. You were saying, Miss Penhale? About the weight?"

Mr Cummings could not contain himself. "This young lady, sir, is mistaken in her calculations. To effectively support the important work of the brain, the flying body ought to be larger."

"And how much space do you think we have for a flock of these in each ship?" the Prince inquired. "No, I think she has the right of it. One can fit more pigeons than albatrosses in a cage. Pray continue, Miss Penhale."

Loveday thought she might suffocate on her own breath. But this was why she and Celeste had been included. Why they had won the Prince's prize. She must not give way to the vapors now.

"To begin, the brain's brass cover may be eliminated and only the works incorporated into the body," she said, focusing on the problem now that the surprise of his arrival had dissipated. "That will remove half the weight. To balance its presence in the bow, the propelling apparatus at the stern may be slightly larger, but only slightly, and made of the lightest material we can find, as Celeste has shown here." She picked it up and handed it to the Prince.

"We heard that French air ships were spotted off the coast, sir," Celeste said. "Surely, we must move ahead with all speed."

"I agree with you, Miss Aventure." He nodded to them. "Mr Guelph, will you favor me with your company on a tour of our prototype? You may show me your progress and estimate its completion date."

The two men went out, and Loveday sagged against Mr Davy's bench.

"Well done," he murmured as he tapped his papers into order.

Mr Cummings shot her a poisonous look as he returned to his workbench.

"Do not give the brain back just yet," Celeste whispered. "I want a look at it. It almost worked, you know. If it had not turned turtle, I believe it would have flown true. He has something here."

By the time the Prince and Mr Guelph returned, Celeste had filled two pages of her oxblood-red notebook with thoughts and speculations, and Loveday had sketched a revised body for the pigeon.

But the Prince had one more surprise for the day. After conferring with Mr Guelph, he returned to Loveday and Celeste's work area with a roll of plans.

"These are the latest drawings by Mr Guelph," he said. "I want the two of you to review them. Granted, you are moving quickly here, but I believe improvements may still be made along the lines of what you suggested for your flying dispatch box. Weight, aerodynamics, that kind of thing. We have no time to lose, and better you fix the improvements on paper than once we have built the fleet."

"And how do they progress in Portsmouth, sir?" Emory asked.

"The hulls are ready to be built out, once Mr Barnes's protective layer is on," the Prince replied.

Mr Barnes looked ready to faint at this unanticipated attention.

"Decking and piping will be next, the moment our colleagues here have reviewed the plans and new ones are drawn. The corsets have been constructed separately. Then all that remains for all six will be envelopes and rigging. I am of a mind to bring my engineers down to Portsmouth for the final fitting-out. There is no room for error. Even though my shipwrights are talented men, we cannot take chances."

Mr Guelph bowed. "We are, as always, at your disposal, sir."

"I am glad to hear it," the Prince said. "Sorry to have missed your do the other night, Guelph. This ruckus at the coast demanded my attention, I am afraid."

Loveday translated: The Princess of Wales having to move house demanded his purse be opened, and right smartly, too.

"Think nothing of it, sir. There will be other opportunities."

The Tinkering Prince left them, then, clearly wishing to stay, but already two courtiers had popped their heads in the door looking for him.

To Loveday's astonishment, when she rose from her farewell curtsey, she found Mr Cummings behind her.

"I will adjust the size of the apparatus to fit the present body, as His Royal Highness suggests," he said stiffly.

I suggested it, you potted wilkie! But while he may have read it in her face, Loveday closed her lips on the words. "And I will reform the body to accommodate it," she said instead. "If Celeste and I do that today, will you be ready for the demonstration Thursday?"

"I will. Allow me." Without fanfare, he untied the apparatus from the pigeon, turned, and went back to his own bench with it.

Loveday and Celeste exchanged raised eyebrows at his shift in behavior. Then again, when a prince of the royal blood told you to buck up and get on with it, only a fool would stand upon ceremony—or pride.

ON THURSDAY, after having dined with Loveday, Celeste, and Arthur the previous evening, when Emory brought the little boiler up to pressure, and the wings began to buzz, thank *le bon Dieu*, Celeste could feel the anticipation around the meeting table. Loveday tossed the pigeon toward the high ceiling of the workroom with both hands.

It sank—recovered—wobbled—

And then flew like an arrow to the bench of Mr Cummings, where its target address was concealed under the top, to emulate the hull of a ship.

"Hurrah!" Mr Barnes shouted, throwing his notebook into the air.

Celeste grabbed Loveday's hands, jumping up and down and barely managing not to shriek in triumph.

Emory had leaped to his feet and opened his arms, as if he would hug them both. Propriety rose in his face in the form of

Mr Guelph, who clapped him on the shoulder. "Well done, all!" the latter cried.

While Celeste recovered from almost having hugged Emory in public, Loveday dashed to Mr Cummings's bench. "Well done, indeed, sir! You have solved it!"

"I believe we all four solved it." His face actually relaxed into a smile. "Now we must build a flock of them. Say, four per ship?"

"That is a good number to begin," Celeste said, disinclined to contradict him when he looked almost happy. The aeronauts would tell them soon enough how many they would need.

As it was, she could barely concentrate for the rest of the day. It was so tempting to tinker with the pigeon, to make improvements to it now that they knew its basic function worked. But they must remember the Prince's charge to review the plans for the fleet's ships, including the prototype that waited in the courtyard outside.

Time and speed were of the essence. But so was care.

They were still poring over the plans on Friday, so Loveday brought them home to compare to their previous work. Madame Racine tutted about Celeste and Loveday's squirreling themselves away in the butler's pantry-turned-workshop on Saturday morning, and Mrs Heath sent them increasingly disapproving glances every time she passed along the corridor.

It was early afternoon when Celeste glanced up to find the white-haired housekeeper in the doorway. "A gentleman is here to see you," she announced, gaze lingering on the plans spread out on the top of the articulated sideboard.

Celeste straightened. "Sir Emory Thorndyke?" Oh, could

she sound any more breathless? Even though she had been working near him all week, it seemed she could not get enough of him. That almost-hug of jubilation seemed to have set her all aflutter.

Mrs Heath shook her head, dousing her hopes. "A Mr Barnes. Madame Racine would like you to join her in the withdrawing room."

"Bother," Loveday muttered with another longing look at the plans.

Celeste shrugged. "He is pleasant company, and perhaps he has something of interest to tell us. We will be fresher after a moment of distraction, in any event."

Loveday slipped the plans into the top drawer. The articulated sideboard appeared to think they had done enough today as well, for it began stacking itself against the wall. The plans' location was now less obvious, in the bottommost drawer. Celeste could not help but smile. Truly, one could almost think it was alive, so sensitive were its internal movements and pulleys.

Jacob rose as Celeste and Loveday came into the withdrawing room a few moments later. He looked like a man about town today, with a fitted navy coat boasting shiny silver buttons and buff-colored trousers tucked into gleaming boots.

"Ladies!" he enthused, sketching a bow. "What a welcome sight on this dreary day."

Celeste was not so sure they were all that welcoming. Both she and Loveday had donned dresses they had brought with them from Hale House. Hers was a chambray donated by Gwen with a hem beginning to show signs of fraying. Loveday's was a pretty wool with the obligatory grease spot on one cuff. She turned that cuff into her lap as she sat beside Celeste on the sofa. Jacob resumed his seat on the chair next to Madame Racine's.

Their chaperone at least looked like the prosperous lady she was, gowned in grey lustring with a white ruff framing her elfin face.

"Monsieur Barnes has proposed an outing," she explained. "I knew you would wish to thank him."

"Very kind of you," Loveday said. "But we had thought to stay in today. As you know, the Prince has charged us—"

Another gentleman might have acquiesced, but Jacob's grin only grew. "Ah, but you haven't heard where I plan to take you. I've obtained permission from the curators at the Royal College of Surgeons for us to be given a tour of Dr John Hunter's Museum."

The name meant nothing to Celeste, but Loveday immediately perked up. "The collection of the anatomist? But I thought only physicians and surgeons were allowed."

Jacob winked at her. "Physicians, surgeons, natural philosophers… and engineers. Who better than the Prince's Own?"

Loveday was on her feet. "I'll fetch our pelisses."

Madame Racine rose more slowly. "You and Celeste will change. I will ask Mrs Heath to have our pelisses ready. You can wait a quarter hour, Monsieur Barnes?"

Jacob rose and bowed again. "I would wait an eternity for a moment with you and your charges, madame."

"This museum is exciting?" Celeste murmured to Loveday, who was climbing the stairs at a surprisingly fast clip. "More exciting than adding to the improvements we have already listed on the plans?"

"It is held to be the finest collection of anatomical speci-mens in the world," Loveday told her. "I cannot believe Mr Barnes found a way to allow us to be admitted."

"He has the charm, that one," Celeste said with a shrug.

She still wasn't sure what all the fuss was about, but she was quite willing to escape the house for a little while. Their review of the air ship plans, while coming along, had been making her head swim. Accordingly, a little more than a quarter hour later—but not by much—they all climbed into Jacob's coach and headed for Lincoln's Inn Fields. That their colleague could afford his own carriage, and the horses and coachman it required, spoke of how high he'd climbed in the world.

Once again, an elderly curator met them at the doors. Oh, but these English attempted to guard their treasures, like a dragon hoarding gold. She did not remember being escorted in the Louvre, but then, she was the daughter of *La Blanchard*. Perhaps the curators there had reasoned she would not possibly steal from them when they could find her at a moment's notice.

This museum was as open as the British Museum had been closed. The long hall to which the curator led them was easily three stories tall, with a glass roof that let in the light. A wide aisle ran down the center, and smaller aisles edged the walls. In between were glass-topped cases and pedestals holding the most amazing collection of animal and human life. More bottles were arranged on shelves along walkways that stood out from the second and third floors. Celeste put her hand to her bonnet and looked up and up.

"Nearly fourteen thousand preparations," Jacob said exultantly. "From the simplest forms of life like a shrimp up to man himself, embalmed or preserved in spirits for all to see."

Ah, so that was the odd scent to the air, musty and cloying.

"Indeed," said the curator, who had introduced himself as Dr Monk. "It seems you have visited us before, Mr Barnes."

"A few times," Jacob said with humility. "I find it fascinating, so of course I had to introduce my colleagues as well."

Dr Monk glanced down at the paper he held in his gloved hand. "A Mr Penhale and a Mr Aventure, I believe." He looked up to frown at the ladies as if suspecting they had come in without their husbands or brothers.

"Miss Penhale and Miss Aventure," Jacob corrected him, "the winners of the Prince's prize in engineering and the newest members of the Prince's Own."

Dr Monk's craggy eyebrows rose, then he swept them a bow. "Miss Penhale, Miss Aventure, a great honor. Allow me to acquaint you with our little collection."

It was hardly little. As they wandered up the center aisle, he pointed out the skeletons of a rhinoceros from Egypt and ostriches from the southernmost colonies. The massive air sac hanging overhead belonged to a giant beaked squid brought back from Captain Cook's voyages in the Pacific.

"A shame we could not use that for our gas bag," Celeste murmured to Loveday, who nodded. "The horizontal shape is efficient in the water. I wonder if it would be as efficient in the air, like my little propelling device?"

"And what is this?" Madame Racine asked, stopping before a collection of bones nearly as tall as they were.

"We believe it is a creature that lived many centuries ago, before the Flood," Dr Monk said. "You will not find its like today."

With jaws like that, edged with razor-sharp teeth, Celeste was just as glad.

Jacob sidled closer to her. "What do you think, Celeste?"

She kept her gaze on the skeleton of a massive horse standing next to that of a tiny pony. "I think you are too bold, sir. I do not recall giving you permission to use my first name."

He put a hand to his embroidered waistcoat, where presumably his heart lay beneath. "Ah, and here I had hoped for a reward for my efforts. Only smile on me again, and it will be enough."

Celeste shook her head, but she couldn't help a smile.

Jacob's grin popped back into view.

Another curator had come in with a group on tour, so Dr Monk led them up to the second floor and along the walkway. Bottles filled with pale yellow liquid gleamed in the rays from the skylight.

"These specimens are ordered, as you see, according to their purpose," he said. "Feet and the like for locomotion, eyes and stalks for sensing surroundings."

Madame Racine took one look at the embalmed paw of a monkey and fainted clean away.

It took some minutes to revive her, with both docents running back and forth with bottles of spirits that were nearly as effective as smelling salts, while the other tour wandered rudderless below. And then she insisted on a moment to herself to restore her equilibrium.

"What a very accommodating chaperone," Jacob said, offering Celeste his arm. "Shall we see what trouble we can get up to on our own?"

"*Non,*" Celeste said, moving closer to Loveday instead. "I

must discuss these preparations with Loveday. *Excusez-moi.*" She seized her friend's hand and led her back down the stairs to the main hall.

Loveday raised a brow, but she remained at Celeste's side until the tour had ended, they had been conveyed home, and Jacob had left them at last.

CHAPTER 9

"ood heavens, Emory, look here, at the society column. I never thought to see familiar names there." Arthur folded *The Times* and slid it across the breakfast table in his and Emory's modest but comfortable lodgings near St James's. It was Sunday, and the prospect of a quiet day after services was welcome indeed. He had never suspected that debate in Parliament could be at once exhilarating and exhausting.

Emory swallowed his mouthful of sausage with a gulp and addressed his attention to the society page.

This writer has been agog with impatience to see if the rumors were true—that the famed lady aeronauts who have so captured the attention of our beloved Tinkering Prince have actually arrived in Town. Our readers may be assured that the news is quite true, and reports of their beauty and grace have not been exaggerated. Of their intelligence and ability, which are beyond this writer's obser-vations, readers will have to wait for further demonstration.

Indeed, we are happy to report that Miss Loveday Penhale of

Hale House, Cornwall, and Miss Celeste Aventure, a guest at Hale House, have taken up the honor bestowed upon them and have commenced their duties with the Prince's Own Engineers. This column has reported on the gentlemen making up this elite group, including the recently elevated Sir Emory Thorndyke. The young ladies were spotted alighting from a carriage at St James's Palace, whereupon several observations were eagerly noted. Miss Penhale is of a slender yet regal carriage, her trimmed bonnet hiding tresses the color of wheat at harvest, if one may be so bold as to allude to her country upbringing. She is the daughter of a gentleman, and is quite the tinkerer, but of her no more is known except that His Royal Highness holds her in the highest regard. Miss Aventure is small and slight, with quick movements, and her fashionable jockey's cap concealed dark curls of great abandon. But then, she must be forgiven her fashion-forward ways—it is rumored she is French and escaped that country alone in a balloon to avoid marriage with one of Napoleon's lackeys. The young bucks of the ton will be devastated to learn that she is affianced to the aforesaid Sir Emory Thorndyke, a gentleman of Truro in Cornwall.

This publication looks forward with interest to Miss Penhale's proving herself as adept in the ballroom as she is in the royal work-room. One would hope that a young lady of such fair aspect would not mar her prospects by proving herself to be that saddest of creatures—a bluestocking.

Emory tossed the folded paper back so that it slid neatly under the rim of Arthur's plate. "Did you have to sully my brain with that nonsense?" he complained. "Bluestocking, my foot. I hope Madame Racine does not take *The Times*. Our friends deserve better."

Arthur could only agree. The nerve of a newspaper

making remarks about those two young women! Why, they had done as much to preserve the freedom Englishmen took for granted as Wellington or any of the toffs in the House ever had.

He took up the paper again, flipped the society pages aside with a satisfying slap, and turned instead to actual news.

"Emory, listen to this."

"Not more society claptrap?" His friend looked pained.

"No, indeed. But this is interesting."

Theft at Hunter's Museum

It is with moral outrage and sorrow that this publication must report that Dr John Hunter's Museum, one of the intellectual lights of this City, has been robbed.

Yesterday afternoon it was discovered that several specimens of incalculable value to researchers and historians had been removed from their cases. It is not known how the miscreants might have secreted these specimens about their persons, only that it is likely the specimens will be desecrated by being sold.

The College of Surgeons begs the reading public to use all their powers of observation when they are out upon the town, and report to them any sight of the objects. The specimens include the skeletal wing of an ancient lizard of a size that could fit in the hand, a jar of poisonous mushrooms from the Colonies, and an infant Pacific squid preserved intact in alcohol, the much larger version of which hangs from the ceiling in the main exhibit hall.

When the thieves are apprehended, the museum curators vow they will suffer the greatest penalty allowed by the law.

Arthur finished reading aloud and lowered the paper to

regard Emory once more. "I feel sorry for the fool who removed those mushrooms and squid. The point is, weren't Loveday and Celeste there just yesterday?"

"They were," Emory said, clearly uncertain whether this was good or bad. "Yesterday afternoon, in fact, according to Mrs Heath's information. I called to ask if Celeste would like to walk in Hyde Park and was informed Mr Barnes had already taken them out in his carriage."

Emory spat the final word as though it were a bit of eggshell in his breakfast.

"Not a friend of Mr Barnes, then?" Arthur did his best to iron the smile out of his tone.

"Not at all." In Emory's eyes, normally so calm and observant, jealousy battled with apprehension. "But I find it deeply disturbing that these thefts may have occurred while our friends were right there in the museum."

"It is disturbing," Arthur agreed. "Do you think they might have seen something?"

"I hardly know. But I find one fact even more disturbing, Arthur. According to the gossip among the other engineers, Mr Barnes had a very humble start in life. Born on the south bank beyond the pale of good society."

"You can hardly fault a man for that," Arthur pointed out.

"Nor would I. But what disturbs me is that for a time he made his living as a thief."

Arthur sat back in his chair as though Emory had pushed him.

"And this man is elevated to the Prince's Own Engineers?" he asked in disbelief. "Permitted to call upon our friends?"

Emory reported what he knew of the man's history, and concluded, "I am the last to blame someone for their humble beginnings. Not when my own grandfather was a tin miner. But I cannot help but draw a line between the presence in the museum of a reformed thief, and the disappearance of these valuable artifacts."

And any connection with Mr Barnes, should he be the guilty party, would taint Loveday and Celeste forever in the eyes of society. "Is he punting on the River Tick?"

"And driving our friends about in a carriage?" Emory countered.

"The two do not contradict themselves here, at least," Arthur said dryly. "Why, half the young bucks at the Guelph ball the other night were drowning in said river, and yet they arrive in a carriage with a set of matched greys, sporting the very latest in bespoke pantaloons from Bond Street, and proceed to gamble away a month's allowance in the card-room. I should die of heart failure from stress were I to try such a thing—to say nothing of what my father would do once he got wind of it. As it is, this stay in London will strain my pocketbook to the breaking point. I hope my time here does not last long."

"You cannot mean that you would go home, leaving Loveday and Celeste here?"

At least Arthur had managed to distract his friend from the unhappy subject of Jacob Barnes.

"For even were I not employed at St James's until we win the war," Emory went on, "I do not think I could desert them."

No, Arthur did not mean that. Not at all.

"Nor could I," he confessed. "I should seek an additional assignment from the War Office in that case. But would Loveday miss me if I did go?"

"You know she would. At least *you* are not deceiving all of society with a false engagement."

"I suspect there are degrees of falsity." Arthur eyed his friend. "I think the veneer is very thin, on your side, at least."

Emory shook his head. "There are moments when I believe wholeheartedly that her affections are real. One warm glance from those eyes, and I am lost." He sighed and mopped up his cooling eggs with his toast. "Unfortunately, I am not alone."

They were back to Jacob Barnes again.

"You must rise above your dislike of him and put your trust in Celeste," Arthur advised his friend, though he was in no position to be dispensing advice of *that* particular kind. "Easier said than done, I know, but she is too precious a jewel to be marred by anyone's thinking she could be so easily taken in by another man's blandishments."

"I know you are right. And I take some comfort in the fact that she has yet to call off this so-called engagement."

Arthur folded up the paper and sent it to join its fellows in the box next to the fire. "Now, let us talk of happier things, such as those objects upon the mantel. Do my eyes deceive me, or are we the unworthy recipients of vouchers to Almack's?"

Emory groaned. "Have mercy. I was on the point of forgetting the odious things were there. I had much rather receive a squid in a jar, thank you very much."

EMORY HAD JUST DELIVERED Loveday and Celeste to their door in Mayfair on Monday evening and was still saying his farewells in the foyer, when a knock sounded—a knock much more imperious than any the front door had likely received in some time.

"Could that be Arthur?" Celeste wondered aloud as she handed her pelisse and bonnet to Maisie.

"Never mind, Maisie," Loveday said. "I will answer it."

Upon the step stood a footman in livery so elaborate it positively creaked as he bowed. "Am I addressing Miss Loveday Penhale?"

"You are," she said, wondering what on earth this apparition portended.

"Allow me to give you these." He proffered an envelope. "They are vouchers to Almack's, beginning this Wednesday, with Lady Jersey's compliments."

He bowed and was conveyed away in a carriage, leaving Loveday and Celeste standing in the open doorway, stunned to speechlessness.

Maisie closed the door, and Emory gently drew them into the sitting room, where Madame Racine was at the window watching the carriage depart. Loveday opened the envelope with shaking fingers and there they were—their entrée to that most hallowed of halls.

Ladies' Voucher
ALMACK'S

Deliver to
Miss Loveday Penhale and chaperone
Tickets for the Balls
On the Wednesdays in November and December 1819

The other voucher bore Celeste's name and the same dates. She took the card, thick and creamy, with reverence and whispered, "I think I am about to faint."

"Pray do not, for my knees are too weak to bend and help you." Loveday looked up from her unbelieving study of the card. "Oh, how Gwendolyn would weep to know I hold this in my hand!"

"I am on the point of weeping, myself." Celeste clutched her arm. "Today is Monday. This is for Wednesday. Good heavens, Loveday, only two days to prepare ourselves!"

Emory laughed. "And here I was thinking I had two more days of precious obscurity. For Arthur and I have received vouchers also."

"Have you indeed?" Loveday felt such a wash of relief and happiness that tears actually sprang to her eyes. She blinked them back, hoping her friends had not seen. "I shall not be quite so terrified, then, if I know the two of you will be there."

Arthur had said that they would take on the terrors of Town together. How good it was to know that he would be able to keep his promise even at Almack's, where the lady patronesses held absolute sway and where one's success or failure in Society could be determined merely by a smile or a frown.

On Tuesday, Loveday could barely concentrate on the list of improvements to the air ship plans, but at last it was done and submitted to Mr Guelph. Madame Racine had exchanged the vouchers for tickets, so Loveday could not doubt the things were real, even if they seemed entirely surreal.

The next day, she confided to Celeste, "I am sorry now that I spoke with such disdain of Wednesdays being taken up with obligations to Society instead of our obligations to the

Prince. Now the very minutes seem to be whisking by when we need every one of them."

"Thank the merciful heavens that Madame Vermeil completed our order and delivered them in—how do you say? The cut of time?"

Loveday laughed. "The nick of time. And I agree whole-heartedly, or we should be making our bows in chambray work dresses!"

Madame Racine, her maid Honore, and even Mrs Heath were dragooned into helping to sew and pin the trimmings Celeste had chosen on their ballgowns.

"How lovely you are," Madame Racine said when the winter sun was sinking behind the buildings and all had been completed. They took turns before the cheval glass in her bedroom. "That sea-green silk is perfect for your coloring, Celeste, and the single peacock feather in your hair sets it off well."

"*Merci, madame,*" Celeste said, looking pleased. "I am glad that as an engaged woman, I may choose colors other than white or pastel."

"But I will say that this pale blue of an August sky suits our Loveday very well," Madame Racine went on. "I particularly like what you have done with the lace on the bodice. Her neck and shoulders rise out of it as though it were clouds, and the pearl beads in her hair add to the effect."

Goodness. Such compliments from Madame Racine, who vouchsafed a favorable word much more grudgingly under normal circumstances. But then, these circumstances were far from normal, weren't they?

A shame they had only a hack to carry them to their desti-nation, but they arrived precisely as they ought, and then it was time to mount the stairs and present their tickets at the door. Loveday felt quite certain everyone present could see her skirts trembling from the force of her shaking legs. And here were two of the lady patronesses, seated like queens receiving the adulation of their subjects.

Saint Piran, help us!

She and Celeste sank into curtsies as deep as though they were being presented to Queen Charlotte herself. Behind her, she heard Madame Racine's stays creak as she did the same.

"Very pretty, for engineers," Lady Castlereagh said. "Do you not agree, Sally?"

"Indeed. Rise, ladies, and let us have a look at you."

Loveday did not dare glance up to see Lady Jersey's expression. Instead, she clasped her gloved hands together and out of the corner of her eye, spotted Arthur in the doorway.

Unbidden, a smile came to her lips, and her shoulders relaxed.

"Not a spot of grease to be seen," Lady Jersey remarked. "His Royal Highness speaks very highly of you, Miss Penhale, Miss Aventure."

"His Royal Highness is kindness itself," Loveday managed. "We are most grateful to him."

"And he thinks these girls will help England win the war?" Lady Castlereagh said, as though pretty dresses and youth would negate all their accomplishments.

"So he has indicated, your ladyship," Celeste said.

"Never trust the French!" came an acid whisper from someone in the back of the room. Arthur looked around sharply, as though he might spot the speaker from where he stood.

"Indeed," Lady Jersey drawled. "Perhaps even in the ball-room the French tendency to shocking behavior—to say nothing of an invasion—may be seen."

Oh no. Oh, surely not. Surely they had not been invited just to receive a crushing rejection and be shown the door? Loveday could bear the loss of the good opinion of anyone in this room, but to be so disgraced in front of Arthur was unbearable. And here was Emory, joining him in the doorway, looking as though he would spring to their rescue given the slightest encouragement.

She could hear Celeste's breath scraping in her throat.

"Miss Aventure," Lady Jersey said, raising her voice to quell the rushing wind of whispers. "I have heard rumors of a most scandalous dance performed in the French court. One in which men and women may touch more than their hands. Perhaps you and Miss Penhale would be so good as to proceed into the ballroom, and you may demonstrate it for us?"

DEMONSTRATE? Here? From the first time she'd attended a dance in England, at the Midsummer Ball in Cornwall, Celeste had wondered how the English preferred their dances. Now she knew—traditional, carefully choreographed, and well separated. She wasn't sure they were ready for the waltz.

She dropped her gaze in the full knowledge that, while they might have been accepted by the lady patronesses—barely—it came at a price. "I would not dare to presume, your ladyship."

As she dared to glance up, she saw Lady Jersey wave an elegant hand. "Fah! I have asked you to dance. There is no presumption, only acquiescence."

Abject obedience, more likely. Every eye in the room was on them, every gaze expectant—disdainful—avid. Madame Racine wiggled her fingers as if urging Celeste to agree. Lady Castlereagh narrowed her eyes, clearly hoping for scandal. Celeste wanted to sink through the polished floor.

But she was her mother's daughter. If *La Blanchard* could rally herself before Napoleon, surely Celeste could rally before this petty titled tyrant.

"But of course," she said. "Would your musicians know a song with a three-quarters meter?"

Lady Jersey trained her sharp gaze up to the quartet's alcove above the door. The violinist promptly began a song, and the others took up the music.

Jacob Barnes—what was he doing here?—stepped forward and bowed. "Allow me the honor of being your partner, Mademoiselle Aventure."

Not much of an honor if they could still be banished from polite society once people saw for themselves what the *scandalous dance* really was. But she would not snub Emory.

"*Merci*, Monsieur Barnes," she said before turning to her *faux* fiancé. "But of course it must be my future husband, Sir Emory."

She was asking him to risk his social standing as well, but the sweet man never hesitated. As they had in Paris, he set one hand on her waist and clasped her other hand in his. Someone gasped.

She ignored them. With a nod, she took a step, and Emory

fell into the pattern with her. Side, back, turn; side, back, turn, until they were gliding about the floor.

A thump sounded over the music before the cry of, "She's fainted!"

Celeste flinched.

"Do not give them the satisfaction of looking," Emory murmured. "You and I are dancing. That is all anyone needs to know."

"Do you know how dear you are to me?" Celeste murmured back.

"No," he said. "But feel free to tell me after we've survived this torture."

Celeste laughed as they glided into another turn. She felt as though she were flying, safe in Emory's arms.

And suddenly, they were not alone in the middle of the floor. Loveday and Arthur moved past, the latter with a nod of approval to Emory. A moment more, and the diminutive Countess Lieven was gliding past on the arm of a young war hero, who looked as if he were ready to conquer the enemy's dance as he had the Emperor's soldiers. Others ventured out as well, until at least a dozen couples were spinning about the room, skirts belling and tailcoats swaying.

Finally, the music stopped, and Emory released Celeste to bow to her. The other gentlemen followed suit. Celeste realized they had ended the waltz within speaking distance of Lady Jersey, who was watching her, those dark eyes not missing so much as the flicker of an eyelash. That smile could only be called satisfied.

Celeste curtsied. "And that, your ladyship, is how you dance the waltz."

Lady Jersey eyed her a moment more, then she put her

gloved hands together and applauded. Stunned, her syco-phants hurriedly joined in, until the room sounded as though a flock of pigeons had been startled into the sky.

Celeste met Loveday's gaze and grinned. Their star was indeed rising.

~

EMORY STOOD at Celeste's side as various ladies and gentlemen requested to make themselves known to her and Loveday. Her poise, her confidence, her intelligence! She was amazing, but he had concluded that long ago. From the start, having her beside him made his spirits lift higher than the marvelous air ship she and Loveday had invented.

But she'd claimed she found him equally dear. Was he such a coxcomb that he could not wait to hear more?

The supper room was opened with great fanfare, and he escorted Celeste inside and steered her to a table in the corner. Arthur—he would never become accustomed to calling him Lord St Ives—followed with Loveday, and Barnes brought Madame Racine.

"You are all to be congratulated," the émigré said with a smile after they had been seated. "You have acquitted your-selves very well in such august company."

Countess Lieven inclined her dark head in their direction as she sailed past with her Army captain.

Celeste giggled. "Who would have thought the waltz would be so popular here?"

Emory would have wagered it hadn't been the waltz. It had been her joy in the moment that had drawn all gazes to her.

"Who would have thought *we* would be so popular here?"

Loveday countered, returning the smile of a lady and gentleman who were passing. "For a moment, I was convinced we would be shown the door, with a future of nothing but snubs until the end of the war."

"Your popularity is not only here, in these rooms, which I heard someone say were *more difficult to get into than heaven itself,*" Arthur put in. "I stopped by the War Office yesterday, and one of the captains asked me about you two. It seems he'd like you to help me interview the soldiers they are considering to pilot the new air ships."

"Soldiers?" Celeste asked with a wrinkle of her nose. "What do they know of air currents and the like? You would do better to consider sailors and those trained in navigation."

"At the very least, if it must be soldiers, then let it be those with some experience with the steam behemoths," Loveday added.

"I'll be glad to help as well," Barnes put in, leaning over the table. "I can bring our two esteemed colleagues to the War Office in my carriage."

Ah yes, the carriage. It irritated Emory to be reminded of it. He had brought some funds with him from Truro, but he'd nearly exhausted them on food and lodging before his first stipend arrived from the Crown. Even now, he must count his pennies to get by until the next quarter, what with the expense of living in the capital.

The fact was, Jacob Barnes was entirely too accommodating. He acted as if he were intent on courting one or both of the ladies. What was the fellow doing? Celeste was supposed to be betrothed to Emory, and it was clear that Arthur was bellows to mend over Loveday.

As Loveday, Arthur, Barnes, and Madame Racine debated

timing and the servers began circulating with the food, Celeste leaned closer to Emory.

"Having Mr Barnes take us to the War Office troubles you?" she murmured.

She could not tell he adored her, yet she sensed his growing frustration with their colleague. "Forgive me. It is merely that he seems too friendly."

She cocked her head, her gaze on his so intently it was as if she wanted to see inside him. "You cannot be jealous. You know how I admire you. And I am engaged to you."

Not really. Or at least, not yet. But it was clear that if he wanted this pretend engagement to become real, he must find a way to act, before someone else stole a march on him.

Barnes was certainly trying. He told one entertaining story after another as they partook of the thin slices of ham, stewed oysters, roasted eel, and other delicacies offered, until Celeste's gossamer giggle sounded. Oh, to earn another such smile from her as she'd given him during the waltz! Emory wracked his brain, but nothing witty or amusing came out.

As they rose to return to the main assembly room, Barnes hurried around the table to put himself in Emory's path.

"A moment, if you please, Sir Emory," he said. "I could use a few pointers on the waltz, in case the Countess decides to issue another challenge."

Celeste dimpled at them both before following Loveday back into the other room.

"Hold your partner lightly, and follow her lead," Emory told him. "That's all you need to know."

Barnes shook his head, threatening those oh-so-artfully arranged curls. "There seems to be more to it than that, old chap, but very well. While we have a moment, I thought it only fair to tell you that I have tumbled to your secret."

Emory frowned at him. "What secret would that be?"

Barnes leaned closer and lowered his voice. "You and Miss Aventure are not truly engaged. If you were, you wouldn't allow a miscreant like me anywhere near her. Why the lie?"

His heart was sounding in his ears. "I have no idea how you formed that opinion, sir, but I assure you that I hold Celeste Aventure in the highest esteem."

"Who would not?" Barnes agreed, straightening. "But it is clear that you are not willing to take your esteem to its logical conclusion."

"Logic and love, I find, have yet to become acquainted," Emory told him.

"On the contrary," Barnes insisted. "Logic points us to the perfect candidate, someone who is our equal in many ways and our better in others. Miss Aventure is a rare find. If you cannot screw your courage to the sticking point, don't be surprised when others show interest."

With a mocking bow, he turned for the assembly room.

Leaving Emory standing alone.

CHAPTER 10

The War Office wasted no time in canvassing the ranks of both army and navy for men willing to do what had never been done before—serve king and country in the air. In fact, it was testament to the emergency session of Parliament that orders had gone out with such dispatch. As soon as crews were chosen, they would go down to Portsmouth and then to Cornwall for actual training in the air.

"For it soon became clear," Arthur said as they bowled toward Millbank in his hired carriage, not Jacob's after all, "that the flight of the Princess of Wales has frightened more of those old men in Parliament than any of them are willing to admit. At least they show it in their support for the Prince's proposals—including funding for our air ships. They begin with six, and the Prince plans six more."

"From Parliament's lips to our workshop's ears," Loveday quipped. "Once Celeste and I suggested improvements to the design, suddenly we were tripping over extra men on hand to carry them out."

"And they are coming for the prototype on Tuesday," Celeste said. "It will go down to Portsmouth, where the shipyards are waiting to rig it and fill the balloon."

"It is such a pity you could not fly it there yourselves, my dears." Madame Racine was seated facing forward next to Arthur, as was only proper. "Imagine the sensation the unexpected ascent would cause as you rose above the roofs of St James's!"

Loveday laughed, but it was tinged just a little with regret. "We tried," she said. "But Arthur said the War Office was firm. With a crew to rig and fill her, and provide the example for the other ships, the work would go days faster in Portsmouth than even the Prince's Own could do, working from dawn until dusk in London."

Celeste squeezed her gloved hand. "Arthur did prevail in one respect—we are allowed to assist him in his choices today."

"They would be fools not to allow it," Arthur said with the brevity of a man who knows his facts. "Their first test will be to see how the candidates respond to questions posed to them by female aeronauts."

Loveday nodded. "I am looking forward to that part. For if they cannot bear to be questioned by a woman, how will they manage to take orders from one?"

The War Office was housed in a discreet Georgian building in a dignified neighborhood near Lambeth Pier. Arthur was recognized at once and waved through the gates by the guards, and they were ushered upstairs. Through the large windows, Loveday could see the parade ground to the rear, with a company of new recruits going through maneuvers.

On either side of the wide corridor, nearly a hundred chairs had been arranged in two aisles, turning it into a waiting room. Every seat was filled. Some of the men wore their uniforms; some might have been invalided out at the beginning of the war and were now willing to try their hand at flight. Some wore no uniform at all. And there, to Loveday's astonishment, to one side were seated two women.

"I wish to see them first," she whispered to Arthur.

"As do I," he whispered back.

In the spacious office through the door, she, Celeste, and Madame Racine were introduced to Commander Sir William Edwards. They curtsied, and Arthur explained, "Sir William is above my chief in the Walsingham Office, ladies. He will be observing us today and giving final approval of our choices."

"Observing, and doing my best not to interfere, more like, Cap—er, my lord. Bless me, it seems strange to call you that."

"It is equally strange to me, sir," Arthur said with a smile. "Please call me Captain. No need to confuse the issue for the men outside. They will be confused enough when they are drilled like schoolboys by our aeronauts here."

"I am quite looking forward to that," the commander confided.

"Then with your permission, sir, we shall begin. Ensign, please show the ladies in."

They were slightly older than Loveday and Celeste, and the moment they stepped over the threshold, Sir William blurted, "Bless my soul, Diana, Emily. What are you doing here? Do your mothers know?"

The taller of the two crossed the room and kissed him on the cheek. "They think we are shopping. But what will clothes signify if we are invaded? We wish to be aeronauts, Grandfather. When Uncle Henry said the call had gone out, I made up my mind then and there, and Emily agreed."

Her companion nodded.

"You are to go home at once!" Sir William ordered.

"I beg your pardon, Commander, but Celeste and I would like to speak with her and her companion," Loveday said.

"Absolutely not! Aeronauts? Ridiculous."

"We are aeronauts, sir, and, far from being ridiculous, we have the respect and support of the Prince Regent himself," Celeste said. "If these young women are capable, why should they not have the same opportunity as we?"

"Because I forbid it!"

The taller young woman, well dressed and stocky of person, turned to Loveday and Celeste, clearly perceiving they were allies. "My name is Diana Edwards—my late father was the commander's only son. I am twenty-five and have not a marriage prospect in sight. From the time I was a girl, I have studied every treatise on the subject of flight published since the Montgolfier brothers took up the first balloon. I am proficient in mathematics and physics, having read all my father's books from Cambridge, and can tell the difference between a cirrus cloud and a cumulus." She nudged the woman next to her.

"I am Diana's cousin Emily Stratham," the other said. Her clothes were past the pink of fashion, but well made and well kept. "My mother is the commander's daughter. Diana and I grew up together. I too have studied the treatises on flight and have attended every lecture that Mr Babbage and Mr Davy have given. While I cannot drive four in hand like she can, I can sail a boat in choppy weather and bring her into harbor safely." She glanced at Diana, then said simply, "We want to fly, like you."

Loveday gazed at them, nodding slowly. Except for the driving four in hand, their qualifications were nearly identical to her own. "I believe you would be good candidates for training. If Lord St Ives agrees, we will put you on the list, provided you can talk your grandfather round."

Celeste added, "For we would not want you to disobey him and risk a rupture in the family. I know to my sorrow that our service to our country should be a matter of pride, not contention."

"Leave Sir William to me," Arthur murmured. Then, more loudly, he said, "Thank you, ladies. Please write your names and direction using the materials on the desk there. Ensign, send in the next man."

While the commander fumed, his granddaughters kissed him and departed. The first male candidate was rejected out of hand when, upon seeing the females in the room, he remarked, "Are we in the War Office or Almack's?" Only one candidate in every few men bowed politely to Loveday and Celeste after they were introduced by Arthur. Most ignored them, even when they were asked direct questions. Those who replied to Arthur instead of Loveday or Celeste were politely dismissed.

Several of the sailors had heard their names before and were happy to discover that they were to be questioned by the young lady aeronauts. The flirtatious ones were ushered out after a glance at the ensign, who was becoming quite adept at reading the expressions of Loveday and Celeste—and if he missed a frown or a raised eyebrow, Arthur did not.

One young man elicited a squeak of surprise from

Madame Racine, who had up until then been sitting quietly behind Sir William. Celeste glanced at her in alarm.

"Madame? Is anything amiss?"

"Of course not, dear. *Merci*. But I am all astonishment. Paul, is it you, so tall, and in uniform, too?"

The young sailor gaped in surprise. "*Tante Louise!* Whatever on earth are you doing here?"

"I am chaperone to these young ladies, your interlocutors. Miss Penhale, Mademoiselle Aventure, may I present Paul Grenville. He is the son of the house to which I fled after the Terror. His family saved my life, made me part of their family, and made it possible for me to find sanctuary in Cornwall."

Loveday shook his hand warmly and found his answers both civil and knowledgeable, especially as they pertained to the weather conditions in the English Channel. It was clear his experience in the navy would benefit any air ship crew. He was added to the list.

"It is good to find someone known to Madame Racine," she said in a low tone to Celeste and Arthur. "If by this we may repay him for his family's services to our friend, then I shall be satisfied."

"Consider it done," Arthur said as the young man bowed himself out.

In all, by the time the sun was caught in the branches of the leafless trees, they had a list of seventeen candidates who, along with those already managed by Lord St Aubyn, were enough to crew six ships.

And that list included the names of the commander's granddaughters.

For over tea at midafternoon, Arthur had confided to the gentleman some of the details of their actions behind enemy lines, which were already known to the Walsingham Office and above from his reports. Celeste told him of Wintzen, Dupont, Amélie, and Josie, all of whom were doing their part to bring the Emperor to his knees despite the fact that they were women.

"Perhaps you are right," Sir William said at last, burying his nose in his teacup. "It's not as if they're becoming governesses, is it?"

"The world is changing, sir, and our Prince is prepared to lead that charge," Loveday said, daring to lay a comforting hand on the gold braid of his wide navy wool cuff. "Your granddaughters may bring themselves to his notice even as you have during your career, on their own merits, for their bravery and commitment to their country."

He grumbled under his breath, and Loveday, sensing victory, said no more.

When they came out into the courtyard, she took a deep breath of cold November air. They had been cooped up in that office all day, and if it had not been so far, she would have been tempted to walk back to Mayfair.

"Come, my friends," Arthur said, indicating one of the carriages waiting for hire. "You have had a hard day's work. I'll see you home."

Another carriage rolled in—a familiar one they had been in only days ago, to go to Dr John Hunter's Museum.

"Why, Mr Barnes," Madame Racine said as he opened the door and jumped down without waiting for the tiger to lower the steps. "Are you come to volunteer for the Aeronautic Corps, too?"

"Indeed not, madame." He bowed over her hand, then inclined his head politely to Arthur. "I somehow missed you all this morning, but I am come to take my fellow engineers home."

"I shall see them safely to Mayfair," Arthur said gravely.

Honestly, the nerve of Jacob Barnes. What was he thinking, to push himself upon them in this way? Loveday saw Madame Racine into the carriage Arthur indicated, and he waited for Loveday to be seated before he swung himself up into the forward-facing seat next to her chaperone.

"Celeste…?"

Jacob Barnes's carriage made a sweeping turn and bowled out of the courtyard before they even had time to realize Celeste was no longer there.

"The nerve of that boy!" Loveday exclaimed. "He has practically abducted her."

"She is an affianced woman," Madame Racine said in soothing tones. "He is no danger to her when her heart belongs to Sir Emory."

"But madame, she has no chaperone," Loveday protested. All that fuss to have one, and a young woman might be plucked off the street with no greater reaction than this? What would Mama say?

"*You* are not engaged. I am needed here," Madame Racine said complacently.

"And if they are not waiting in front of your door by the time we arrive," Arthur said grimly, "young Mr Barnes will find himself eating grass for breakfast in Hyde Park."

"THAT," Celeste said, "was badly done."

Jacob leaned back against the squabs, looking so pleased

with himself she was tempted to give him a good poke with her hat pin to deflate him. "On the contrary, I thought it masterfully done. I have the honor of your company all to myself."

"What honor, when you threaten my reputation by doing so? I would be within my rights to demand that you set me down on the next corner."

"But you won't," he said with a gentle smile. "It's far too long a walk back to Mayfair. And I promise to be a gentleman."

She shook her head. "You are no gentleman. That, I am beginning to believe."

He heaved a theatrical sigh. "Alas, I cannot seem to outrun my past. I'm sure Thorndyke has regaled you with my sorry beginnings."

He had, but Emory was a fair-minded fellow. She felt him fretting over Jacob's attentions, but he had said nothing that might diminish her opinion of her colleague.

"It is known among the Prince's Own that you were a thief once," she allowed, crossing her arms over her chest. "But you have obviously reformed."

"Do thieves ever truly reform?" he asked, head cocked so that his top hat slipped the slightest on his curls. "No, I believe I have moved on from being a master at picking pockets to a novice at stealing hearts."

"You," Celeste said with a roll of her eyes, "are no novice."

His laughter pealed. "You are wasted on Thorndyke." He sobered. "I, on the other hand, am prepared to lavish my attentions on you in the hopes of winning your regard."

"Then you are wasting your time," Celeste told him. "I am in love with Emory Thorndyke and no other."

"How fervent you sound. Yet I have it from him that your engagement is all a sham."

Celeste's heart kicked in protest. "He said that?"

He smiled as if he had heard the astonishment in her voice. "Indeed he did. Oh, I had guessed as much. He is not nearly as solicitous as he should be for one betrothed."

"He is solicitous enough for me," Celeste insisted. "And you are too bold, as usual. I stand by my words. I love Emory Thorndyke. Master thief or novice, you shall not steal my heart. Now, if you would prefer I step out, have your coachman pull aside."

"I may not be as much of a gentleman as you'd like," he said, "but I would never dump you on the curb like yesterday's rubbish. I will see you home. Just know that when I set my sights on something, I do not look away so easily."

Celeste met his gaze. "And know that, once given, my love does not waver."

"All the more reason to wish that love directed my way," he assured her.

CHAPTER 11

One week later

*I*n the airy workroom at St James's, Mr Guelph looked as though he would burst with his news as Loveday and Celeste removed their bonnets and Emory carefully placed his new beaver hat upon his workbench. "Gather round, ladies and gentlemen." He flourished a letter with a crest and seal. "I have news." When they had all taken their places at the meeting table, he cleared his throat.

Sir George Campbell, right honorable Commander-in-Chief of Portsmouth, hereby begs His Royal Highness George Augustus Frederick of the United Kingdom of Great Britain and Ireland and of the British Dominions beyond the Seas, Prince Regent, and the detachment of men and women known as the Prince's Own Engineers to inspect the first vessels and aeronauts in His Majesty's service, hereafter known as the Royal Aeronautic Corps.

The inaugural flights will take place on December 6, 1819, at ten of the clock or as soon thereafter as weather permits, at the Portsmouth shipyards.

Accommodations have been arranged for the Prince's Own Engineers at the George Hotel, which is convenient to Admiralty House.

Loveday was barely able to contain a squeal of excitement—held back only because she had caught Mr Cummings's critical eye.

Emory's breath, however, was coming fast as he asked, "Has His Royal Highness accepted, sir?"

"I have had information that he has, and will, of course, be staying at Admiralty House," Mr Guelph assured them, unable to keep an enormous grin from his face. "May I inform the Commander that all present are able to go?"

Loveday's glance at Celeste confirmed that even had Madame Racine expressly forbidden it, they would have found a way to go, too. Not see their ships ascend? Impossible!

"Will we be permitted to crew the ships ourselves, Mr Guelph?" she asked.

"I expect that you and Miss Aventure will," he allowed. "I would be forced aboard at sword point, myself. I cannot even look down my own stairwell without feeling as though it will throw me into the basement."

"Then I believe we shall be a full complement," Jacob Barnes said. "I for one am going solely to see our lady aeronauts take to the skies."

Loveday absolutely would not acknowledge this bit of flummery.

"We shall have our share of work to do, no doubt," Mr

Cummings said. "Last-minute adjustments to sensitive equipment, gauges, lines, that sort of thing. But we have not much time to prepare—it is already the second of December."

"I propose we abandon our posts and hasten home to pack," said Mr Babbage. "The next time we see one another will be in Portsmouth!"

Loveday could hardly get home fast enough, to the point that she was rude to Jacob when he offered his escort, and even Emory protested the pace she set along the now familiar streets. Once they reached their own door, Madame Racine at once apprehended how important this journey was and began to issue orders. "Sir Emory, if you would be so kind as to go to Fleet Street and buy five places on the stage coach, we may leave from the Bolt-in-Tun Inn and be conveyed directly to Portsmouth. We have then only to decide whether we wish to break our journey in the middle or travel the whole way in one day."

"The whole way," Loveday and Celeste said together.

"I suspected as much," Madame Racine said with a smile. "Honore and Maisie will assist our packing. I suggest one trunk between the two of you. The coach will be crowded."

"Are we to go also, ma'am?" Mrs Heath looked apprehensive. "I cannot say I have ever been outside London, but I am willing if I am needed."

"You are needed here more," Madame Racine said, to the housekeeper's obvious relief. "I do not want the house to appear unoccupied, not when our young ladies are working on papers that may well involve state secrets. You and Maisie will stay, and Honore will attend the three of us. If Sir Emory will escort us, I shall be content indeed."

Sir Emory lost no time in assuring her that he would

countenance no other plan. Loveday wondered if this might have something to do with Jacob, whom she devoutly hoped would find another way to get to Portsmouth. Perhaps the heavens would smile on them, and he would oversleep and miss the coach.

That evening after supper, she was surprised to find Madame Racine in the foyer, pulling on her gloves.

"Madame!" she exclaimed. "Surely you do not mean to go out—why, we have ever so much to do."

"Honore knows what to pack for the two of us," their chaperone informed her. "I am committed to cards at the home of the Chevalier de Chalmy's widow. I should not dream of slighting her by breaking up the tables she has so carefully arranged. By the time I learned of our so unexpected journey, it was too late to send round a note."

"Oh… of course you must go," Loveday said rather lamely. "Enjoy your evening, madame, and we will see you in the morning."

"I forget that madame has friends here and a life in Society that does not include us," Celeste confessed when Loveday told her of this unexpected departure. "I hope that does not make me thoughtless and selfish."

"If you are, then I am, too," Loveday said with a rueful laugh. "I am glad, though, that she is able to see her friends and re-establish old ties. I should do the same if I had to live here and had the chance to return to Cornwall to see everyone."

"Perhaps there is someone here who will tempt you to such a life?" Celeste asked with a wink.

Loveday snapped a petticoat between them, then folded it

carefully into their smallest trunk. "You know there is no such person. The only—" She stopped.

"The only man who is remotely interesting to you is still, thank the saints, a resident of Gwynn Place," Celeste finished.

Loveday felt the heat flood her cheeks. "Am I that transparent?"

"I know it is not the custom for a woman to tell a man that she cares for him," Celeste said slowly, folding one of her new day dresses carefully so that it would not crease. "But in order for a friendship and comradeship to ripen into something more, someone must take action."

"At least you have the advantage of being with Emory with all Society's approval," Loveday said. "Here we are, off to Portsmouth, and goodness knows where Arthur is."

"If I may hazard a prophecy," Celeste said with a smile, "Emory will tell him where and why we are going. Arthur is not a man to let such an opportunity pass."

Loveday could only hope she was right.

The next morning found them at the Bolt-in-Tun coaching inn well before the sun ever thought of rising, and after a journey that was indeed as crowded and uncomfortable as Madame Racine had feared, they reached Portsmouth in the late afternoon. And there in the innyard was a tall form that made Loveday's breath stop in her throat.

"Arthur!" she exclaimed as he lifted her down from the coach. "I mean, my lord, what are you doing here?"

"Strangely enough, I heard about this jaunt of yours before Emory told me of it," he said as Emory lifted down Celeste, and then assisted Madame Racine and Honore. "Commander Sir William Edwards would consider nothing else but that I should accompany him here to see his granddaughters acquit themselves. They have been here a week and have been sending letters every day to apprise him of their progress. And," he said, leaning closer and lowering his voice, "I am here in an official capacity, too. As a sort of secretary to the Commander, and to produce a full report for my own chief at the Walsingham Office. Parliament has been obliged to spare me for a few days."

Loveday remembered what Celeste had said. Someone had to take action. "I am glad." She dared to look into his eyes. "Whatever happens, I am glad we are here together."

"I am, also," he said with a smile. "Our foursome shall not be separated, even by royal command."

He turned as a private coach and four rumbled into the yard and must not have seen her smile congeal on her face. She had meant *we* as in the two of them. And he had heard *we* as in they four. Clearly she had her work cut out for her.

The occupants climbing down out of the coach turned out to be Mr Guelph, Jacob, Mr Davy, and Mr Babbage. And in the flurry of greetings and the necessity of helping Celeste avoid Jacob's attentions, no one suspected that Loveday's spirits had deflated like Celeste's original balloon, sagging into the sea without hope of rescue.

PORTSMOUTH COULD NOT SEEM to make up its mind what it wished to be. In that way, it reminded Celeste a little of Paris. The High Street boasted stone houses as fine as any in London, including the elegant Admiralty House, home of Admiral Campbell, the Commander-in-Chief, Portsmouth. Nearby shops carried any manner of items, some brought in, no doubt, by sailors returning from far-off ports. But soldiers in mismatched common dress roamed the streets and found their way into the grog shops off the back alleys, and sailors ate and drank with abandon, as if glad to be on solid ground again.

His Royal Highness and the obligatory company of guards were staying at Admiralty House. Just the sight of the Royal Carriage trundling through town had been enough to bring the inhabitants out onto the streets to wave flags and cheer, even in the cold, brine-scented air. The Prince's Own and Arthur had been given rooms in the George Hotel (what was it with the British and naming things George?) with its bow windows overlooking the narrow street. Both the innkeeper and the chambermaid had already informed Loveday and Celeste that Admiral Nelson had left the George Hotel on his way to his death at Trafalgar. Celeste merely smiled and nodded. No sense upsetting them with a French accent when it had been French *sous-marins* that had defeated their hero.

It was too late in the afternoon to begin their work, so everyone settled into their rooms or took a turn about the town. Loveday and Celeste had a room that looked out on the dockyards, with Madame Racine just across the corridor. Their chaperone seemed to wish to keep her watchful eye on Loveday and Arthur, for she followed them as they strolled about the hotel, out across Green Row, and onto the Governor's Green beyond. Once again, she appeared comfortable with Celeste and Emory walking together, thinking them happily engaged.

Celeste could imagine herself so as she accepted Emory's arm and took a turn about the green as well. The grassy sward lay just outside the city's brick walls on a flat leading up to the harbor. The golden stone of the Governor's House and the church, Dormus Dei, glowed in the cool November sunlight. At the edge of the lawn, the land dropped to the blue-grey waters of the English Channel, choppy now in a rising breeze. The masts of sailing ships looked like winter-bare trees in a vast forest.

Ever since their waltz at Almack's, Emory had hovered over her like a surveillance balloon on the battlefield. At first, she'd found it endearing—and very helpful for keeping Jacob at bay—but lately, she'd begun to wonder at his purpose.

"Sir Emory is attentive," Madame Racine had mentioned the other night over dinner, as if she'd noticed the change as well.

"He is underfoot on occasion," Loveday agreed from across the table. "And I detect a return to the bossiness he used to display before you arrived in England."

"He told Mr Barnes to mind his own affairs," Celeste explained to Madame Racine, "when all he was doing was asking me why I had settled on silk instead of another material for the envelope. Material properties are his specialty, but, in truth, I did not mind that Emory sent him on his way."

"It must be difficult for Sir Emory to face a challenge for your affections," their chaperone commiserated. "In Cornwall, there are few his equal. In London?" She shrugged.

As if there were men of his stature on every corner.

"He has no reason for concern," Celeste said. "I am his betrothed."

Loveday tilted an eyebrow but said nothing.

"Ah, well," Madame Racine had said. "These English gentlemen like to think they rule—from the corridors of the castle to the halls of industry. You must accustom yourself to it if you wish to be happy as Lady Thorndyke."

She had not found a way as yet.

Emory cleared his throat now, and Celeste glanced up into his face. His cheeks were turning red, but she did not think it entirely due to the wind.

"Is something wrong?" she asked.

"No," he allowed, tucking her arm a little closer. She wore her wool pelisse and he, his multicaped greatcoat, but being closer was nice for other reasons.

"We have had little time for private conversation since that night at Almack's," he continued, "and I have been wanting to ask you about something you said ever since. Now that I have the moment, I cannot think how to phrase the question."

What could she have said to concern him so? "I am always happy to listen to anything you wish to tell me," she said, hoping this would encourage him.

He smiled. "So I've noticed. And you are unique in that ability." His smile faded, and his gaze dropped again to the brittle grass beneath their feet. "You must know that I care for you, Celeste."

Ah. Yes, she had said something of the sort at Almack's. "And I care for you as well."

"Do you?"

She stopped, and he turned to face her fully. Never had she seen such doubt etched on those chiseled features.

"*Oui*, Emory. I do," she told him. "You have been a good friend to me."

"A friend." He bent and picked up a stone, then hurled it hard enough that it plunked into the water foaming below. "Is friendship between us what you hope for your future?"

Her heart *would* start its frantic beating. "What do you hope for *your* future?"

"I have been giving it considerable thought," he admitted. "I am not fond of London. Too large, too noisy, too difficult to think. I believe I will be happier in Truro. Perhaps not managing the mine," he hurried to assure her as if she had said the words aloud, "but with my own workshop, developing devices that could aid the nation in other ways besides winning a war. I can dream of a home, a wife, children. Even a measure of standing in the community."

In other words, domestic bliss. It was the dream of many a gentleman, she was certain. But the way he had said it—home, wife, children—as if they were so many items he must accumulate to count his life well led. Did she wish to be something he checked off a list? And in his mind, was the only role for the wife to tend the house and raise the children? What if she had dreams of her own beyond the domestic sphere?

La Blanchard had never successfully managed motherhood, not in the way a child wanted and deserved. Celeste had always prided herself on being her mother's daughter. Was she truly any different that she could consign herself to so narrow an existence, for him?

"They are goals held by many men," she allowed. "I can see why they appeal to you."

"And do they hold any appeal for you?" he asked, gaze trained out toward the sea, as if he feared to find the answer written on her face.

"I don't know," Celeste said. "But I promise you, I will also give the matter considerable thought."

As if she could do anything else.

CHAPTER 12

The next morning, a brisk tailwind from the east drove them all across the green for the dockyard, skirts and greatcoats plastered against their bodies. The entire compound was enclosed in a stout brick wall, and they must enter through a tall gate, where soldiers came to attention and scowled.

"State your purpose," one barked to Mr Guelph, whom he must have taken for their leader.

Their colleague had supported the navy for a sufficient number of years that he didn't so much as balk. He didn't stop either, though now three air-crank repeater rifles were aimed at his broad chest.

"We are the Prince's Own Engineers and Lord St Ives of the War Office," he declared with a wave of his meaty hand. "We are expected. Stand aside."

The rifles wavered, then fell, and the guards moved back from the gate to allow them to enter.

"I sincerely hope they recognize us in the future," Loveday

murmured to Celeste. "I do not want to face *that* every morning."

"And I do not wish to face this walk," Celeste murmured back as they passed a massive pond where long logs lay floating, waiting to become seasoned enough to serve as a mast on one of His Majesty's ships. "Perhaps we can construct new velocipedes."

Loveday grinned. "Can you imagine their faces?"

The walk took them past long stone storehouses and tall brick offices. The scents of tar and freshly cut wood hung in the air. Jacob attempted to walk next to Celeste, but Emory cut him off. She took her fiancé's arm to make her position crystal clear.

"A large complex," Emory ventured. "I cannot wait to see how they have improved the steam works to accommodate the air ships."

In truth, neither could Celeste, until she spotted steam from one of the smaller buildings off to the side. Disappointment was as bad as a pinched shoe.

"Is that it?" she asked Emory.

"No, that's the kiln." He nodded toward a larger building—new, by the white of the stone. "This is the steam works—you are more familiar with its appearance from above, no doubt, when we flew over it in August."

Mr Guelph pulled open the brick-red door, and the welcoming sound of machinery chugging drifted out with a cloud of steam.

Celeste and Loveday followed the other engineers into the cavernous building. Multipaned windows high on the second story sent down feeble light on monstrous engines being constructed for the steamships. Some were apparently being tested, for pistons were chugging, and steam hovered in the air. Steel gantries holding pulleys and winches crisscrossed the space. Workbenches lined the walls, with tools in easy reach. The dozen or so men working all looked up as the Prince's Own came to a stop.

His Royal Highness trotted forward. An older gentleman paced him, his gut leading, thick white hair waving back from a face with the jowls of a bulldog.

"Admiral Sir George Campbell," the Prince said, "allow me to introduce my own engineers. You know Mr Guelph."

Admiral Campbell inclined his head. "Sir."

"And you will have heard of Mr Humphry Davy."

The Admiral beamed. "Laughing gas. Jolly good fun."

Mr Davy's smile seemed riveted to his handsome face. "It was intended for an anesthetic, sir. For medical purposes."

"Yes, yes," the Prince said, his attention already moving on. "I sent you Babbage's paper, Georgie. Here's the man himself."

"Cabbage?" the Admiral asked, a frown forming.

"*Babbage*, sir," the mathematician said, looking every bit as pained as Mr Davy. "The clockwork sextant?"

"Ah, yes," the Admiral acknowledged. "Very clever, though I'm still unsure how useful it will be with all those gears."

"Sir Emory Thorndyke," His Royal Highness continued, undaunted. "Invented the pump that's clearing seawater out of the Cornish mines."

"I'd like a word with you about bilge pumps," the Admiral told him, and Emory bowed, expressionless. Celeste hid a smile.

"And of course, Mr Jacob Barnes," the Prince said, "renowned for his discovery of the magnetic properties of ceria, and Mr Stephen Cummings, who is exploring the potential of electromagnetism."

Both gentlemen bowed as the Admiral acknowledged them.

"And I see Mr Barnes and Mr Cummings brought their ladies," he said before the Prince could introduce Loveday and Celeste. "You may stay for the tour, my dears, but I will have my men escort you out immediately afterward. It isn't safe for you here."

His Royal Highness cleared his throat. "No, no, Georgie. Miss Aventure is affianced to Sir Emory, but they are here under their own steam." His blue eyes twinkled behind his spectacles. "I say, that's rather good. In any case, Miss Penhale, Miss Aventure, allow me to introduce Admiral Sir George Campbell. Georgie, Miss Penhale and Miss Aventure are the winners of my prize for engineering and the inventors of that air ship your men have been studying—the progenitor of my fleet."

As the Admiral's frown returned, the Prince waved toward the far end of the room. There, surrounded by workers, stood *Lark Deux*, the ship in which they had sailed to France and back. She'd been stripped of her gas bags and propped up in wooden ways, as if her captors had been determined to keep her from the skies. Lines and rigging straggled down like forlorn locks of hair, and the helm lay on the ground beside her.

"Oh, Loveday," Celeste murmured. "What have they done?"

❀

LOVEDAY FELT RATHER as she had at the age of ten, diving for the first time off the rocks below Hale Head and neglecting to account for trajectory and aerodynamics. While Jory shouted a warning, a second too late, she hit the water in a belly flop. It had taught her a great many lessons about physics and had felt rather like this—a blow, followed by a persistent tingle of pain.

Arthur glanced at her, his brows crinkling into a frown. To spare him concern, she bore up under the blow, as she had done that sunny August day, swimming to the surface to assure Jory she was unharmed.

"Admiral," she said, "do you anticipate that *Lark Deux* will again serve His Royal Highness and fly?"

"Too slow, and too fragile, I'm afraid," he said. "She was a fine beginning—the two of you did well. But with the improvements the Prince's Own have made to the ships we're building here, she won't give them much competition now."

"Miss Aventure and Miss Penhale were responsible for many of those improvements, Georgie," the Prince said, walking on. "At my request." Their group followed him like so many sheep after their shepherd.

"Remarkable," the Admiral said. "The flying snuffboxes were an inspired touch. Even useful. We've been testing 'em between ships."

"We call them *pigeons*," Celeste managed, clearly as irritated at the *even useful* as Loveday herself. "Because they return to their source."

"What will you do with *Lark Deux*, since she is not able to fly with the rest of the fleet?" Loveday persisted, forced to walk behind the Prince Regent and the Admiral as protocol demanded even in here, but speaking to his left shoulder.

"Hasn't been decided," the Admiral said. "We might scrap her—use her for parts, don't you know. Or auction her off. The veterans' widows' fund is always looking for things like that. She'd cause quite a stir if we got her rigged up again."

Scrap her! Auction her off! The ship that might have turned the tide of the war?

"Or you might return her to us," Loveday said clearly, even as the navy man, who had moved on from the subject, raised an arm to point something out to the Prince. "She might be unsuitable now for military purposes, but when air ships become commonly used by the general public, she will be a fine demonstration of their capabilities."

The Admiral laughed. The Prince merely looked thoughtful.

The newly minted Viscount St Ives said, "Miss Penhale, as is her wont, is looking to the future. I see from that stack of barrels over there that you have accepted Sir Emory's and my gift of the lifting gas for these initial tests."

"Indeed, my lord," the Admiral said. "Dashed fine of you, since our only other source of supply would be old Boney himself!" He laughed again, as if this were a fine joke on the Emperor.

"My point exactly, sir," Arthur went on with respectful yet relentless logic. "It is our view that travel by air is not so far off. And Cornwall is well placed, both with regard to natural resources and in the talent—may I say genius—in her sons and daughters."

"Well said, St Ives," the Prince told him, clapping Arthur on the back.

Loveday was still not used to hearing Arthur called St Ives.

But the more it happened, the better it seemed to suit him, as though he was growing into it.

"I'm afraid the widows will have to make do with sea chests and trinkets at their next fund raiser, Georgie," the Prince told him. "*Lark Deux* must go back to Cornwall to act as a bellwether. She will signal that the times are changing."

The terrible pressure on Loveday's chest, rather like not being able to breathe underwater, began to ease. She dropped back to walk beside Arthur.

"Thank you," she said in a low voice. "For standing up for us. And poor dear *Lark Deux*. She does not deserve so ignominious an ending, even for the sake of the sailors' widows."

"I must agree," he said, bowing his head to keep their conversation to themselves alone. "She saved our lives and may have changed the world. She deserves to fly in Cornish skies. To be recognized for her accomplishments."

She had a feeling he was not speaking only of the air ship.

Blushing, she turned his compliment aside, just a little. "To accustom Cornishmen to the sight? Especially if the detachment does come to be stationed at St Michael's Mount permanently."

"Cornishmen must get used to aeronauts in their midst," he said. "Male and female. And I must admit that two young ladies of your stature in the Prince's eyes, sailing above the rooftops, will go a very long way toward the new Corps's recruiting efforts."

She couldn't help but laugh, and without thinking, slipped her hand into the crook of his elbow.

His warm, gloved fingers covered hers, as though the movement were so natural he had not thought to stop himself, and he hugged her hand between arm and body.

Madame Racine, whom Loveday had completely forgotten was walking behind them, cleared her throat.

Loveday stiffened, and then wished she hadn't. But Arthur didn't seem to mind. He squeezed her fingers and then released them, the cool air inside the manufactory flowing between them as they once again walked an acceptable distance apart.

The Admiral hailed a man who reminded Loveday forcibly of Thomas Trevithick, so large and muscular was he. But here there was no red hair and a beard to match, but a mahogany face that sported a black, wiry beard, and eyes and movements that snapped with energy as he crossed the stone floor to meet them.

"Your Royal Highness, you've met Mr Terwilliger, Master of Works for the air ships. The man who chivvies all these navvies into order and gets our birds in the air, eh, Henry?"

The Master bowed low, and the Prince raised him to shake his hand. "We have met. It is good to see you, Terwilliger. Did that air-propelling device in this last revision give you any trouble?"

"Not at all, sir," the Master said in a voice like a bass fiddle. "You'll see the results during the test flights tomorrow." His gaze found Loveday and Celeste with unerring speed. "Are these the young ladies you told me of?"

"Indeed they are." The Prince turned and introduced them.

Master Terwilliger's face split into a grin, and he shook their hands in a grip like iron. "It's pleased I am to meet the minds behind that air ship. I hope you're as proud of what we've produced as I am."

"I have no doubt we will be," Loveday said, unable to keep the smile from her own face. Suddenly, between Arthur's warm elbow and this man's regard, the morning had regained some of its sparkle. "I do not think I can wait until tomorrow."

"Ah, but you must. Last-minute details, you know," he said, apparently thinking his tone was confidential, though it was audible to everyone within a dozen feet. "We don't want our birds diving for hake in front of their Prince, now, do we?"

"Certainly not," she said, laughing. "And you may blame any difficulty with your air propelling devices on Miss Aventure here. It was she who turned the steamboat paddles on their ear and put them on the stern."

"Inspired," he said with emphasis. "You'll see, I promise you. Why, in speed and maneuverability alone they should be able to—"

The Admiral clapped him on the back. "All in good time, Master Terwilliger," he said. "We'll have nothing left to say tomorrow, at this rate, and I must give my charges the rest of the tour before I take them home for their dinner."

The Master bowed once more, winked at Loveday and Celeste, and strode back to his crew.

The rest of the tour included the green where they had landed *Lark Deux* on their spectacular return from France, and a windy stroll along the ramparts of the old fort overlooking the Channel.

"My wife Eustacia and I will see you all for dinner," the Admiral told the Prince's Own as they took their leave. "Eight o'clock, eh?"

"We look forward to it, Sir George," Mr Guelph said.

"Capital," the Prince said. "Lord St Ives, if I might have the pleasure of your company at Admiralty House, there are a number of matters George and I would like to discuss with you and Sir William."

They strolled away, leaving Loveday feeling distinctly at loose ends. But she dared not show it, or Jacob would make it his mission to show them about the town, and that she could not bear.

So when Madame Racine expressed the wish to return to the inn, she and Celeste leaped at the opportunity. Emory escorted them, and the others scattered to visit friends or otherwise satisfy their curiosity about other areas of the shipyards, leaving Jacob to tag along after whomever he willed.

"Do you really think we will be allowed to take *Lark Deux* home?" Celeste asked when at last they were enclosed in the comfort and privacy of their own chamber at the George.

"The Prince has said so, and to my mind at least, that is as good as a command." Loveday laid down her pencil, before she'd even made a single note or sketch about what they had seen. "Oh, Celeste. To be broken down for parts! How could they do such a thing?"

"Thank *le bon Dieu* for Arthur, who spoke up to help you," Celeste said. "And for knowing exactly how to phrase it so that it did not sound like they would be returning a toy to a weeping child. He is a brave man as well as clever, my friend. He would not put himself forward before royalty like that for just anyone."

"No," she agreed softly. Then, "Celeste, will you do my hair tonight the way you did at the Guelph ball? I wish to look my best."

Celeste must know her too well, for she was not deterred by the apparent change in subject. "You know he thinks you lovely even in your old dress with the grease spots on the hem."

"He does?"

"If he doesn't, he will once you are married." Celeste pulled up a chair next to hers at the little writing desk. "Now, did you see that internal corset they had hanging in a harness at the very back, near the big doors? If that isn't to support a horizontal envelope, I don't know what is."

"I did, and you're quite right." Loveday's pencil began to fly, and so absorbed did they become in their work that it was a shock when Madame Racine came in to tell them it was time to dress for dinner.

The evening was a success by any measure, and the worry lines that had marred the Prince's forehead earlier in the day smoothed out in the company of mechanically minded people like himself. There was no dancing or cards, but the conversation was so stimulating that Loveday, at least, did not miss either.

And Arthur insisted so politely on seeing her home while Emory escorted Celeste that even Madame Racine was content to take his left arm while Loveday had possession of his right, despite the tiresome presence of Jacob on the street behind them.

Loveday climbed into bed, finding sheets smelling of sea air and lavender. She snuggled down next to Celeste to talk over the events and the conversations of the evening. She had barely opened her mouth to speak when the window on the other side of the room rattled.

"Good heavens." They both sat up, Celeste already halfway out of bed. "Surely a storm couldn't have come in so quickly. We must latch this at once."

A thump came at the window.

"That is no gust of wind." Celeste leaped for the washstand just as someone shoved the window wide.

CELESTE SNATCHED up the empty pewter water pitcher even as Loveday raised her hands in the way their former bodyguard had taught her in France.

But one look at the man who jumped down into their room, and the pitcher clattered to the floor.

"Marcel!" Celeste threw her arms around her old friend, then disengaged to shove him back. "What are you doing? You could be shot as a spy!"

"Keep talking that loudly, and I will be," he said, turning to close the window and latch it as if he thought another fellow might climb up after him.

Celeste took a deep breath to control her emotions as Loveday came to join them.

"Pardonnez-moi," Celeste murmured. "But you should not be on English soil. Unless you have renounced the Emperor?"

"Not yet," Marcel hedged, facing them fully. He was much improved since the last time she'd seen him, haggard from captivity in Napoleon's dungeon under the Tuileries. His dark locks sprang from a dusky red scarf tied around his head, and his slender frame once more filled his smocked shirt and trousers. "But Etienne and I are not far off from that day."

Etienne was his brother, a smuggler who plied the waters between Calais and Dover. Usually. What had brought him this far down the south coasts?

"And Josephine, Amélie?" Celeste asked, suddenly as hungry for news of her friends as she often was for one of the little meat pies Mrs Kerrow baked for breakfast.

"Both well," he promised her. "They send their love to you and Mademoiselle Penhale."

"Why are you in Portsmouth, Monsieur Delaguard?" Loveday was clearly as perplexed as Celeste herself.

He inclined his head. "First, I came to thank you. You saved my life, and I will always be grateful."

Loveday smiled. "Celeste's friends are mine also, and brave and skilled to boot. No innocent should have to endure Napoleon's prison."

"Traveling on a smuggling vessel does not make me exactly innocent," he told her. "But I hope I am not such a villain as to fail to warn you. We have been anchored to the north for a few days, waiting for a promised cargo. When we ventured into the town, we saw the report in the paper about the Prince's visit—and that of his so famous engineers. That he would recognize you in this way gives me hope."

"We are making progress," Celeste allowed. "But why the warning?"

"Things are changing," he said, dark eyes glittering. "The device of your Job, the Pisky, is no longer able to stop the *sous-marins* from finding us. Smuggling vessels have been sunk as often as your British naval ships. We think it is because they are using another form of guidance now."

Loveday met Celeste's glance. "Surely Monsieur Patenaude has not returned. Not after the Emperor's treatment of him."

"The Grand Inventor is still in hiding," Marcel reported. "And rumors say that the Emperor is livid. At least he has abandoned the idea of automatons flying air ships."

Had he, now? Celeste could only hope their defeat of the prototype had convinced him, even if so much money and planning had gone into the scheme.

"And La Croix?" she asked. "Did he succeed me as Chief Air Minister?"

"*Oui*, and he is more determined even than *La Blanchard* to see England invaded."

"His standing is at stake," Loveday said, clearly remembering the man all too well. "And likely his life."

Marcel nodded. "He and the Minister of War are working together. France now has more than a dozen air ships. I have seen some of them attempt to cross the Channel. And there are enough of the benighted *sous-marins* to carry the Emperor's forces to England. Invasion is no longer a matter of if but when. If your Prince wants to stop Napoleon, he must act soon or risk being overpowered on his own shores."

CHAPTER 13

The three completed air ships had been moored in one of the enclosed docks, as if they were to sail into the Channel like the ships anchored outside Portsmouth Harbor. They hovered just off the water, gangways leading down to the planks of the docks, which were filled three deep with the Royal Guards, the steam works staff, and the Royal Marines, along with dignitaries from the city and shire. Breaths rose in the cold air in puffs like so many boilers.

Celeste was merely glad to be stationed with the other members of the Prince's Own, off to one side, true, but at least only in the second row. Loveday stood on one side of her, Emory on the other, with Jacob just beyond and Arthur, as one of the representatives of the War Office, in front of them. By tilting to one side, she could see the Prince as he paced up and down the narrow strip of dock left for him, as restless as Rhea, the Penhale carriage horse, let out of her traces.

It was the closest she had come to him since Marcel had left them last night. At least her friend had managed to quit the inn with no one, including Madame Racine across the corridor, the wiser. She and Loveday had debated how they might share the news with His Highness. With the ceremony in progress, he was surrounded by officials—from Admiral Campbell to the Mayor of Portsmouth to the local aristocracy. None of the Prince's Own had had an opportunity to get within four feet of him, much less have a conversation about something so important as Napoleon's plans.

Farther down the dock, the naval band played a rousing anthem. As they finished with a roll of the drums, the Prince stopped his pacing and turned to address the crowd.

"A glorious day for England," he declared, squinting through his spectacles. "Three marvelous craft, unlike anything we have developed before. The ingenuity, the precision…" His voice trailed away as he glanced wistfully back at the floating air ships.

"The ability not only to defend, but to take the fight to the enemy," Admiral Campbell, resplendent in his dress uniform, suggested.

"Yes, yes," the Prince agreed, turning his gaze back to the assembled audience with obvious difficulty. "But it is the progress we must celebrate and honor, Admiral Campbell. Not just our military prowess."

The mayor stepped forward to present the Prince with a bottle of wine. "Shall we christen them, Your Highness?"

The Prince absently set his fingers around the neck of the bottle, then strode to the first ship. "In the name of His Majesty and the powers he has vested in me, I christen thee *His Majesty's Air Ship Royal Eagle*."

Applause rang out as he smashed the bottle against the gleaming hull. Red wine ran down the planks like blood.

Celeste shook off the ugly thought. His Royal Highness

was right. If these ships must be used for war now, someday they would be used for a higher purpose—carrying travelers all over the world in search of family, health, and prosperity.

A local baronet, spindly of leg and pointed of nose, stepped forward with his bottle. "And now the next, Your Highness."

The Prince shook himself out of his reverie and moved down to the next vessel. Repeating the ceremony, he christened her *HMAS Royal Falcon*.

"How very original," Loveday whispered to Celeste, who could only agree.

Now Admiral Campbell was given a bottle and stepped forward with a proud grin to offer it to his future sovereign.

The Prince took it, fingers rubbing at the dark glass. He looked to the final ship, then to those waiting, and then finally directly at Celeste and Loveday.

"Miss Penhale," he called. "You and Miss Aventure were the ones to bring this design to our attention so memorably. I wonder, would you care to christen our third ship?"

LOVEDAY THOUGHT her heart would beat right out of her chest as she slipped from her place past Arthur and into the full view of everyone present. She curtsied to the Prince and the Admiral and took the bottle with hands that shook.

"Give it a good whack," the Admiral said encouragingly. "Bad luck if you don't break it, you know."

Little did he know how many sheets of copper she had pounded into submission in the steam works at home. Breaking the bottle was not so much a concern as how they would react to the name that had just come to her for this beautiful ship.

A name that would have meaning for both her and Celeste.

She took a deep breath and raised her chin. "I name this ship *HMAS Lady's Triumph.* May God bless her and all who fly in her!" She broke the bottle over the prow, and wine poured onto the dock as the crowd cheered.

"Well done, Miss Penhale," the Prince said. "May I invite you, Miss Aventure, Lord St Ives, and Sir Emory to crew one of the vessels, along with Captain Ellis and our first contingent of aeronauts?"

The naval band struck up a brisk march as a dozen of the men they had interviewed and—oh, well done!—two women marched down the dock in pairs.

It seemed perfectly reasonable and practical for her and Celeste to assume command at once. If they left it up to the Admiral or even the captain bringing up the rear, the officers would spend an hour dithering about who was crewing where, and who had precedence, and they would lose the sunlight.

"Welcome, Miss Edwards, Miss Stratham!" she cried as Diana and Emily reached her. Both wore newly assigned and rather large naval coats over their dresses, making it clear to Loveday that Celeste's designs for uniforms were needed sooner rather than later. "Miss Stratham, if you will board the *Royal Falcon* with Captain Aventure and Sir Emory, and Miss Edwards, if you come with Lord St Ives and I in the *Lady's Triumph,* the other aeronauts may divide themselves among all three ships. Captain Ellis," she said to the man with the gold braid on his tricorne, "I assume you will take command of *Royal Eagle* as His Royal Highness's flagship?"

"Indeed, miss—er, Cap—er, ma'am."

She might have smiled at his rather stunned acquiescence had she not seen Admiral Campbell puffing up and getting ready to let out a protest at her arrangements like so much steam from a boiler. Hastily, she saluted the Prince in farewell and boarded.

In the ship in the next dock, Celeste crossed at once to the boiler, ignited it, and began to give orders. Loveday did likewise, both making it clear what each person's task was to be and finding it natural to instruct them in how best to do it. As he had on *Lark Deux*, Arthur took his place at the vanes, now improved so as to be almost automatic, a pair of hydraulic levers controlling all that canvas and consequently the steering.

Lady's Triumph and *Falcon* were the first to be ready to lift, the boiler's pressure gauges a little high, but well within the range of safety. Loveday's crew stood at their stations, young Paul Grenville practically vibrating with excitement at the momentous occasion.

"All right, Captain?" Celeste called to their counterpart in the third ship.

"All right, er, Captain. We need but a moment to prepare our engine." It was no wonder the *Eagle* was behind. The captain may have been briefed on what his crew was to do, but it was plain as the nose on your face he was short an engineer who knew her business.

Loveday made up her mind. "Miss Edwards, will you disembark, please, and act as the *Royal Eagle*'s engineer on this flight."

"At once, Captain," Diana Edwards said, and leaped to the dock in one graceful move. *Lady's Triumph* bounced gently, tugging on her ropes.

In two minutes Miss Edwards had one aeronaut at the firebox, a second with an eye on the gauges, and had stationed herself at the instruments to follow their progress. In the next minute, if the steam was any indication, the boiler was coming up to the correct pressure. Before her proud grandfather could even inform the man beside him that she was a relation, Diana signaled that the captain might take the helm. "Ready to lift, sir," she said.

"Ready all," Loveday shouted. "Up ship!"

The navvies darted in to loose the ropes, and the three ships fell up into the air to the cheers of everyone on the dock and those waving flags from shore and rampart. The band launched into "Heart of Oak" with gusto, its stirring strains fading behind them as the ships sailed out over the harbor.

With a *crack!* she could hear across the empty air and heaving waves between them, the apparatus controlling one of *Falcon*'s vanes broke, and Loveday heard Emory shout as he struggled to guide the ship manually.

A sound like a banshee's scream sounded from *Eagle* as the silk of the envelope tore, leaving the gasbags naked inside their corset and hundreds of yards of fabric snapping like demented wings in the wind, dragging down their speed.

Loveday made a whirling motion with one arm. *Come about! Go back!*

And then her own deck tilted so suddenly from stern to bow that she could only grab the gunwale or slide down the planks in a heap—looking overboard just in time to see the air propeller Celeste had designed plummet into the sea.

It had fallen off.

How had it fallen off? How had these mistakes, these accidents, been permitted to occur, and in front of the Prince and all this company?

This was a disaster! At this rate, they would all be in pieces in the sea and die of the cold before they could be rescued.

"Go back!" she shouted. "Come about—return to shore!"

Lady's Triumph, to her credit, came about in a smooth turn to port, with *Royal Falcon* limping after her in a much wider turn, since Emory's vane on the starboard side had ceased working at all. *Eagle* plummeted rather faster than safety advised. It was nothing short of a miracle when they regained the safety of the docks.

The naval band had not even reached the fourth stanza.

Some in the audience groaned, as if they had been expecting an aerial display of acrobatics. Some were simply confused.

Loveday disembarked and, with Celeste and Captain Ellis, dared to approach the Prince.

A silence fell that was broken only by the dying wheeze of a cornet and the snapping of flags.

She took a breath. "We have work to do, Your Royal Highness."

"Yes, I should say so," he said mildly. "Was that the air propeller you lost?"

Celeste muttered something that Loveday pretended not to hear.

"It is clear that we have somewhat to overcome," the Prince went on. He raised his voice. "I and my engineers will stay on in Portsmouth until these problems are solved and my fleet is ready to fly sound and true. What say you?"

"Huzzah!" cried one of the aeronauts. "We are with the Prince's Own!"

"And we shall put you to work," Celeste said, eyes sparkling and back straight. "An aeronaut must know his or her ship from keel to corset. No one shall defeat the Royal Aeronautic Corps!"

Cheers broke out, and quite on its own, the aeronauts formed an advance guard for the Prince, Admiral Campbell, and the rather dazed dignitaries who had not expected the party to be over quite so soon.

As they marched down the docks in as much triumph as if they had actually shot Boney out of the sky, Loveday took Arthur's arm with more urgency than propriety.

"Arthur, you must help us," she said quietly.

"I am no engineer, but I will do whatever you need to prevent such a debacle occurring again," he said. "Those vanes of Emory's were tampered with, I will swear to it."

"We will soon find out. But it is not the ships I must speak of. We have received information from Marcel, the smuggler we brought out of Napoleon's prison, that Napoleon has abandoned the unmanned air ships of the kind that attacked Celeste and has thrown his resources instead into *sous-marins* that can carry troops. What's more, Old Job's Pisky no longer works on them. They have made improvements to the *sous-marins*, rendering our devices ineffective, and are preparing an imminent invasion."

Arthur's arm tightened against her hand, his whole body protesting this news.

"You are best placed to convey this to the Admiral and the Prince. They must know as soon as possible."

He nodded. "I will see it done."

For the first time that day, she let out a breath of relief.

"Thank you, Arthur. I have never been so glad to have trustworthy friends around me than today."

"Nor I," he said. They were nearly to the end of the dock, the crowd shouting huzzah for their prince. "But I fear we have enemies among us as well. Promise me you will be careful over the next two weeks."

"I will," she assured him. And somehow, her hand found its way into his, and his fingers entwined with hers and held on. "You, too," she whispered.

And only the pushing of the crowd and Madame Racine's appearance at her elbow could have forced her to let go.

Dear Papa, Mama, Rosalind, and Gwen,

You may have read in the newspapers that the Prince's Own Engineers, as well as Lord St Ives, have accompanied His Royal Highness to Portsmouth to prepare his fleet of air ships against Napoleon's impending attack. The rumors of the Princess of Wales's flight inland were quite true, and in fact, circumstances have caused the Prince to request that our entire company remain here for two weeks to speed our preparations.

You may imagine the rejoicing in the town. In our small corner of it, the George Hotel, where the Prince's Own are all staying, such a number of invitations have arrived that the innkeeper is quite at a loss to manage them all. Fortunately Madame Racine is equal to the task of accepting this mayor and rejecting that baronet. Indeed, Mama, we chose very wisely when we approached her all those weeks ago!

Since we are to be so much closer to you, and may not get away for a visit for some time, I write to beg that you come to us, even for a few days' time. Celeste and I miss you very much, and I know that for Sir Emory and Lord St Ives it would be quite like seeing their own families again if they could hear news from home.

If you decide to come, there is a delightful inn close by that can accommodate you, called the Star and Compass. And if you come before Tuesday, it will be within my power to secure invitations to Lord St Aubyn's reception, where all the aeronauts trained thus far will attend to offer their salute to his kind patronage. I know Ros and Gwen will not like to miss that.

Be assured Celeste and I are very well, and you may tell Mrs Trevelyan that his lordship is walking now with barely a hint of his injury. To be sure, His Royal Highness and Commander Sir William Edwards of the War Office keep him very busy, but we see him often and are glad for it.

Let me know of your plans by return post, and if you can come, I will make arrangements at the Star and Compass.

With all my love and best regards to Mrs Kerrow, Pascoe, and the staff,

Loveday

News that His Royal Highness, Lord St Ives, and the Prince's Own Engineers would be staying at least another fortnight swept Portsmouth, and invitations indeed arrived so frequently the innkeeper begged leave to put them in a basket for Mr Guelph to pick up once a day. Their colleague handed it to Celeste for Madame Racine with a wrinkle of his large nose.

"If Lavinia were here, she could handle these in a trice," he confided. "You and your chaperone will know what to do about them."

"As if I understand Portsmouth society," Celeste complained to Loveday that night as they sat with Madame Racine in a corner of the private parlor where they had been taking their meals. The gentlemen had retired for the evening, and the three ladies had spread out the various pieces of vellum on the polished wood table.

"It is not so difficult," Madame Racine assured her, scanning today's offerings with a practiced eye. "The mayor's wife —yes, we must answer her favorably. And of course the Admiral. He has the possibility of making your work easier. And certainly this one, from the wife of the Master of the Steam Works. He has been so kind to you."

In the end, it became clear they could attend no more than one event per evening, except for the reception for the visiting Lord St Aubyn put on by the Royal Aeronautic Corps, which they could pair with the Admiral's dinner since he and Lady Campbell would probably attend as well. Celeste hoped the Hale House family would arrive in time.

With the possible exception of Jacob, none of them were particularly looking forward to the social whirl. Celeste could only be glad that he had seemed more focused on their work than on winning her hand since they'd arrived in Portsmouth. Indeed, he spent more time with the Master of the Steam Works or one of his associates than with the engineers. And that meant Celeste could continue to keep company with Emory in the evenings.

It had been no hardship. If perhaps the topics of discussion often centered around their work, it was only to be expected. Everyone knew why they were in Portsmouth. And if perhaps their hosts were more eager to speak to him than her, that too was to be expected. He was the man who had invented the famous steam pump that was revitalizing the fortunes of many in the West Country. She was the Frenchwoman who had helped Loveday Penhale win the Prince's prize. She could not speak of her training, her experience, without revealing that she was the daughter of their enemy's once cherished Chief Air Minister. Or that she had briefly held the post herself.

Still, most days, Celeste was happiest in the steam works. She could not deny that it seemed more like home than any other place in the city.

"I expect to see Thomas Trevithick's face every time we walk into the building," she told Loveday as they approached the steam works the day after the disastrous test flight. "Though perhaps that is because Master Terwilliger brings him so strongly to mind."

All the members of the Prince's Own were there ahead of them today. They had decided to compare plans to actuals to see if they could spot any discrepancies that might have caused the failures. The others had already begun, with plans rolled out on the workbench and heads bowed in study, while all around came the bang of hammers, the whir of pulleys, and the hiss of steam as the workers continued fitting out the next three ships.

Mr Cummings made way at the sight of Loveday and Celeste approaching. She moved in next to Emory. The walk over had been brisk, but as his hand slipped down and cupped hers, she was quite warm indeed.

"I'm sure you'll spot it right off," Mr Cummings said to Loveday with a sigh and a wave at the parchment.

Loveday glanced down at the plans, then bent closer. "These are not the plans we reviewed in London, sir."

Celeste frowned. So did Mr Cummings as the others exchanged glances.

"They look identical to me," he said, half bluster and half doubt.

"No," Loveday insisted. She pointed to the strips of copper running from the steam engine to the instruments. "See here? This piping was to go under the decking, not above it. The exhaust system was moved under the hull on either side of the keel so as not to interfere with the air propeller. And this vane has no connection to its steering apparatus." She glanced up. "Please tell me this isn't what they used to construct the vessels."

Mr Guelph flapped a hand at the Master of the Steam Works to beckon him closer. "Are you certain these are your working plans, sir? Already we spot irregularities."

The Master came to frown down at the parchment as well. "Those aren't our plans. They'd be spotted with grease and curled by steam if they were." He raised his head. "Ho, Prescott! Bring the Prince's Own the plans we used to build the ships."

Mr Prescott, a burly fellow with a beard standing out at attention from his chin, approached, wiping his hands on a rag. "I did, sir. First thing. Aren't those they?"

"Apparently not," Mr Cummings said, puffing out his chest. "And I for one should like to know what you've done with them."

Both the Master and his mate looked less than amused, their faces turning ruddy and their bodies stiffening with affront. "You'll have them immediately," the Master promised, and the two stalked off.

"A ball tonight?" Emory murmured to Celeste as they waited.

"A dinner," she answered. "In a private parlor at the George, so at least we will not have to borrow a hack. And the aeronauts have been invited."

Jacob must have been listening, for he leaned around Mr Babbage. "I'm particularly looking forward to dinner this evening, Miss Aventure. I'd like to give these aeronauts a look over, become acquainted with the sort of people you and Miss Penhale chose."

A scowl settled on Emory's face like a rain cloud over the Channel. Celeste gave his hand a squeeze.

"We had the same thought," Loveday told Jacob. "But if they cannot find the plans, we may be working this evening, and so will you."

She might have the right of it, for, after a quarter hour of searching, the Master and his mate had to admit defeat.

"I don't like it," Master Terwilliger told Loveday, Celeste, and their colleagues, his brow beetled. "They were here, rolled up and in my desk, only yesterday. Instead, I find these older copies, from before the problems were corrected."

"I would not expect the navy to misplace something so important," Mr Cummings drawled with a shake of his head.

"Nor did we," the Master assured him grimly. "I can think of only one way for those plans to have disappeared. They were stolen." His glare took in them all, as if he dared them to argue with him, or suspected them to be the thieves.

Mr Davy spoke up. "We must inform His Royal Highness. In the meantime, Sir Emory, if you and our esteemed ladies would look over *Lady's Triumph*, Mr Guelph and Mr Cummings can review *Royal Eagle*, and Mr Babbage and Mr Barnes can study *Royal Falcon*. If we cannot find the fault in the plans, we must find it in the execution."

The approach agreed, they split up, the chemist walking with the Master to locate the Prince Regent.

"I cannot like it," Celeste told Loveday as they and Emory left the workshop and headed for the docks. "First thefts in London, now here. It is as if we brought the thief with us."

"Even among the Prince's Own," Loveday murmured with a glance back at Jacob.

CHAPTER 14

"Q u'est-ce que c'est? Loveday—Emory—look at this." Celeste beckoned them down to the stern, where her air propeller had once held pride of place on the keel. "You can see where the steamwrights had to change the exhaust system, and where the Archimedean beam is. But look!"

She pointed, her finger trembling, at where the air propeller had been attached. Loveday leaned in. "Are those scratch marks? And look, the threads of the screw have been stripped halfway down, as if—as if—"

"It was loosened by force before the test flight," Emory said soberly.

"And so it spun itself right off the beam." Celeste's face was a study in outrage. "After all that work, someone dared to do such damage!"

Emory's hands formed into fists, giving silent testimony as to what he'd like to do to the saboteur.

"Celeste, can we build another?" Loveday asked. "Time is not on our side, as we all know."

"I will ask Master Terwilliger if Mr Barnes and his metal-wrights can do the work. That is, provided no one has taken a sledgehammer to the molds."

"Let's board now and see what else we can find," Emory suggested, "and then we'll return to the steam works to give the Master a complete list."

In the next dock, Mr Babbage and Jacob were bent over the vane that had snapped on *Royal Falcon*, making notes amid murmurs of outrage. Loveday paid particular attention to the vanes on either side of *Lady's Triumph*, examining every inch of the arms controlled by hydraulics and where the canvas was roped to each arm.

"It seems our saboteur is a person of restraint," she reported grimly sometime later. "Only one major destructive act per vessel."

"And at least one incompetent one," Celeste said, pointing at the firebox. "This weld is terrible. It would have failed on the second voyage, if not the first, had we been aloft much longer."

"That would have been dangerous indeed," Emory said. "Fire on the deck—and the gasbags hanging not eight feet above."

They had come closer to certain death than they had previously believed.

A minute examination of the boiler and the piping below deck revealed that all was in order there, at least. "And," Loveday said, wiping her hands on her handkerchief, "built according to the set of plans we reviewed in London. At least we may be thankful for that. Repairs are one thing when one is so short on time, a rebuild quite another."

They reconvened on the docks with the other ships' teams,

to find that they had determined much the same thing. Mr Babbage looked grim. "As you say, Miss Penhale, one major destructive act and one seeming carelessness that, given time, could have proven fatal."

"A thin patch in the exhaust pipe of the *Falcon*," Jacob said, his eyes having lost all their sparkle, his mouth set more firmly than Loveday had ever seen it. "The heat would have caught the hull on fire."

"And an unfastened rope in the yards containing the forward gasbag," Mr Guelph said. "While the cuts that began the rending of the envelope could have been spotted from the ramparts had anyone thought to look, the other was easy to miss—until the rope snaked out of all its grommets and allowed the bag to sag forward, throwing off the trim in a way that could not be repaired."

"They are clever, our saboteurs," Mr Babbage said. "They have some training in mechanics—or at the very least, are connected to someone who does."

Loveday had been keeping Jacob in sight during their examination. Either he was an actor worthy of the London stage, or he was truly as angry as the rest of them about the way they had been set up to fail.

Fail fatally.

Who hated them so completely that they would risk so much?

The Prince's Own lost no time in making their report to the Master of the Steam Works. His face settled into equally grim lines. "This brings my entire yard into further disrepute," he said, voice rasping with anger. "I won't have it. We will get to work at once on these repairs and finish the next three ships even if I have to keep men here around the clock. I will request a company of Royal Marines from the Admiralty to guard the ships night and day."

With a solution in safe hands, Emory escorted Loveday and Celeste back to the George to prepare for the dinner that evening.

"The last thing I wish to do this evening is make scintillating conversation," Loveday groaned to Celeste as they dressed after having bathed. "Is it too much to hope that my dinner partner will prefer a woman who is seen and not heard?"

"That would disappoint us all," Celeste said and gave her a squeeze. "I am certain our new recruits will be so awed by being at table with Admiral Campbell and Commander Sir William—to say nothing of Lord St Ives—that they will be incapable of speech, too. The navy men will have the floor and never know it was by default."

That was the only light in this evening's darkness—that Arthur would be among the company. And when they walked along the corridor to the private parlor, which had been set with a long table, crisp white linens, and sparkling glassware, her spirits lifted when she spotted him near the window, deep in conversation with Emory.

"He is reporting this afternoon's events to Arthur," Celeste whispered. "I am glad. The Walsingham Office needs to know."

They had just joined the two, Madame Racine going to talk with Mr Guelph, when from their new vantage point, Loveday saw a carriage roll up outside. A very familiar carriage. In a moment, a woman in a Lunardi bonnet was handed down, then two young ladies wearing stovepipe bonnets Loveday had never seen before.

"Mama—Papa!" she exclaimed, cutting off Emory in midsentence. "It is my family—they have arrived. I must go down at once!"

She and Celeste hurried from the room, but once in the corridor, Loveday picked up her embroidered skirts and ran down the staircase.

"Loveday!" her mother cried. "And Celeste! Oh, we were so hoping you would be at home."

Nothing had ever felt so good as her mother's embrace, and then her father's. Even Gwen hugged her with actual enthusiasm.

"It has been so dreadfully dull without you," Gwen confessed as she released her. "And the neighborhood is positively empty without Lord St Ives. Is he here?"

"Yes, but—"

Rosalind hugged her, too. "Oh, do tell me you are not engaged for dinner. We must hear everything without delay."

"I am afraid we are," Loveday said, "but I will see if another table can be set. You must certainly join us—it is in honor of the new aeronauts. Lord St Ives is upstairs, and Papa, you will be glad to see Sir Emory again. Come, you may leave your things in our room. Oh, how happy Madame Racine will be to see you!"

Arrangements were swiftly made, introductions completed, and Loveday was so delighted at seeing her family again that it didn't even irritate her when Gwen flirted with not one, but both aeronauts on either side of her at table. The greatest topic of conversation was, naturally, the disastrous test flight and what had been done to assure nothing like it would happen on the second trial. The Admiral's wife, Eustacia, took a shine to Loveday's mother, which as far as she was concerned, sealed her opinion of Portsmouth as the most congenial place ever to have the privilege of her daughter's skills and talents.

Though thankfully, Loveday did not hear her say that out loud to anyone but Papa, in the corridor before they made their way downstairs for the short walk to the Star and Compass.

Other than those first hurried words by the window, Loveday did not get another chance to speak with Arthur. News of his family must be communicated by her parents another time, since Sir William would have nothing but that Lord St Ives must be at his side constantly, giving counsel on this latest development.

"Saboteurs on my watch!" he said in a low voice that carried perfectly well throughout the room. "I won't have it. My lord, I trust your ability to bring this to an end before our aeronauts take to the skies again."

"I will do all in my power," Arthur promised solemnly.

But it was Loveday on whom his gaze fell. He might not be able to speak to her, but his eyes told her all she wanted to know.

I want to be alone with you, and it maddens me that I must dance attendance upon my superior officers.

I feel the same. Be safe, while you are off pursuing saboteurs.

His answering smile made her warm all over, and she had to move away from the fire.

THEIR LIVES BECAME an endless stream of activity over the next few days. Besides spending long hours at the steam works, they were expected at events nearly every night. Unfortunately, the Prince did not seem inclined to participate. He had thrown himself into the work, moving from ways to steam works, questioning everyone, staying after others had gone. Madame Racine had more than once charmed her way past the guards and marched into the steam works, with much hand waving and words like *reputation* and *obligation,* to wean him away for a few of the balls, dinners, and soirees his future subjects were so anxious to give.

At the steam works, Emory and Mr Babbage were helping with issues concerning the rigging on *Royal Eagle,* while Jacob and Mr Cummings focused on materials questions with *Royal Falcon.* Mr Guelph and Mr Davy were advising on the final three ships to make sure all the latest changes were being implemented in them as well. That left Celeste and Loveday to work on *Lady's Triumph,* which had been moved back into the steam works for retrofitting the piping and the firebox.

"Insufficient shielding," Loveday was explaining to the metalsmiths. "We cannot have a crew member bump against the copper and be burned. These are not installations underground or in isolation. We must have room to move about safely and at speed."

"We," Celeste heard one of the smiths mutter as he began removing the pipe from its casing. "As if she intends to fly it herself."

"She did, you gumpus," his colleague told him, bending to help. "You saw her, before the air propeller fell off. Don't you know she and Miss Aventure were the ones who flew *Lark Deux* from Paris right to this very port and landed her at the Prince's feet?"

He did not mutter after that, except to say, "Yes, Miss

Penhale. No, Miss Aventure. Right away, Miss Penhale," with a bowed head and the utmost respect.

They were inspecting the next iteration two days later when Mr Davy poked his wavy-haired head up over the gunwale and smiled apologetically.

"Pardon me, Miss Aventure, Miss Penhale. Did you perhaps borrow the list of corrections?"

Loveday looked up from the gleaming piping. "Not I. I committed them to memory."

"I did not commit them to memory," Celeste confessed with an answering smile, "but neither did I borrow them. Perhaps Sir Emory?"

"I tried the others first." He puffed out a breath. "Troubling. Things go missing so easily here, it seems, despite the presence of the Royal Marines. I will ask the Master." He disappeared below the gunwale.

"What if that list has been stolen, too?" Celeste murmured to Loveday. She moved to the gunwale and gazed about at all the movement. The scents of hot metal and burning coal singed her nostrils. Clouds of steam from working engines gathered under the rafters. It took a moment to locate the chemist with the Master framed in the open doors to the docks. The latter's posture was becoming more rigid and truculent with every word Mr Davy said.

"This is becoming impossible," Loveday agreed as she joined her. "One would think the Portsmouth steam works as plagued by spies as Napoleon's court. Shall we discover passages behind the walls next?"

"We are entirely too interesting to be left alone," Celeste replied, remembering something their bodyguard had once said. "But there cannot be so many spies here, when it is known we are under the Prince's protection. Can you see these hardworking men as traitors to their country?"

Loveday gazed from side to side as if studying the men anew. A cluster of steamwrights were clustered around one of the newer ships as they lowered the boiler into her. Others were busy installing piping or running rigging. Everyone seemed so industrious. So focused. So proud of their work.

"No," she said. "Besides, what does stealing profit them? They have few opportunities to sell what they steal. Marcel might be the only smuggler daring enough to climb into the navy's pocket, and he certainly isn't going to carry their ill-gotten gains to Napoleon."

"Unless someone here knows a French sympathizer," Celeste reasoned.

Loveday shrugged and turned away from the scene. "Sympathizer or no, you would have to be a master thief to manage this many thefts, in all these places, to say nothing of the actual destruction."

A master thief. Who was also a master at his more honest trade.

Jacob Barnes had claimed himself a master thief before he had been plucked from the gutter and raised by a curate's family. He had also claimed that no thief was ever truly reformed. She glanced to where their colleague was chatting with one of the metalwrights working on plating for an unfinished ship. How easily he invited confidences. Was it really the work they had been doing, or the opportunities their work afforded, that kept him here so long?

"*Pardon*," she murmured to Loveday before hurrying down the gangway and wandering closer to their fellow engineer.

"And these welds," Jacob was saying, laying a hand on a piece of copper. "A new material, you say? Who invented it?"

Who indeed? Celeste sidled closer. "I would very much like to hear as well."

The wright turned redder than a radish and stammered out an explanation.

"How very clever," Celeste said when he had finished. "And how well you explain it. I can see you have given Monsieur Barnes much to consider. You must share your insights with me, my friend." She linked her arm in Jacob's and led him away.

"Finally decided to throw Thorndyke over, have you?" Jacob's eyes were bright with triumph when she drew him to a stop against the wall behind a hull, in one of the few places of privacy the steam works afforded.

Celeste dropped her hold on him. "Never! But I am wondering about throwing you to the wolves, as you English say."

Jacob blinked. "Why, my dear, what have I done to displease you?"

"I am not your dear, nor the one you should be pleasing. What have you contributed to our efforts?"

He reared back. "What have I contributed? Why, I was the one to suggest the insulated pipe housing. And I had a hand in settling the construction of the boiler as well."

She had not noticed that. "Indeed," she said, putting her hands on her hips. "And your purpose in questioning the wrights now?"

A frown was gathering on his handsome face. "To understand the way they work. I thought at least some of the flaws might lie in process rather than product."

Possibly. How irritating. Celeste lowered her hands. "Do you not find it odd that so many things have gone missing, first in London, then here?"

"Not in the slightest," he said. "Thieves are everywhere."

"Apparently even here, under the noses of the Royal Marines," Celeste said.

He raised his dark brows. "What are you saying?"

"Something I should have considered before now. We all know how expensive it is to live in London, yet you manage the finest clothes. Your own carriage. You must earn the same stipend we do, so your income cannot come from your work. Napoleon's agents would gladly reward you for your aid. Furthermore, you were everywhere the crimes were committed, and by your own admission you are a skilled thief."

"It wasn't me," he said flatly. "My income is through my adopted father, who left me a small inheritance, which I have shamelessly squandered." He pressed a hand to the chest of his oh-so-fine, silver-shot waistcoat. "You wound me deeply by entertaining any thought that I would endanger king and country by aiding the French."

Oh, but he looked so sad! Those deep brown eyes turned down at the corners, and his lips sagged, as if he could not draw breath.

"And you insult my intelligence if you think I would *not* consider it," Celeste informed him. Then she sighed. "I do not want you to be guilty, Monsieur Barnes. At moments, I have believed us to be friends."

As if she had confessed she adored him, he glanced to where Emory was working. Her *faux* fiancé was watching them. She blew him a kiss, which set his face to flaming.

"And only friends, it seems," Jacob said.

Celeste shook her head. "I told you who holds my heart. But I care enough about you to warn you. Do not attempt to steal anything else or run, or I will take my theory to the Master. He may not be so willing to give you the benefit of the doubt."

He bowed to her, and she returned to Loveday's side.

"That did not look pleasant," her friend said.

"It was not," Celeste said with another sigh. "But it had to be done. It appeared to me that only Jacob had a possible reason, the opportunity, and the skill to commit these crimes. He denies it. I do not know what to think."

Loveday gripped the gunwale, eyes narrowing. "Then let us consider further. Reason—to help the French. Opportunity—access to the museums in London and the Prince's Own here in Portsmouth. And what of the one who stole our plans in Cornwall? We must add access to the steam works in Truro and our workshop at Hale House. Skill? Of that I cannot be certain, but it is possible, with assistance." Her gaze met Celeste's. "Mr Barnes could not have done all this. There is another."

Celeste stared at her, a terrible certainty making her blood chill in her veins. "Do not say it."

"I must." Loveday swallowed as if she could not bear to say the words. "Madame Racine."

$\mathcal{C}$eleste's hand rose as though to cover Loveday's mouth, before it fluttered down again. "It fits, does it not?"

"Horribly well." Loveday felt sick. "But we cannot convict her on speculation alone. We must ask her to her face, and if she is guilty, we—we will—" Do what? Hand her over to the Royal Marines?

How could she do that to the woman whose presence here had made it possible for them to fulfill their dreams? Who had been so supportive of Loveday's efforts at the steam works in Truro all these years? Who had given her French lessons as a child, for goodness sake!

"We must talk to her," she concluded lamely. "Now, without delay."

Emory took one look at the pair of them throwing on their pelisses and tying the ribbons of their bonnets with shaking fingers, and abandoned his duties to snatch up his hat and follow them out. "What has happened? Loveday, is something amiss with your family?"

She told him, laying out both suspicions and circumstantial evidence as clearly as if she were reporting it to the magistrate.

Oh, help us, what if I actually have to do so?

She shook away the thought. "Please come with us, Emory. This is bound to be a very unpleasant interview."

"Would you like me to do the talking?" His steps were as rapid as theirs, as they pushed against the wind.

"No, I know her best," Loveday said reluctantly. "Though if she becomes upset and lapses into French, Celeste must speak to her."

Loveday half hoped they might put off the evil moment by finding Madame Racine had gone out. Indeed, there was no answer to their knock on her chamber door, though the innkeeper had assured them she was upstairs in her room. Loveday pushed open the door, biting her lip at this intrusion into their chaperone's privacy.

"Madame? I'm so sorry but—" She stopped and pushed the door wider. "Madame? Are you here?"

The room was empty. Truly empty—not a pelisse or a dress or so much as a handkerchief was left inside. The bed was neatly made, the curtains open.

"Has she changed rooms?" Celeste asked in astonishment.

"The innkeeper would have told us," Loveday said.

"What are the chances she has got wind of our suspicions somehow and fled?" Emory examined the dressing table, the washstand, the floor under the bed. "Nothing. Not a clue as to her whereabouts. And the fire is out—wait."

He fished a bit of paper out of the ashes in the grate, took one look, and handed it to Celeste. "It's in French."

She frowned down at the burned remains. "It is but a corner of a letter. It says, *keep you here* and then *wherry waiting* and then something I cannot read."

Loveday took it, but even with her knowledge of French, the last word was indecipherable. *"Wherry waiting?"*

"The word could also mean *rowboat* or even *gondola*, as in air ship," Celeste said. "I do not understand. Why would she leave? Where has she gone?"

"If that means *air ship* and not *wherry*," Emory said, "we can only conclude that she and at least one other mean further mischief at the docks. We must find the lady at once and put these questions to her."

"We need help," Loveday said. "Emory, if you send to the Admiralty for Arthur, Celeste and I will gather my family and the Prince's Own. We must search the town, paying particular attention to the docks. Whether wherry or air ship, it is our only clue."

Within the hour, Arthur had joined them, and they fanned out from the George Hotel to the docks. Mrs Penhale had refused to participate, vowing that their friendship with Madame Racine would be ruined forever by such groundless suspicions. She took to her room and would have made Gwen and Rosalind stay with her had not their father intervened.

"If she is innocent, then something may have happened and she will need feminine assistance," he said. "If she is not, then she must face her neighbors and realize the gravity of her loss and betrayal."

Papa, clearly, was not about to forgive Madame Racine for putting his daughter in jeopardy, if their suspicions turned out to have substance.

He and the girls went one way down the street, Arthur and Loveday another. Celeste and Emory told the Prince's Own that the chaperone was missing and might be in danger. Word spread through the steam works and thence to the docks, until it seemed every man under the Master's command was battling the wind and rain and turning over everything from stones to bellows to find the older woman.

But she was not to be found.

"Could she simply have decided to change lodgings?" Arthur raised his voice against the wind. "Or met a friend who invited her to stay?"

"She knew her duty to us—and would never abandon it under my mother's very nose," Loveday said. Her voice trembled with frustration and worry. "Arthur, I am so afraid that what we suspected is true. Where is the most likely place for a person to find a wherry?"

"Besides the foot of Hale Head?"

The dear man, trying to raise her spirits. "That was a coracle, and I did manage to steer it, if you recall."

"You did better than I. When it overturned on my head it became clear to me that the navy was never going to be my career." He took her hand, and somehow the wind seemed less harsh. "I think we ought to search nearer the docks. The navy uses longboats and wherries to supply the ships at anchor."

It was not the first time Loveday had blessed his instincts —the instincts of a man who had been a spy in enemy territory and could put himself into the mind and thoughts of another. For on the second long dock, they found her, wrapped in a blanket in a wherry, struggling with the oars in the heaving sea, and clearly determined to row out to a ship barely visible in the rain and mist.

"Madame Racine!" Loveday shouted down the short ladder as rain pelted her. "Are you all right?"

"Foolish child," came the answering shout. "Go away. I am going home, and nothing you can do will stop me."

The wind blew her blanket up over one shoulder, and Loveday gasped.

For gathered close around her feet were any number of strange objects. A glass jar containing a baby squid in alcohol. A long tube of sturdy leather in which the plans for the air ships were typically delivered. A clock—or what appeared to be a clock, but was probably one of Old Job's Piskies. And several things Loveday had never seen before. Madame Racine tore the blanket off and used it to secure the objects. Then she seized the oars once more and leaned into them, pulling farther away from the dock.

"Madame, it's not too late!" Arthur called, his voice rising with fear for her. "You can put those things back and we'll say nothing, I promise you. You must only change your allegiance and forswear the Emperor."

"*Jamais!*" Madame Racine cried, fighting the swell, the oars digging into the water. "I am taking them to him. Nothing I have sent before has been enough, but surely one of these will do. He will finally reward me, after all my years of service in this benighted place." She was twenty feet farther now, pulling hard for the ship anchored in the deeper water outside the harbor walls.

"We can't let her get away!" Arthur cast about for a rowboat tied within reach.

Loveday drew in a breath as the mist thinned just enough to reveal the waiting ship.

A familiar ship, low of gunwale, sleek of hull, and with two masts.

The *Marguerite*.

"Arthur!" She grabbed him even as he pulled a rowboat closer on its mooring line, hand over hand. "Arthur, wait! That's no ship full of Napoleon's men—it's a smuggling vessel —Etienne's. She thinks she's going to France, but she won't. Once he realizes who she's betrayed, Marcel will turn her."

"And if he doesn't?" Arthur gazed down at her, rainwater dripping off his chin and ears. "If Celeste's friends have been lying to us all?"

She shook her head, and droplets of rain flew off the brim of her sodden bonnet. "You know Marcel as well as I. He would never have risked his life to climb in our window—to make sure we warned the Prince of the invasion—unless he was on our side. You'll see."

All the same, Loveday found her breath backing up in her chest the closer Madame Racine drew to the French smuggling ship.

Then the mist closed in, and they could see nothing. Loveday shivered in her soaked pelisse, the December winds cruel and finding every bit of exposed skin. Arthur opened his greatcoat and tucked her against him, planting his feet against the buffeting wind and enabling her to lean on him.

"We should return to the George and notify the Marines," he murmured.

"Not until we know for certain," she said against his shoulder. "We must not allow them to think that Marcel and his brother are involved in her treason."

He had taken a breath to reply when his body stiffened. "A longboat. The wherry is tied on behind."

As though they might witness her familiarity with Arthur from out in the harbor, Loveday hastily stepped free of his comforting warmth.

And sure enough, here came a longboat with a huddled female form amidships. One of the men waved, and Loveday heaved a sigh of relief at the welcome sight of his dusky skin and red bandanna. "Marcel!"

In minutes, the longboat was tied up, and Marcel and four sailors were climbing the ladder. One carried all the objects Madame Racine had stolen, still wrapped in the blanket. Marcel bowed to Loveday and Arthur.

"I believe you have lost something," he said, normally cheery voice heavy.

"Several somethings," Arthur said. "Among them trust and friendship, it seems."

Madame Racine sniffed, then had to wipe the water running off her nose. Etienne handed her a bandanna from his pocket, and reluctantly, she took it.

"I hereby turn this lady, by her own admission a spy in the service of Napoleon, over to you," Marcel said.

"I thank you for your loyalty, and for your prompt action," Arthur said. "I will see you and your brother pardoned for this."

"What about us?" The other boatmen murmured amongst themselves. They were keeping an eye on the naval ships, far too close now for comfort.

"All of Captain Delaguard's crew will be included," Arthur promised. "In fact, it would benefit us all if those who engage in the Channel trade were to rally to England's defense as much as they see fit. For if Napoleon were to succeed in his invasion, this lucrative trade would end, and every man Jack of you would have to return to his plow and crab traps."

The men looked at each other, disgust at such a fate written plainly on their faces.

"Someone has to keep the *sous-marins* busy," Etienne said with a grin. "We might not have the Piskies to help us, but we have a few other tricks to play."

"Tricks come to us by way of Flanders," Marcel said with a meaningful glance at Loveday.

Ah, so Monsieur Patenaude, the Grand Inventor, had established a workshop somewhere and was busy doing his part to foil the Emperor's plans. This was good news indeed.

"When the time comes to launch our air ships for France," she said, "we will depend on your help. It will not be long. Before Christmas, I'll wager."

"*Marguerite* will be reefed close," Marcel promised. He dug in his pocket. "I came by this not so long ago, in the market in Saint Malo. Give it to Celeste, would you?"

In a velvet bag tied shut with a bit of thin rope, Loveday could feel a small object. "I will." Loveday went up on tiptoe and kissed his cheek, then slipped the object into her rather damp reticule. "*Merci*, Marcel. Be safe."

Amid the laughter of his fellow sailors at his bemused face, they climbed back down into the longboat and before long had disappeared into the mist. Arthur hefted the makeshift sack and its contents clanked. "Come along, madame," he said to the Frenchwoman. "You must answer for your actions."

She tilted her chin with disdain and shook his hand off her arm. "Lord or not, you may not touch me."

As she followed the two down the length of the dock,

Loveday could only grieve. Even the lowering sky seemed to mourn the loss of a woman once held in such high regard.

"So, Madame Racine was indeed our spy and saboteur?" Celeste couldn't quite make herself believe it, though she and Loveday had both suspected it.

Loveday nodded. From the Admiralty, where he had taken Madame Racine, Arthur had sent word to the others to break off the search, and everyone had returned to their lodgings.

"She was sent here by Napoleon when he first came into power," Loveday explained, settling her skirts about her on the edge of the bed. "I gather from her rants that she was none too pleased to be stationed in such 'a backward place as Cornwall,' to use her words. She was convinced nothing good could come of it, until Richard Trevithick invented his steam engine and Thomas and the rest of us continued the work." She shook her head. "No wonder she was so happy to help me. It gave her entrée to the steam works and no one to question it. She had no idea we would develop the air ship, but she was quick to take advantage of it."

"Advantage of all of us," Celeste murmured, coming to perch beside her. "I trusted her to send word to my mother and friends that I was safe. Instead, she must have corresponded with the traitor Toussaint and sent our original set of plans from the workroom at Hale House." Her throat closed, and she had to swallow. "And my mother went to her death thinking I had gone before her."

Loveday must have heard the catch in her voice, for she

put an arm about her shoulders. "I am so sorry, Celeste. I wish we had considered her sooner."

Celeste dashed a tear from her cheek with the back of one hand. "We thought she was our friend. We could not know her treachery. At least we are rid of her now."

"Thanks to Marcel. He gave me something for you." Loveday rose and fished in the reticule drying before the fire. "He said he found it in the market in Saint Malo."

Nonplussed, Celeste opened the ragged little bag that once must have been elegant. An oval object fell into her palm. She turned it over and inhaled a shocked breath.

It was a miniature of her mother, so delicately painted the artist must have used a brush with a single hair. Her complexion was flawless, her eyes triumphant as she looked out at the world. The miniature was framed in plain silver, tarnished now, with a metal loop at the top where someone might have worn it upon a ribbon at their throat, or hanging from a chain.

The tears, never far away, overflowed.

"How lovely she looks," Loveday whispered, handing her a handkerchief and taking the tiny painting.

"And he found it in the market?" Celeste marveled. "I suppose, with her being in disgrace, its value was next to nothing. And yet, I feel he has given me something priceless. I had no image of her, you know, and fled Paris with only the clothes on my back. And my memories."

"Yet there comes a time when memory fades." Loveday wiped a tear from her own cheek with the heel of her hand. "She will never fade now. Besides this, she lives on in you, *chère amie.*"

Celeste sobbed on her shoulder as they both grieved for

two older women, one who had never quite mastered motherhood, and one who had stood in that place and thrown it away.

At length, they must blow their noses and return to that unhappy subject.

"We have suspected, have we not, that Madame Racine had at least one confederate," Loveday said on a shuddering breath. "She caused the damage and took our plans in Cornwall, but I do not believe she was often enough in the steam works here, or had the knowledge, to have caused all the damage to the air ships. Someone must be helping her."

Celeste squeezed her arms closer to fight off a shiver. "Then we must remain watchful."

"If we remain at all," Loveday said. "The loss of Madame Racine presents us with a different sort of problem." She met Celeste's gaze, and Celeste's stomach sank.

"We have no chaperone." Of all the ridiculous concerns at this moment!

Loveday sighed. "You can be sure my mother will remark on it."

She did, at dinner in the private parlor there at the George Hotel, and at length. A young lady's reputation was her true treasure. They could not possibly consider remaining.

Even if they had considered nothing else all afternoon. When war was imminent, and they had work vital to the nation yet to do.

"We must find a solution," Loveday's father put in when her mother ran out of steam. "Loveday and Celeste have done yeoman's work. His Royal Highness clearly depends on them. And there is Cornwall's honor to consider."

"There is *our daughter's* honor to consider," Mrs Penhale

said, nose in the air. "I am certain Emory Thorndyke can uphold that of Cornwall perfectly well."

"Sir Emory is a fine fellow," her husband agreed. "You won't find me arguing that. But he didn't invent an air ship. And he should not be given the glory for it."

Loveday's mother raised her brows. Clearly, she had not considered the matter from that direction.

"Perhaps, Mama, you could stay with us," Loveday ventured.

The lady's lips tightened, as if she could not bring herself to consent.

"Oh, but how wonderful," Celeste said, clasping her hands together. "There is no lady more respected, more admired—why, to hear Lady Campbell tell it, you are already the best of friends. To have a chaperone who understands us so well, who is well educated not only in the social graces but the history and culture of England."

"Doing it too brown again," Loveday muttered under her breath.

Mrs Penhale's lips relaxed. "I am glad you find my presence such a comfort, Celeste. But I must think of Gwendolyn and Rosalind, too."

"It's only days until Christmas," Mr Penhale reminded his wife. "We can stay here until then. It wouldn't be Christmas at home without Loveday."

She softened further. "There is that. Very well. I will stay for now. Until the Prince relocates to London again." Even as Celeste and Loveday exchanged glances, she held up one finger. "But you will need to find another chaperone, a married lady preferably, who will watch over you and your household in London. Either that, or come home."

⁓

THE SECOND TEST flight was scheduled for just before Christmas. Crews at the shipyard and steam works had been working around the clock. Six air ships now floated in the docks, although only the newest three would launch on this flight.

"Yes, yes," His Royal Highness said, stalking up and down the dock, boots thudding against the planks. "Coming along nicely, I see."

In the biting winter wind that put the red in everyone's cheeks, Mr Babbage, Emory, Jacob, Loveday, and Celeste trailed him like the tail of a kite, while the Royal Guard maintained a watchful distance. Mr Davy, Mr Cummings, and Mr Guelph had declared themselves perfectly happy to wait inside the steam works with Master Terwilliger for the Prince's verdict on their work.

His Royal Highness stopped in front of the air ship that had been christened *Prince's Pride*. It tugged on the ropes holding it in position as if eager to fly. With a copper-covered hull and blue silk covering the corset that held the triple gas bags, the vessel was both sleek and powerful.

"This one, I think," he said.

Jacob, who had been taking notes about anything the Prince wanted changed, looked up from the oxblood-red journal in his hands. "This one what, Your Highness?"

"This is the one I will fly," he said.

Emory's head jerked up, Celeste clutched Loveday's arm, and everyone else stilled, except the captain of the Royal Guard.

"I must advise against it, Your Highness," he cautioned,

stepping forward. "I know you flew with your lady engineers a few months ago, but these craft are, well, unfinished."

The Prince drew up his considerable height. "They are as finished as the prototype that carried us. Nay, even more so! Besides, how can I command my valiant troops into the air if I have not traveled there first myself?" He turned his gaze back on the air ship, and his smile returned. "Ah, to fly again. There is nothing like it, eh, Miss Aventure?"

Celeste summoned a smile as his gaze brushed hers. "Nothing like it at all, Your Highness. But me? I am easily risked on prototypes. You are far more important to England."

The Beefeater nodded once, as if that were that.

His Highness glanced at Loveday. "And you, Miss Penhale? Do you agree that I must stay hopelessly earthbound for the good of the Empire?"

"I do, sir, alas," she told him. "We can, with effort, replace an air ship. We cannot replace you."

He looked to Emory. "And you agree, Thorndyke?"

"Yes, Your Highness."

His eyes narrowed behind his spectacles, and he glanced to Jacob, who stood with pencil poised. "Well, Barnes? Your thoughts?"

Jacob grinned at him. "Nothing would keep me out of the air, Your Highness."

Celeste nearly groaned aloud.

"Ha!" the Prince declared, slapping Jacob on the back. "Do you hear that? I will take this beauty out, and you shall come with me, Barnes, along with its crew. You will tell me if anything is amiss and witness this great flight."

Jacob bowed. "It would be an honor, Your Highness."

"Your Highness, I—" the captain began, clearly aghast, but the Prince held up his hand.

"Enough! The decision is made. On Christmas Eve, we will take these three out and see how they fare. And I will hear no more arguments."

He stalked down toward the next ship.

Emory shook his head at Jacob. "Now you've done it."

Celeste caught the wretched man's arm before he could follow. "Talk to him! You must see the folly of it."

Jacob shrugged, removing her hand from his arm in the process. "There must be some advantage to being Prince Regent. Don't worry. I'll tell you all about it when we come back." He winked at her and hurried after the Prince.

The man was maddening! Could he truly not see the damage that would ensue in the country should anything happen to the Prince?

"We designed them well," Loveday said beside her. "They will fly perfectly."

"The Prince will be safe," Emory agreed. "And likely even more supportive of our work."

Celeste nodded. They were probably right. There had been no more accidents or vital parts stolen since Madame Racine's capture. Perhaps her accomplice had lost courage and gone to ground. Or perhaps there had been no accomplice at all, and the lady was much more clever than they had thought. Chances were good that the Prince would indeed be safe on a mere test flight.

But, truth be told, she envied Jacob. What wouldn't she have given to rise into the sky again! Their test flight had been so short—too short! But the crews must be sent up to familiarize themselves with the vessels they would fly in battle. This time, it would not be her and Loveday's place to do so.

Once the war was over, would she ever again have the opportunity here in England? *Lark Deux* had not yet been made flightworthy, the wrights' days and nights being wholly occupied by completing the Prince's six ships. Were she and Loveday to be grounded permanently after all, once the Prince had his fleet in the sky?

CHAPTER 16

$\mathscr{A}$ll of Portsmouth seemed to have turned out on Christmas Eve morning to see the test flight—especially when the news got out that the Prince himself intended to captain his own ship. Cheering people lined the ramparts and clogged the roads. Little boys swarmed up the spars of fishing boats tied up at the docks, heedless of their owners' shouted warnings.

As Celeste had gloomily predicted, she and Loveday were not invited to assume command of either *Phoebus* or *Power of Portsmouth*. Admiral Campbell had stolen a march on them and assigned the captaincy of both ships before the two more experienced aeronauts—themselves—had even arrived. *Prince's Pride* was to be crewed, as the Prince had commanded, by Jacob Barnes and four of the aeronauts who had gone up before. Diana Edwards, Loveday was happy to see, had clearly impressed her grandfather so much that today she again acted as engineer, this time on *Phoebus*, and Emily Stratham was crew on *Power of Portsmouth*.

Loveday had even had a glimpse of Madame Racine's

young friend as he leapt aboard *Prince's Pride* to take his place at the vanes. She wondered if he knew that the woman his family had taken to their bosom was a spy and a traitor. She hoped not—today, at least, a young aeronaut needed no distractions of that kind.

Arthur had told her quietly that Madame Racine had left the day before for London and the War Office, Commander Sir William Edwards at her side in the coach, two Royal Marines balefully watching her from the seat opposite. She would be questioned closely, for if she had stolen so much in only six months, what other information and technology had she been able to smuggle to France in twenty-five years? Who knew how well informed Napoleon had become about English defenses because of her?

Loveday shook off the dark thoughts and did her best not to show how desperately she minded being left ashore.

"I am trying not to be selfish. Truly, I am happy the other captains are able to share this honor and gain valuable experience," she muttered through her teeth to Celeste, probably the only person within hearing who would understand.

"I, too," Celeste admitted. "But it is not easy. I am, as you English say, feeling quite the dog in the hay about it."

"Manger."

"Yes. That, too."

With a cry of "Up ship!" from the Prince, the navvies ran in, loosened the ropes, and once more three beautiful ships rose above the docks, then the walls of the fort, to a great roar from the crowd. The storm of two days ago had blown itself out, and they could not have wished for a clearer sky nor steadier winds—as Mr Guelph had been at some pains to tell them.

Loveday could hear the faint shouts of the nearest captain —could follow what his commands might be as they headed out over the Channel. Such a beautiful sight they were!

"Four hundred feet," Celeste murmured, as though her soul, too, were aboard and reading the instruments. "Take her higher. Put her through her paces."

As though they had heard, the ships rose another hundred feet, then executed a maneuver that took them in a graceful circle, one after the other. The ships turned their shoulders into the wind and came about in the other direction, in an aerial ballet that made the crowd shout its appreciation.

Phoebus and *Power of Portsmouth* came about again and divided, as though *Prince's Pride* were meant to take the center position for their flight back to port.

But *Prince's Pride* kept going, farther into the skies over the Channel.

Arthur broke out of the row of dignitaries on the dock and made his way over to them. "What is His Highness doing?"

The other two ships hesitated, and in a moment, something flashed in the sun and sped away.

"They've released a pigeon," Celeste said excitedly. "Oh, look, it is heading straight for the Prince's ship, just as it was designed to do."

"They weren't supposed to test the pigeons," Loveday objected. "I heard Admiral Campbell give them their orders. Head out for a mile, execute the turns, and come back. *Phoebus*'s captain is being cautious, lest something go wrong while the Prince is aboard."

Phoebus and *Portsmouth* peeled off in opposite directions and came about, once more facing out to sea, then steam puffed as they laid on coal and began to pursue *Prince's Pride*.

Arthur pulled the far-scope from the pocket of his great-coat and peered through it. "I don't like this." He lowered the far-scope and handed it to Celeste. "I must speak to the Admiral. Something is wrong."

"Has *Pride* malfunctioned?" Loveday asked, her voice rising as she watched Arthur push through the crowd. "If it is the vanes again, I am going to insist that someone be sacked!"

"I do not think it is the vanes," Celeste said, the far-scope to one eye. "I think all of Portsmouth has just given a wonderful sendoff to our spy. Jacob has engineered this debacle. He is not only a thief—he is an agent of Napoleon."

Loveday clutched her arm. "I do not want it to be Jacob. I saw his face when we were searching for Madame Racine. The man was furious at the thought of her treason. You could be right—but consider, Celeste. Just moments ago, who was so eager to get aboard he forgot precedence and boarded before the rest of the crew—before the Prince?"

Celeste turned pale. "Paul Grenville. Oh, Loveday, surely not. We chose him ourselves!"

"Because Madame Racine influenced us to do so. We have been well and truly imposed upon, my friend, by either or both of those young men. All we know for certain is that the Prince is in mortal danger!"

"Send them up, all of them!" Admiral Campbell roared, striding down the docks where the three remaining vessels floated, waiting. "I will not allow the kidnapping of our future monarch. We join *Phoebus* and *Power of Portsmouth* in the air, and we bring him home."

They were all still in shock. Celeste clung to Emory's arm, glad for his strength—and for the *faux* engagement that allowed it. Loveday was standing suspiciously close to Arthur, who had returned to their sides after speaking to the Admiral. Now he stepped away from her to block the fellow's furious strides.

"A wise course," Arthur assured him. "Where are your other pilots? We'll send word to them at once."

The Admiral sucked a breath through his nose and let it out in a puff that hollowed his impressive chest. "We can send our remaining recruits up, but we have no one experienced enough to captain the ships."

Before Celeste could do more than grasp the implications, Loveday moved to Arthur's side.

"Then send us," she told the Admiral. "As you have seen, Miss Aventure and I are experienced aeronauts, and Lord St Ives and Sir Emory are experienced crew. If you assign two Royal Marines to the recruits aboard each ship, we will have crew and defense in one."

Celeste held her breath, sure the man would argue. From the first, he had been uncomfortable with their roles in the Prince's Own. How much less would he approve of them at the helm of one of his precious air ships, when they had experienced such unmitigated disaster the first time? Did he hold them to blame for that?

He studied Loveday's face as if her credentials were written upon it. Then he nodded slowly. "Very well. That's two, at least."

"I believe I know a third," Arthur put in quickly as Celeste exhaled. He looked to her. "Would our friends outside the harbor be willing, do you think?"

Marcel? He had the most experience as an aeronaut, and Josie and Amélie could certainly serve as crew.

"Of course he would help," Celeste said with a glance to Admiral Campbell. "If he were allowed."

"Then I appeal to you, sir," Arthur said, gaze returning to the Admiral's. "There is a ship just outside the harbor, *Marguerite*, with Marcel Delaguard as first mate. He and his captain have already proven themselves friends to England, as have the others who sail with them, with the capture of Madame Racine. I must tell you, however, that he was trained at l'Ecole des Aéronautes in Paris, under the eye of Sophie Blanchard."

Admiral Campbell stood taller, blue eyes glinting. "Napoleon's Chief Air Minister?"

Even here, her mother's fame preceded her and her students.

"One of them," Arthur hedged with another look to Celeste.

"If you vouch for them, Lord St Ives," the Admiral said, "I will allow it. But only because desperate times call for desperate measures. Bring them here as quickly as you can. We launch on the quarter hour."

AND SO, in a remarkably short time, Celeste found herself once more with Emory on the deck of *Royal Falcon*, working with two of the new recruits to check trim and supplies. Loveday was doing likewise aboard *Lady's Triumph*, with Arthur again as one of her crew. Mr Davy had convinced the Admiral to send pigeons to call in *Phoebus* and *Power of Portsmouth* to refill their coal and water, and the captains and crew of all five ships had been briefed on the plan. Now, the Master of the Steam Works was lecturing Marcel, Josie, and Amélie on the proper behavior on an English air ship before allowing them to board.

"As if there were rules of etiquette even here," Celeste said with a shake of her head.

"There are," Emory said, checking the gauges as the pressure mounted inside the steam engine. "Make sure your coal bin and water tanks are full. Trim your weight. And always obey the captain."

Celeste grinned at him. "I like the last one best of all."

"I find comfort in it," he said with an answering smile, "so long as you are the captain."

How could she fail to appreciate such a man?

The Royal Marines marched down the dock. Two men split off from their company at each ship and climbed the gangway. Red coats as bright as the brass on their rifles, the Royal Marines made the *Falcon* sway gently as they boarded. They drew to a halt and saluted Emory. "Corporal Felding and Private Jones-Smythe, reporting for duty, sir," the more muscular of the two declared.

"I'm Crewman Thorndyke," Emory told him. Then he nodded to Celeste. "Report to our captain, Corporal."

His grey gaze swung to Celeste, moving from top to toes, as if taking in her serpentine redingote and the spruce wool skirts that peeked out below. There had been no time to return to the George and don her flying costume, and she would likely have given Admiral Campbell an apoplexy had she showed up in *pantalons*.

"Corporal, Private," she greeted them. "Welcome aboard.

Crewman Thorndyke will brief you on your duties. Do not fire those rifles unless I give you leave."

The slender private, who was about her age if the lack of scruff on his chin was any indication, glanced to his corporal, who drew himself up until the feather in his tall felt hat nearly brushed the silk of the envelope.

"We have our orders from Admiral Campbell, ma'am," Corporal Felding said in tones that rang against the copper of the boiler.

"Admiral Campbell will not be with us a thousand feet in the air while we cross the Channel," Celeste informed him. "And he has never captained an air ship. So he might not know that the bags over your head carry lifting gas. If they are punctured by bayonet or ball, we will plummet into the sea or crash to the ground. I am certain you would object to that."

He hastily lowered his rifle until the butt was on the deck. Private Jones-Smythe copied him.

Emory moved away from the boiler. "Let me show you what to do, gentlemen, so you may balance your weight with work."

The two Royal Marines meekly followed him.

Less than ten minutes later, the gauges showed they were up to full steam, and with Emory now acting as engineer, Celeste assigned the two recruits to the vanes. She stood at the helm, gripping the smooth wood. Something was pushing up inside her, like lifting gas, and she was just as ready as *Falcon* to shuck off the ropes and soar.

Admiral Campbell had taken up a position in the middle of the dock, the Prince's gramatophone at his lips.

"Attention, captains," he called, his voice echoing. "*Phoebus* and *Power of Portsmouth*, lead off together. *Royal Falcon*, then

Royal Eagle, and then *Lady's Triumph*. On my mark. Are you ready, Miss—er, Captain Aventure?"

"*Oui*," Celeste said, then, when he shuddered, she quickly called out, "Aye!"

Emory nodded to her.

"Miss Penhale?" the Admiral bellowed.

"Shouldn't that be Captain Penhale?" Arthur called from the deck.

Celeste could almost hear the Admiral grinding his teeth. "Captain Penhale?" he shouted.

"Aye!" came Loveday's clear voice.

"Captain Delaguard?"

"Aye, Admiral, sir!" Marcel called, the words still heavily colored by a French accent.

"Very well." Admiral Campbell swiveled to face Celeste again. "Captain Aventure, take her up."

It sounded wrong, that title. Once she had dreamed of being a captain under her mother in the French Aeronautical Corps. Now she would sail for friends and adopted country.

But she did not have to do so under false colors.

"Captain *Blanchard*," she shouted back. "For England! Up ship!"

CHAPTER 17

And so they had an armada. A small one, to be sure, but there was something fine and deeply satisfying about looking to port and seeing *Lady's Triumph* with Loveday at the helm and looking to starboard and seeing *Royal Eagle* with Marcel in command. Josie and Amélie sent Celeste a wave, which she returned before setting both hands to the helm. Ahead, *Phoebus* and *Power of Portsmouth* were on course for the French coast. But in the expanses of sky between the great golden bags of lifting gas, she could not spy another air ship on the horizon.

Where had their enemies taken the Prince? Was Jacob a prisoner, too, or was he the spy who had helped Madame Racine? Was Paul Grenville innocent, or still doing Madame Racine's bidding, and through her, that of Napoleon? Did the kidnappers intend to hold the future monarch for ransom or something worse?

Their task had seemed so simple in Portsmouth: Locate *Prince's Pride*, surround it, and force it back to England. But none of that would work if they could not find the runaway air ship.

"Vanes horizontal," Emory called. "Speed twenty knots, steady as she goes."

Steady. Like him. And unflappable. And terribly logical.

He must have left his station, for she felt him behind her. He reached around her and tapped a gauge as if he wasn't sure it was reporting correctly.

Celeste peered at it, too. "The pressure in the gas bags is good, *oui?*"

"Quite good," he allowed. "Better than I had expected. It appears the changes we made have indeed been improvements, as we hoped."

"But if it improved our performance," she said, "it improves the performance of *Prince's Pride* as well. How far ahead of us can she be?"

He straightened, and she felt a chill. It was the air and the height. Flying, in a dress! Her mother had done so for performances, but never while working in the Aeronautical Corps. There was much the English still needed to learn about air ships and their crew.

"Assuming the same tailwind and speed," Emory mused, "and a three-quarter-hour head start, I estimate they are fifteen miles ahead."

"Then they will reach the French coast before nightfall," Celeste said, "if that is where they are heading."

"It is almost certainly where they are heading. We will reach it after darkness has fallen," Emory added, "unless we can increase our speed."

"Without depleting our stores," Celeste warned. "We still

have to return. You do not want us coming down in France again."

"No indeed," he said. "My French is still decidedly rusty. And you will likely have a price on your head."

The chill only intensified. "Signal Loveday," Celeste said. "She will have an idea."

They had only one pigeon per ship, and if one of them failed, then that ship would be cut off from any communication but hand signals. He took it from the cabinet in the stern bench inspired by their picnic basket, along with one of the pieces of paper and a pencil stowed there for this purpose. Celeste glanced at it as he wrote.

Est Pride is 15 miles ahead. Must increase speed or risk losing her after nightfall. Ideas?

He enclosed the note in the box, ignited the tiny engine he had designed for short flights, and adjusted the electromagnetic device in its head to find the corresponding target in *Lady's Triumph*. Then he threw the whirring device over the side.

"Blimey," she heard Private Jones-Smythe say as the wings flashed across the empty air between the ships. "What is that? A beetle? A bird?"

"We call it a pigeon, because it always comes home," Emory told him. "It was designed by—"

From a distance came a *whumph*, and the air ship swayed as if slapped by a mighty hand. Someone—Corporal Felding perhaps?—gasped and clutched at the rigging.

"Was that a cannonbomb?" Celeste shouted to Emory, grip tightening on the helm. She glanced his way long enough to see that he was clinging to a shroud as he leaned precariously over the gunwale. The crewman on the port vanes was peering up as well, as if afraid he might lose his head if he stood.

"Only the concussion," Emory called. "It was sent off course by the movement of a sloop below us. From what I can tell at this altitude, it's *Marguerite*."

"Etienne is following us?" Celeste asked, wishing she could see over the side from her spot... but she had designed it for vision on all sides and above, not below. "Of course he is," she answered herself. "His own brother flies with us!"

"And he's working with other smugglers, by the look of it," Emory reported. "At least, I can see two other ships, and neither are flying flags. One more is on the horizon, heading this way. They're tacking back and forth, attempting to prevent the *sous-marins* from rising to fire on us."

Oh, the brave dear men! A warm glow that had nothing to do with the low December sun suffused her. They were not alone out here—the smugglers had heeded the call and were coming to help save the Prince. But... the *sous-marins* had proven deadly to the British Navy. How long would the smugglers be able to outwit them?

LOVEDAY SEIZED the pigeon before it crashed into the boiler and damaged itself, then opened it to scan Emory's note. She turned over the sheet of paper and scribbled a reply.

Clouds at 1000 feet indicate winds southerly. Reef sails and rise, using air propeller only to stay ahead of wind. Notify fleet.

She reset the target on the pigeon's head, then tossed it overboard as she would one of the doves at home and watched with no little satisfaction as it did what it was intended to do. Really, Mr Cummings should be proud of what he contributed to the war effort, and afterward. For along with air ships, these little pigeons could certainly be used in civilian life.

Less than a minute after the pigeon was received on *Royal Falcon*, she saw it tossed out and head off to its target on *Royal Eagle*.

"Furl jib and vanes, Crewmen," she ordered the aeronauts at the levers. "We are taking her up. Engineer St Ives, full speed on the boiler, if you please—we shall ride the upper winds to see if we can catch *Prince's Pride* before they make landfall."

One by one, the fleet rose another five hundred feet, and only one of the *Triumph*'s aeronauts lost his breakfast over the side at the rapid change in elevation. His humiliation was doubled at the jeers of his mate, who was also as white as canvas but refused to succumb.

Loveday felt the moment when the winds at the higher elevation seized the ship and they no longer had to fight the north-to-south flow of those blowing below. "Loose jib and vanes!" she called, and soon even the Royal Marines had to take off their tall hats and stow them in the pigeon compartment, lest they fly over the side and into the vast ocean lying like wrinkled silk far below.

Falcon broke formation, rose just enough to clear their envelopes, and settled into place at the head of the fleet. "Follow Captain Blanchard's lead," Loveday called.

"She means to bypass the fort at Cherbourg," Arthur told

the crew, watching *Falcon* closely for the least change in course. "Stay alert for steam clouds below—it means a cannonbomb is incoming. Captain, we must stay well away from shore—two miles at least."

"Understood," Loveday said and could not help a smile of joy. This was what she had been made to do—well, perhaps not chasing princes through the air, but flying with Arthur at her side. Surely a gift beyond price!

Whumph!

They saw the cannonbomb coming this time. Before she could even shout an order, both aeronauts on the levers had shoved the vanes hard to port. *Lady's Triumph* tilted out of the way and the deadly exploding ball passed them a hundred yards to starboard. Arthur leaned over the gunwale.

"Safe," he reported. "It exploded beneath the waves in a foaming dome of water. *Marguerite* and the others did not follow us. They are clearly intending defensive maneuvers closer to English shores."

They were on their own, then, come what may.

Celeste allowed *Falcon* to drift out to sea a little way, out of range of the land-based steam cannon, and set a course following the coastline north. But how were they to locate *Prince's Pride*? They might follow the coast for miles, but at some point they would need either a sight of the runaway ship, or be forced to cross the Channel to make landfall in Southampton or even Brighton to take on coal and water. And the farther north they went, the greater the likelihood they would run into Napoleon's air ships.

"*Falcon* is changing course, Captain," Arthur reported. "She's heading inland."

"Hoping to find concealment in those clouds, perhaps," offered Private Beaton, one of the Royal Marines.

Clouds? The weather was clear, and any clouds were of the thin cirrus variety.

"Engineer St Ives, take the helm," she said to Arthur. "Steady as she goes, in *Falcon*'s wake."

She joined Private Beaton on the gunwale, then realized what he had seen. She sucked in a breath of cold air.

"Those are not clouds, Private," she said. "It's smoke. And look—there in the distance. It's *Prince's Pride*!"

"It's under attack, Captain," the young man exclaimed, hefting his rifle into the ready position surely more by instinct than necessity at this distance. "I count five enemy ships in the air."

"We must go to their assistance at once!" cried the other Royal Marine. "And—and what in the name of heaven is *that?* Down there, crossing the valley."

Loveday resumed the helm so that Arthur could look.

"That, Corporal, is a steam behemoth," he said tersely. "It is war on the ground."

Loveday tore her attention from the chaotic panorama swiftly coming into view ahead. She could not tell friend from foe on the ground. Only in the air. Which was her job. "Marines, forward positions, if you please, and ready rifles. Fire only on the horizontal, never the vertical, if you want to stay in the air. Engineer St Ives, we need your expertise. Reconnoiter, and give us your analysis of what you see down there."

He needed no longer than a minute at the gunwale, and when he returned amidships so that everyone could hear, amazement battled with apprehension on his face.

"The tide of war has turned. We should never have permitted the Prince to fly," he began. "He is under siege in the air, as Private Beaton reported. From their arms and transport, the British Army seems to be holding the hills running east and west directly south of the town below us. Ten French war behemoths are pitted against them, and the Russian Bears seemed to have finally loped into the fray. They command the plains to the north, where they have clearly been encamped for some time. I do not hold out much hope for Amiens. It will be crushed under the metal fists of three furious forces."

If the crewmen had been pale before, now they were ashen.

Amiens? They were to the north, then, of any of the places Loveday and Celeste had seen on their trip to Paris in the steam wagon. In any case, the ground was becoming more and more obscured as smoke and dust rose to spread itself below, blown by the wind. She hoped the inhabitants had had enough warning to flee before the Tsar's forces launched their attack.

"We can do nothing for the ground forces from here," Arthur went on. "We must do as we were commanded, and force the Prince's ship back and out of danger."

"Are we going to fight the French air ships?" Private Beaton looked elated.

Arthur glanced to Loveday, and in his eyes she saw quiet confidence. "Were it up to me, I should say yes. But I do not captain this ship."

"Never let it be said I declined good advice," she said with a grin. "Crew, to your stations. Engineer St Ives, ahead full steam. Our first objective is the Prince's safety, and if we can scuttle a few French air ships in the course of getting him clear, then so much the better!"

IT WAS CHAOS. Having surrendered the helm of *Royal Falcon* to Emory for a moment, Celeste looked over the gunwale, transfixed. Behemoths bellowed and snorted great gouts of steam, and bombs burst. Steam cannon coughed, and foot soldiers fled, like ants scurrying into their hill. La Croix must have found a way to improve the little bombs her mother had invented to make her performances more exciting, for the packages came flying out from the French air ships to arc dangerously close to the English ships before falling to wreak havoc on the ground below.

Thank God none of the behemoths had been retrofitted as yet to fire directly up into the sky. Bad enough that the steam cannon's range required it to belch its deadly balls in a high arc before falling and destroying its target. Woe betide the air ship caught in the middle.

"Permission to fire, Captain?" Corporal Fielding begged. He had crouched next to the gunwale and aimed his rifle out, with Private Jones-Smythe beside him.

"Not yet," Celeste cautioned. "We must know how many we face. I task you, Private. Give us an accurate tally of our ships now in the air."

"Aye, Captain," he said. His rifle clattered against the copper as he crouched lower. "Two port and starboard, the ones from Portsmouth that rose with us. I can't see *Phoebus* or *Power of Portsmouth*."

At least Loveday and Marcel were still aloft.

"Can you see *Prince's Pride*, the one flying the Prince's flag?" Emory called. Very likely he would need to drop more coal into the box for the boiler. She did not dare look to see how much of the precious resource was left.

"No, sir," Private Jones-Smythe reported.

"I'll check port," Corporal Felding volunteered before ducking across the deck.

The two crewmen on the vanes hunkered lower.

Celeste returned to the helm and nodded Emory to the side. He moved toward the bow and wrapped an arm through a shroud. "I cannot see much of anything, but I believe that's *Power of Portsmouth* straight ahead, tacking to stay out of range of a ground emplacement."

"Five more coming about," Private Jones-Smythe called, and now there was a hint of panic in his voice. "French, by the look of them."

"Five more French ships on this side," Corporal Felding put in. "There's *Phoebus*! The marines are taking on one of them. And here's *Lady's Triumph*, sailing in from the west! There goes their target's envelope! Take that, Boney!"

Another sound rose from the battlefield like a wave.

"The British encampment is cheering," Private Jones-Smythe cried. "We've given them heart. That's right, boys! Let them hear you!"

The crewmen on the vanes exchanged shaky smiles.

The thump from below wiped the smiles from their faces. It felt as if someone had boxed Celeste's ears. She shuddered. So did the *Royal Falcon*.

"Lucky shot from a steam cannon," Emory told her, making his way back to her side. "Swing north."

She turned and gave the order, and the aeronauts at the

levers adjusted the vanes to comply. They came about just in time to see a cannonbomb hurtling directly toward them.

"Emory!"

It was the only word she could cry before the bomb struck, and light and sound exploded around her. The deck canted, wrenching her from the helm. She fell, slid, scrambled to find purchase. A moan came from the ship, as if it hurt as well.

"Hold on!"

Emory grabbed her hand as she slid past. Her feet dangled out the gangway, kicking in empty air. She had the absurd notion that Mrs Penhale would not be pleased to find her limbs so utterly exposed to every fellow fighting four hundred feet below.

She gripped Emory's hand with both of hers as the ship went into a spin. "The helm!"

"You first," he said through clenched teeth. He gave a mighty heave and pulled her up against him. She clung to him, heart pounding, breath hissing faster than a steam pump. Private Jones-Smythe was clutching the gunwale, his rifle swaying from its strap. Closer to hand, Corporal Felding hugged the deck, eyes squeezed shut. Both aeronauts had been torn from their vanes as well, arms wrapped around the shrouds.

"Can you reach the helm?" Emory panted with a jerk of his head upward.

"I must," she said. "Help me."

"Fielding!" he shouted. "A hand!"

The corporal's eyes snapped open, and he inched his way along the gunwale to Emory's side. Together, they managed to shove her up the slant. Her stomach rebelled against the motion of the ship, and she swallowed bile.

She reached out, grasped the base of the helm, then pulled herself up. Hands shaking, she hauled on the wheel, and the ship slowed its frantic spin. The aeronauts released the shrouds, crawled to the vane levers, and began setting them to rights while Emory tended to the boiler. Corporal Felding managed to reach his comrade and hold on. Someone retched. She knew the feeling.

Agonizingly slow, they straightened, though the deck continued to hang at a frightful angle.

"We've lost the starboard shrouds," Emory reported, voice raspy, as if he struggled to catch his breath as well. "But she'll fly."

She had to. After everything they had been through, Celeste fully intended to return to England.

And marry Emory Thorndyke.

Never had that wish been more fervent, nor her purpose more clear. Whatever length of life she was blessed with, she wanted only to spend it with him.

Now, she just had to see that they lived long enough to say their vows.

CHAPTER 18

The two Royal Marines may have been little older than Loveday and Arthur, but they knew their business. She heard them adapting their marksmanship to the new rules of the air, encouraging and inventing strategy on the fly. As they would on shore, one man fired while the other reloaded, then they changed places. The crewmen on the vanes stayed out of their way.

"Aim for center mass, not the crew," the corporal said. "They're not built like ours, with more than one gas bag."

"If we can hole the bag, we can take out the boiler from above." Private Beaton sounded very grim for someone with such a fresh, open face. "That will put paid to them, sir."

This strategy worked terrifyingly well for two of the ten ships. And then horror struck. As she watched, a cannonbomb whistled through *Royal Falcon*, shearing its shrouds amidships and exploding moments later in the sky. Loveday screamed as the deck tilted, nearly throwing Celeste out. And then the shrapnel from the blast landed on the French ship below, tearing through the gasbag with an explosion that temporarily lifted *Falcon* off its course.

"Three!" Private Beaton shouted.

"Four!" the corporal called back to Loveday. "*Portsmouth* hit its mark. Now we are even."

"Vanes horizontal, crew," she commanded, swallowing her fear for her friend. "*Royal Eagle* will protect *Falcon*. *Lady's Triumph* must go to the Prince's defense!"

None of them had anticipated being anywhere near France, to say nothing of flying into the middle of a battle. But she had no choice—she could not leave, for the Prince must be protected at all costs.

Lady's Triumph sailed in at speed to take on the French ship trying to force the Prince down in the thickest of the smoke. Private Beaton and his corporal operated like a well-oiled machine, keeping up a steady fire once they came within range of the French ship. The latter appeared to have some kind of incendiary bombs on hand—which meant certain death if they should catch a gasbag. The entire ship would go up in flames, just like the warehouse on the banks of the Seine a few months ago.

"They are constantly moving," the corporal cautioned Private Beaton. "Remember to lead with the muzzle, as we do on the sea."

Triumph's position at the stern of the French ship gave them just enough cover to hole the gasbag, and the ship began to lose altitude. Faster and faster it fell, as the escaping gas tore the hole wider. But there was no time to see its demise, for Loveday must lay the helm over to escape a cannonbomb. At least the *whumph!* of the steam cannons gave a few seconds' warning—the difficulty was in seeing the trajectory through the smoke before the wretched things struck.

The turn gave her a moment to see below. The behemoths had swiveled to take on the Russian Bears, the Tsar's great armored coaches of which, before this, Loveday had only seen engravings. They were much more terrifying in real life, with steam belching from enormous twin chimneys in the rear that powered them forward. Cannons protruded from the bow, and when they fired, the balls made a whistling sound in the air like a scream.

"Are we winning?" she shouted to Arthur. "On the ground?"

"Not our remit!" he shouted back. "Our orders are to turn the Prince around!"

Did that mean they weren't winning? But there was not a blessed thing she could do about that—not without cannon or at the very least those French bombs to drop upon a behemoth. But now that *Prince's Pride* was no longer being harassed, her task was clear. Stop its crazed flight inland and get it turned about.

"We're going in!" she cried. "We'll cross her bow and turn her!" She brought *Triumph* about. "Vanes vertical!"

Lady's Triumph stooped on *Pride* as though she had been a falcon herself, running across her bow so close Loveday could spot the terrified faces of the aeronauts working her vanes.

In a flash like a tableau, she saw three things.

Jacob Barnes at the helm, his wrists tied to the wheel with what looked like rope cut from the rigging.

The Prince, likewise tied to the shrouds.

And standing in front of him, Paul Grenville with rifle to

his shoulder, clearly having lifted it from the body of the Royal Marine lying on the deck.

He took aim, the muzzle tracking just ahead of their course.

"Loveday!" Arthur shouted and tackled her from behind.

The ball sang over their heads as *Triumph*'s stern cleared *Pride*'s bow.

"Give me a chance at him!" Private Beaton bellowed.

"Arthur—the helm—" Loveday gasped from under him, her cheek mashed into the deck.

"Are you all right? Darling, are you hit?"

"No!"

He hauled her to her feet, and they staggered to the helm. "Are *you* all right?" She touched his pale face, checking for blood.

"Yes. Come about, or Beaton will leap onto *Pride* in sheer rage."

"One moment, my lord," she said, and grabbed him by the buttons with both hands. She kissed him with fierce joy, with relief, with gratitude. He had saved her life—and what's more, he had called her *darling!*

He rocked on his heels and staggered back out of her grip, less from the tilt of the deck, it seemed, than from sheer bemusement.

She seized the helm once more. The English forces below must manage as best they could. With a surge of elation, Loveday *knew* nothing could bring her down. With a feral smile, her teeth bared, she laid the helm over and brought *Triumph* about, this time on a diagonal course that would take them across the bow in a way that no water-bound vessel ever could.

"Vanes vertical!" she screamed. "Rifles ready!"

And as *Triumph* dove from this unexpected direction, both her Royal Marines took aim and fired.

"Vanes horizontal!" she called to the crewmen. "Coming about. Marines reload!"

"No need, Captain," Private Beaton looked as though he would levitate in the air. "We got him!"

"No time for a pigeon—signal Mr Barnes to follow us out of danger."

She came about once more, slower this time, to see Jacob Barnes's mouth drawn back in a silent howl as if he tried not to weep, though whether in shame or relief, Loveday could not tell. But he had anticipated her orders, and already *Prince's Pride* was coming about, heading for the coast and a modicum of safety. Two aeronauts had abandoned their posts and were untying his hands and those of the Prince. Then, without ceremony, they picked up the bleeding Paul Grenville by the hands and feet, and swung him over the gunwale.

Loveday did not know whether he was still alive. Nor did she watch him fall. Her entire being was centered on getting the Prince Regent to safety.

They emerged from clouds of steam and smoke into air that was slightly clearer. The offshore breeze was not strong enough to turn them back, but it would cause them to use whatever coal and water they had left more quickly. Still, she had just a moment to breathe deeply before they made a run for it.

"Loveday, look!" Arthur pointed to starboard. "Air ships ho!"

All the breath went out of her lungs as though she had been struck. "How many did that wretched La Croix make?"

she croaked. "Send a pigeon to the *Falcon* at once. We must retreat!"

But even as Arthur pulled their pigeon out of its cubbyhole, she could see it was too late. There were too many of them. A dozen at least, bearing down on them like so many avenging angels determined to make these their last few seconds on earth.

THE NOISE from the battlefield faded, as if every hand had stilled and every eye strained upward. Celeste stared at the air ships sailing in from the east through rising clouds of steam and smoke. How had France managed so many so quickly? Surely there had been no time to retrofit the ones Toussaint had built, for those had been designed to be flown by a single automaton, not a human crew.

"Five, six, seven of them," Emory said, clearly counting every silk envelope as she was. Only he could sound as if they were a marvel rather than approaching doom. It had been challenging enough to fend off the ships already above the battlefield. Once these joined the fight, even in the air the British forces would be hopelessly outnumbered. And the poor Prince! After all *Triumph*'s brilliant maneuvers, they would never be able to rescue him now.

Of course, he was probably gawking at the fleet just as they were, seeing his own execution coming in like a summer storm.

It was hard not to gawk. Horizontally striped gas bags in gold and scarlet, copper decks long and sleek, they cruised with majestic glory across the pale blue of the winter sky. Yet something about them poked at her, like a dream begging to be remembered.

Celeste dashed the tears from her eyes and peered closer. No, it could not be. How could they bear such a strong resemblance to the final plans Loveday had hastily revised before she and Celeste had escaped France? As far as Celeste knew, only one person had a copy of those plans.

And she was flying the first ship that swept past.

From the helm, *Gardien* Julia Wintzen, or rather Captain Wintzen, Celeste's former bodyguard and spy for the Karlsruhe Confederacy, offered her a salute. Her pale hair had come loose from its pins and flowed behind her in the crisp air, making her look even more like a Valkyrie come to life than she had in the halls of the Tuileries.

Corporal Felding raised his rifle.

"Lower your weapons!" Celeste ordered. "They are friends! We are saved!"

Clearly confused, he carefully uncocked and lowered the weapon.

"I believe that one is trying to capture your attention, Captain," Private Jones-Smythe ventured, and Celeste looked to the other side, where another of the wondrous craft was flanking them. Her heart clenched, and she gave a muffled cry.

Emory must have heard it, for he stepped closer, gaze on the sturdy older woman at the helm of the other craft. "Who is she?"

"I called her Dupont," Celeste managed, tears falling that were not caused by smoke. "Though I might as well have called her *Maman*, for she raised me while my parents were busy performing all over Europe. Napoleon sent her to the front. I never thought I'd see her alive again. Just look at her!"

As if just as affected by seeing Celeste, Dupont's face softened, and she blew her a kiss from the helm.

"But who are they?" Private Jones-Smythe asked, voice hushed and wary, as the other air ships passed in an array of strength. "Why don't they shoot?"

"Because they're on our side!" Celeste cried. "It's the Karlsruhe Confederacy. Loveday and I armed them with plans to build their own air ships. I never dreamed they would be so beautiful!"

"They must have been working around the clock since we left France," Emory said. "There? Do you see that copper protuberance near the wheel? Is that an automatic speaking tube, to allow them to communicate?"

"It must be! Oh, but Loveday will want to examine them as soon as this battle is over."

Emory laid a hand on her shoulder, and she felt the touch to her toes. They would be safe now, surely. With so many arrayed against them, the French forces must admit defeat.

"What about those?" Corporal Felding asked, nodding toward the north.

Emory's hand on her shoulder tightened, and they squinted past the trailing rigging. From over the hills in the distance, more air ships approached, these with envelopes striped vertically in gold and black, with a symbol sewn across the largest stripe.

Who would come from the north? Had the French circled around behind them? Were they trapped anew?

"Look sharp!" Celeste ordered the corporal. "Can you tell

the design? Are they French? From the pirate kingdom in the south? Russia?"

One of the aeronauts made a face. "That looks like the British lion."

Emory strode to the gunwale and leaned over, as if that would give him a better view.

"It is a lion rampant," he reported. "Black on a field of gold." Then he stiffened and looked back at Celeste. "But they appear to have no steam engine, only a complicated set of gears, like immense versions of those little boxes Napoleon favored, the ones that were forever ringing."

Clockwork? Could it be?

"It is the Flemish lion!" Arthur shouted.

"Monsieur Patenaude reached Belgium with a vengeance," Loveday managed, trying not to laugh and cry together in hysterical relief. For a captain, that would never do. "Oh, Arthur, look at the gears in the stern—all the propelling devices they power—have you ever seen their like? I must know how it works."

"All in good time, Captain," he said meaningfully, recalling her to her duty. "We must stay aloft as long as we can to guard the Prince."

"Of course," she said at once. "This battle is not over yet."

Her bloodthirsty crew were hard put to conceal their disappointment at being relegated to guard duty, but poor Mr Barnes could not be expected to keep the Prince out of danger alone. She could not even contemplate what might have happened to the second Royal Marine in *Pride*'s crew.

Not now. Not when hope told her that victory could be theirs.

For this was no test flight—the Confederacy ships had come to wage war. They were outfitted with bombs—and more, with bombardiers who had been trained to frightening accuracy. The ships swooped in with grave dignity, leaving utter destruction in their wake. When a bomb hit the first behemoth, such was the explosion that it blew down instead of up, creating a great crater in the earth. A second behemoth promptly walked into it and fell with an ear-crunching crash.

Arthur, watching closely from the gunwale, gave a huff of amazement. "The soldiers inside those beasts have never seen defeat," he said, rubbing his leg as though it ached with the memory of the shrapnel that had ended his career as a soldier. "On the ground, too, the tide will turn."

So it seemed to Loveday. And with two more direct hits and another fatal fall into a crater, the French mechanicals were down by half. It did not take long for the English cannoneers to take advantage of their disarray, and when the behemoths were down to three, the French called a retreat. From above, the bugle call sounded like the bellow of a wounded bull, and so, perhaps, the French forces were indeed. For they could not withstand the assault from the air. All the French air ships were down, some burning, some merely wreckage. The Russian Bears swept in, and with their greater maneuverability, put paid to the last of the fleeing behemoths.

As the winter sun sank toward the hills in the west, no more steam cannons fired, no more companies of rifles sent fusillades of musket balls at the advancing forces. As the smoke and steam cleared from the skies, Loveday saw the lovely Confederacy ships sink to the wide plain where the

Russian forces had been encamped. The Flemish lions followed.

The English air ships hovered in the now emptying skies, as though uncertain of what to do.

"Captain?" the Royal Marine corporal asked. "Orders?"

"We will take her down also. Signal to Mr Barnes," Loveday said. "I believe the Prince Regent will wish to thank his allies for their timely appearance. We must not deprive him of such an opportunity."

Loveday positioned *Lady's Triumph* on the starboard side of *Prince's Pride*, the battered but still gallant *Royal Falcon* coming about to take up a position on the other. *Royal Eagle*, *Phoebus*, and *Power of Portsmouth* sailed in to take up positions to the stern. And together, as though they had actually rehearsed it, their captains brought the Prince's little fleet safely to rest in the center of the double arc created by the European fleets, like the apple of an inventor's eye.

CHAPTER 19

*R*iding a white horse and bearing a white flag of *parlez* that appeared to be a rectangle of hastily cut canvas, an envoy from the French forces met the Prince of Wales, General von Zeppelin of the Karlsruhe Confederacy, High Commander van Meere of the Kingdom of Flanders, and Countess Viktoria Sokolova of Russia on what had become a *de facto* airfield. Standing to one side, Arthur had not a doubt that the man's original brief from Napoleon had been to declare victory on the Emperor's behalf and take the Prince Regent prisoner, to be conveyed to Paris in chains like some ancient Roman trophy from Britannia.

Now, it was difficult not to feel sorry for the man, who was forced to humble himself and bow before the four victorious commanders of the Battle of Amiens.

"I am empowered by the Emperor Napoleon Bonaparte," the envoy said, leaning on the staff of his flag for support, "to beg your mercy for our brave soldiers, and to convey his devout wish that the controversy between our kingdoms be ended."

The Prince looked amazed at this mealy-mouthed way of putting it. Arthur had to admire the man's courage. The words were certainly not appropriate to the occasion.

"Convey to your Emperor that all offensive forays over the original borders of France are to cease," the Prince said sternly. "All construction of machines of war is likewise to cease. He is to return to the peaceful government of his own kingdom, listen to his Parliament like a responsible monarch, and see to his people, whom he has made to suffer during all these years of war."

The envoy looked miserable.

High Commander van Meere stepped to the Prince's side. "If he does not agree to these terms at once, we will recommence battle operations in the morning and continue until we are floating above the very gates of his palace in Paris."

"I for one will be happy to drop a bomb upon it," Countess Sokolova said coolly.

"I think it safe to say that he will agree," the envoy said hastily. "Arrangements will be made for formal peace talks in some neutral location, with a view to a permanent armistice."

General von Zeppelin nodded. "Vienna, shall we say, in the East Kingdom. Civilized place. Music, good food. Excellent coffee."

The envoy bowed low and got himself on his horse with ungraceful haste. He galloped off toward the hills, where smoke from a burning behemoth was rising like a forlorn flag in the long rays of a fading sun.

The Prince Regent inclined his head to the commanders of their now allied fleets. "My boundless gratitude to you and your forces, my lords, my lady, for coming to our aid in such an unprecedented and magnificent manner," he said. "I should invite you to dinner if I had somewhere to serve it. As it happens, I have not even a flask of brandy to offer you."

General von Zeppelin clapped him on the shoulder and made him stagger. "It is we who ought to thank you, Your Royal Highness. Seems the designs for these vessels of ours came by way of a pair of your engineers. I'm told they are women. Is that true?"

The Prince beckoned Loveday and Celeste over, and without a moment's thought, Arthur and Emory left the small group of the Prince's Own to go with them. Arthur stood back a respectful step or two, lest someone believe there had been a mistake, and the engineers in question were actually male.

The two young women he esteemed most highly in the world sank into curtsies. The Prince raised them and introduced them to the commanders.

"Oh, sirs," Celeste said eagerly to the newcomers, "we should so much like to see how your ships have been constructed. For you have obviously greatly improved on our designs."

"Indeed yes," General von Zeppelin said, looking immensely pleased. "We should be delighted to give you a tour. And then," he added with raised eyebrows to the Prince and the Countess, "perhaps we might convene on my flagship for that tot of brandy. Even on a ship of war, one must have the barest minimum of comforts, *nein?*"

Loveday laughed, and when the general offered her his arm, she twinkled over her shoulder at Arthur and walked away with him.

The group followed. Jacob Barnes made his way back to Celeste, his face red with emotion, his mouth trembling with what Arthur could imagine were the words he felt it most necessary to say.

"Celeste, I am so sorry," he burst out.

She paused, slipping her hand into the crook of Emory's elbow. "It is we who should apologize, Jacob. Until the moment we saw your hands tied to the helm, we believed you at least partly responsible for the kidnapping of the Prince."

"I blame myself," he said desperately. "I have already tendered my resignation to Mr Guelph for my foolishness. I didn't see it. Paul Grenville was so personable, so knowledge-able, it never occurred to me even as we were drinking together that he could possibly be a spy—never mind one so accomplished."

"You must not blame yourself," Arthur said, moving them along. He did not want to lose Loveday to the joys of touring warships. "None of us suspected him. I take it he overpowered one of the Marines?"

Barnes nodded. "Disarmed him and tipped him over the side. With a loaded rifle in the Prince's back, the other could do nothing. Tried to ambush him and was murdered for his pains." He looked up. "Dashed fine shooting from the Marine aboard your ship. The man deserves a medal."

The Prince, whose hearing must be acute, slowed to join them. "I have already made a note of Private Beaton's service to the Crown, Mr Barnes. You did your best, including putting yourself in harm's way, keeping your body between mine and the spy's while you were forced to restrain me. I will not forget it, sir."

At this, Barnes was reduced to incoherence and had to withdraw.

Arthur hoped that Mr Guelph had roundly refused his

resignation. He had a feeling that the happy-go-lucky, flirtatious Jacob Barnes had passed through the fire and come out on the other side a wiser, more tempered man than the one who had so recklessly departed Portsmouth.

The Prince fell into step beside him. Arthur did his best to conceal his surprise, though he noticed that Emory and Celeste stayed not far away as they ambled after Loveday and General von Zeppelin toward the glorious, stately fleets of their allies.

"And you, St Ives?" the Prince said. "What are your plans now?"

Taken slightly aback, Arthur managed, "I—I hardly know, sir. Find somewhere to bivouac tonight. Convey you to England without incident in the morning. Beyond that, I have not thought."

The future monarch smiled. "Let me advise you, then."

"Certainly, sir. I should be grateful."

"That girl," he nodded toward Loveday, whose smile was so bright as she spoke with von Zeppelin it was clear he was as enamored of powered flight as she was herself, "is of the kind that happens along only once in a man's lifetime."

"I agree with you most heartily, sir."

"She piloted that ship as though it and she were one being. Like Athena herself, going to war with nothing but her own skill and, not an owl, but her pigeons. I have never seen anything like it."

"Nor will you again, I hope," Arthur said, beginning to recover. "We were prepared for a test flight, not an act of war that took you into mortal danger."

"And none of you hesitated for an instant." He gave a nod. "Do you have intentions toward her?"

This was no time for prevarication. Not after what they'd just been through together. Not after that kiss. "Yes, sir."

"Good. Don't muck it up. Secure her at once, and I will see about some more land to go with your title. A man should be able to support a woman like that in style."

Arthur lost his breath—not at the land to be added to what he had already so generously been given, but at the royal command to do what he most wanted in the world.

"The little manor near St Ives is all very well for setting up housekeeping," the Prince mused, "but I understand there's a collection of derelict mines not far from you, there on the south coast. The old Earl of Falmouth's property. Title's extinct. Land is played out and awful for farming, but with Thorndyke's pump and my plans for a larger fleet, the lifting gas ought to change the economy of the neighborhood for the better."

"Yes, sir," Arthur croaked. "Thank you, sir."

"I have faith in you. You've proved yourself today. You'll go far, St Ives, if you wish it, with that young lady by your side."

"Yes, sir. I'm most grateful, sir. I will speak with her father the instant we return to Portsmouth."

"You do that." The Prince patted his shoulder and moved up to join High Commander van Meere, leaving Arthur feeling as though he needed a flag staff to lean upon, too.

Up ahead, Loveday pointed at some protuberance on the hull of the Confederacy flagship and clapped her hands in delight.

Secure her at once.

Mr Penhale's permission would have to wait. Far be it from him to disobey a royal command.

CELESTE WAS JUST as interested in those flying the craft as the wonders of the craft themselves. Knowing Loveday would tell her all, and that the English aeronauts were already tending their vessels, she turned to Emory. "I must find Dupont and Wintzen."

He nodded. "Of course. I'll speak to the army commander and see what can be done about taking on coal and water." He tilted his head toward the Royal Marines, who were walking behind them as smartly as if they were on parade. "As captain, you are likely expected to relieve them of duty."

Celeste squared her shoulders and turned to the two men. "Corporal, Private, you have served your country well. You are relieved of duty for now. You might find the commander in charge of this camp. I'm sure he will appreciate your reports to add to his own."

They both snapped to attention and saluted her smartly. "Captain."

"And thank you for saving our lives up there," Private Jones-Smythe said with a wistful glance up at *Falcon*'s gas bag.

Corporal Fielding was already heading for the commander's tent in the distance. She had a feeling he couldn't get away fast enough from anything that flew.

Celeste leaned closer to the young pilot. "I understand they are training pilots on St Michael's Mount in Cornwall. If you enjoy flying, you might request a transfer."

He grinned. "I might at that, ma'am." With a final salute, he followed his comrade, and they were soon lost to sight.

Now that both Jacob and the marines were settled, and Emory off to find coal and water, she made her way across the camp toward the magnificent ships of Flanders and the Karls-ruhe Confederacy. The British soldiers immediately straight-ened as she passed, doffing helmets and saluting or even bowing. Two elbowed others out of her way with devoted smiles. Well, perhaps there was something to be said for skirts after all. They gave a lady a certain *éclat* entirely missing from *pantalons*.

The air ships of the Confederacy had settled in a well-spaced arc on the flat acres of the field, and already fires had been lit for a celebratory dinner. Still, they were taking no chances, for soldiers who must have sailed with the air ships were on guard duty around the camp perimeter.

One leveled his air-crank rifle at her. "Halt! Who goes there?"

Celeste inclined her head. "Captain Blanchard of the Royal Aeronautic Corps."

They evidently had not yet heard about the fledgling branch of the King's service. He narrowed his eyes. "*Captain* Blanchard?"

"One of the persons responsible for this victory," Wintzen said, cuffing him alongside the head as she approached. He staggered and lowered his rifle. She stepped around him and enfolded Celeste in such a hug that the breath whooshed out of her.

"Do you like what we did with your plans?" she asked, releasing Celeste and waving a hand at the row of ships.

"Very much," Celeste said, managing to find her breath again. "Loveday and the other members of the Prince's Own will likely be along shortly to study them, if you are willing. She is with General von Zeppelin."

She shrugged. "You two designed them. You have every

right to see them. And you? How are you faring? Captain Blanchard, eh?"

Celeste smiled. "By accident, I assure you. We were on a mission to rescue His Royal Highness. I have no doubt I will be back at the workbench again once we return." She leaned closer. "I understand from Loveday that you were a close friend of Monsieur Patenaude, Napoleon's former Grand Inventor. I did not see him in the fray, but could it be he has sailed with the Flemish ships?"

Her former bodyguard flushed red up into her blond hair. "Perhaps I will find out and speak with him."

"You should," Celeste said, treading the fine line between encouragement and presumption.

"And I hope you have spared time to speak with me," Dupont said, coming around the gondola of the nearest air ship.

Celeste ran to her and threw her arms around her for a hug as fierce as Wintzen's. "Oh, Dupont! How I have missed you!"

Dupont held her close. "And I you, *mon ange*. Why did you not tell me you intended to fly to England? Did you think I would try to stop you?"

"*Oui*," Celeste admitted, drawing back to look up into her dear face. There were more wrinkles around those steely grey eyes, more silver working its way into the iron grey tresses, than the last time she'd seen her companion. She did not like the idea she might have had a hand in those changes.

Dupont sighed. "You are probably right. But oh, how your mother and I grieved your loss."

Tears were gathering again. "I know. And I grieved hers and yours."

Dupont looked away, the memory obviously painful. "I promise you, Celeste, I tried to tell your *chère maman* not to go up that night. But she would not listen."

Celeste sniffed back her tears. "She did not take advice well. She did not give it well, either. It always sounded more like an order."

Dupont slipped an arm about her shoulders. "She would be so proud of what you have accomplished, *ma petite*. You rival her brilliance in the skies."

"Never," Celeste whispered. "But I like to think she and Papa would be pleased to see this war end and their inventions returned to use for the good of all."

"Now, there is a future we can all agree on," Dupont said.

"But you," Celeste said. "What does the future hold for you?" When Dupont hesitated, she hurried on, "Come back with me to England. I am a member of the Prince's Own Engineers, as is Loveday, my good friend. You can work beside us, serve as our chaperone as you did for *La Blanchard*."

"Ah, nothing would give me more pleasure." Dupont's round face was wistful. "But I have pledged myself to the Karlsruhe Confederacy. Much damage has been done there by these bombings. I want to help them rebuild."

Celeste swallowed. "Then will I ever see you again?"

Dupont released her to spread her hands in a shrug. "Who knows? We fly where the winds blow. Perhaps they will blow me to England one day, or you to the Confederacy."

Perhaps, but she doubted that.

She took her companion's hand. "Then come with me now. There is someone I want you to meet."

"This is the young man who has captured your affections?"

Dupont guessed as they walked through the grass back toward British territory.

"Yes," Celeste admitted. "We have been pretending an engagement for reasons that are too convoluted to explain now, but I hope we may find a way of making that engagement real."

"Bon," Dupont said with a nod. "I will see if he is worthy of you."

Celeste laughed. "You have been spending too much time with Captain Wintzen. You sound just like her!"

They located Emory back on *Royal Falcon*, resupplying the ship. Planks had been set for a makeshift gangway, and soldiers were ferrying buckets of water and loads of coal up to the boiler, donated, one informed her, by the local populace in gratitude for their helping to end the war. A Flemish sailwright was busy in the rigging with new lengths of rope.

Emory straightened from his task as Celeste and Dupont climbed aboard. Coal dust had caught in the scruff of beard that was just beginning to grow, making it appear that someone had sprinkled him with salt and pepper.

"Madame Emeline Dupont," Celeste said, as they came to stop in front of him, "allow me to present Sir Emory Thorndyke. Emory, this is the woman who cared for me when I was young."

Emory took both of Dupont's capable hands in his and bowed over them, apparently failing to notice that he smeared them with coal dust at the same time. "Madame Dupont, thank you. You have raised a fine and marvelous woman whom even a prince is honored to know."

"So I have," Dupont agreed, retrieving her fingers from his grip. "I have yet to determine, however, whether she has found a fine and marvelous man. What should I know of you, Sir Emory?"

Emory lifted his chin, sending sprinkles of coal dust down onto his already bespeckled waistcoat. "I am a member of the Prince's Own Engineers, and I invented the pump that is presently emptying the Cornish tin and copper mines of seawater and lifting gas."

Another lady in Dupont's position would have been more impressed to hear of heraldic prowess and ancestral lands. Her companion broke into a grin and pulled him into a hug. "An inventor? My dear Sir Emory, I think we will get along just fine."

CHAPTER 20

Since the warships were designed for short-haul flights and not for the accommodation and feeding of a crew, the aeronauts of the three nations were billeted in the villages surrounding the town of Amiens, and within the town proper.

Loveday and Celeste, as well as Emory and Arthur, were billeted in a coaching inn facing the square of the town. As they walked in that evening, it seemed the entire populace turned out to cheer the Prince and the allied generals. Dupont, who had consented just this once to add *chaperone* to her duties, still wore her scarlet and gold redingote. Bemused, she accepted the cheers for the Karlsruhe Confederacy, which continued in the distance, heralding the progress of the generals to another hotel.

They were all to meet for dinner with the Prince shortly, there being no clothes to change into or anything but a good wash to wait for, but Arthur laid a hand on Loveday's arm.

"May I speak with you a moment?" he asked.

"Of course." She hoped it was not about some matter of

etiquette in dining with royalty. She knew even less on that subject than he, and besides, how could one stand upon ceremony when even the royal shirt was stained with gunpowder and smelled of smoke?

She let Celeste and Madame Dupont know that they would be walking in the garden in the rear of the hotel and followed Arthur through the arched stone passage.

The sun was down, but between the brief winter twilight and the lamps that had been lit over the passage, there was still light enough to see by. The herb beds were mostly dormant for winter, though on the south side she could smell tarragon, mint, and thyme. Arthur turned in that direction, as though they might find it warmer.

"The scents of home," he said. "I did not know how welcome they would be until this moment. I needed to wipe away the smells of battle."

"You will still need to tolerate those for some time," Loveday said ruefully. "I suspect there is no laundress, and we are on our own."

"I can tolerate anything as long as we share it." As they paced the gravel walks between the herb beds, he tucked her hand into the crook of his elbow and folded his other hand atop it.

"I saw you speaking with the Prince," she offered, in case this was the subject on his mind.

He huffed a chuckle. "Indeed I was. He thinks very highly of you and gave me to understand I had better do the same."

She could not help but laugh. "He is very generous. Perhaps I should choose my moment, and request that *Lark Deux* be outfitted again before we leave Portsmouth."

"Perhaps I should choose my moment, too." He stopped

and drew her down on the benchlike rim of a bed of mint. The scent rose up around them, refreshing and sweet. "Loveday, during the height of the battle, you gave me reason to hope that you might view me as more than merely a comrade in arms—more even than a good friend."

The heat bloomed in her cheeks. "You are not going to let me forget that, are you?"

"No indeed. In fact, it is my hope that I may tell my children about it, and my children's children."

"Heavens, what a reputation I will have in your family." She hardly knew what she was saying, so fast was her heart beating.

"In *our* family," he corrected her softly. "Loveday, we have known each other all our lives. Yet it has only been since Celeste's arrival that I have seen the woman you really are. A woman a man would be both proud and humbled to have at his side, through storm and shadow, sunlight and gale."

She could not reply. She had forgotten how to breathe.

"The fact is… I cannot envision a future without you in it." He took her hands in his. "Will you do me the very great honor of accepting my hand in marriage?"

She caught her breath in a gasp. Her nostrils filled with the scent of mint, and she knew she would never pass by the herb again without remembering this moment.

"Yes, Arthur," she said.

She cuddled up against his side, and he passed his arm about her shoulders.

"I could not imagine being married to anyone else," she confessed. "I cannot tell you how unheroic I have been, wishing all manner of dreadful things upon every duke's daughter and knight's niece you have danced with since we came to London."

He laughed. "I have much to be ashamed of on that account as well. I shall have to apologize to Mr Barnes for the things I thought of him every time he smiled at you."

"You—you will not mind being married to a tinkerer?" She raised her head to look into his eyes. "I do not think I can give it up, dearest Arthur, even for you."

His smile could have lit the little garden all on its own. "Since the Prince has ordered me to secure your hand at once because of his utter admiration for your skill as an aeronaut *and* a tinkerer, I do not think I will have a choice in the matter."

"Has he really?"

"In exactly so many words."

Goodness. "But royal commands aside, I must know if in your heart you accept me as I am."

He did not hesitate. "I do. You accepted my wounded leg when I could not accept my own future. Even yet I may not be able to dance every dance at our wedding."

"As long as you can stand without pain at the altar, that is all I ask."

Smiling, he lowered his head and kissed her. Not the way she had kissed him, daring fate, with death and destruction all around them, but sweetly. Gently. Possessively. And yet with a spark that told her he had been serious about those children.

At length he raised his head, his breathing as fast as her own. "Perhaps we should go in. I did not realize darkness had fallen, and I do not want to give Captain Dupont cause for concern."

Together they rose, retracing their steps along the path,

the scent of mint now stronger in the air than the smoke of a battle long past.

The next day

"Yes, very good," Celeste told one of the young Royal Marines. "Keep her on a steady heading for the next few leagues."

The English general in command of the Amiens camp had insisted he should help fly them back to England. Their crews would be at a minimum so that they could ferry the worst of the wounded to the naval hospital at Portsmouth without compromising the weight in the ships. Though a groan lifted here and there from the soldiers lying on the deck, she knew those aboard *Lady's Triumph* would be rejoicing, for Arthur had not been able to keep his engagement to Loveday a secret. Her friend looked happier than when she was building something, which said a great deal for her feelings this morning.

"Call me if the wind should change," she told the Royal Marine.

"Aye, Captain Blanchard," he said, gaze trained out over the wide blue of the Channel. The other marine nodded, hands gripping the controls of the vanes so hard his knuckles stood out.

Celeste moved through those of the crew tending the wounded to the stern, where Emory was lounging on the aft seat, caped greatcoat slung about his shoulders and long legs outstretched.

"The lieutenant shows promise," she told him.

"You should speak to the Prince," he said as she sat beside him. She still found it amusing that, in all the Prince's improvements, he had insisted on keeping the storage cupboard containing a hamper under the bench at the rear of the craft, as if he too saw the delights of a picnic in the sky that Celeste had once promised Emory. Mind you, the hamper now contained pigeons, not food, but still.

"If you think it would help Lieutenant Vickery," she said. "Though perhaps it would be wiser to praise him to his commanding officer."

"Not about that," he hedged. "About your future. I've been giving it some thought. You taught at l'Ecole des Aéronautes in Paris. You should be the one teaching the new aeronauts at St Michael's Mount."

She caught her breath. Oh, to teach again! She had been only fourteen when she'd started at l'Ecole. Then her mother's illustrious name had been enough to silence any whispers about Celeste being too young or a female. Perhaps, after this victory, the name of Blanchard would carry weight in England as well.

But… if she taught on the Mount, she would be in Cornwall, while Emory would be in London with the Prince's Own.

She would have sworn the ship lost altitude, but it was her spirits that plummeted. She wrapped her hands around each other and forced herself to study them. "Then you would like to end our pretend engagement."

"The purpose of it seems to have fallen by the wayside," he said apologetically.

She sighed. "Yes, I suppose it has. But I shall be sorry to see it go. It gave me an excuse to be close to you."

He shifted, bringing his lean body next to hers. "Do you need an excuse, Celeste?"

She could not help the laugh that bubbled up. "*Mais oui!* There are too many rules in England. I may not wear this, I may not say that. I may not live on my own without a husband or chaperone. I may not say the things I wish for fear of appearing rude—or worse, forward."

"And what would you say," he asked, voice soft, "if the rules no longer applied?"

"Oh, so many things! That I admire you above all men. That you are wise and clever and caring. That you deserve the very best of wives. That—that I wish I might be that wife."

Goodness! What had opened the valve and allowed all that to escape?

She chanced a glance at him to find his face somber. Had she finally shocked him? Did he realize they would never suit?

He rose, then went down on one knee on the deck in front of her. "In that case—Celeste Blanchard, would you do me the honor of marrying me?"

She searched his face, from the sea green of his eyes to the lips that had kissed her so sweetly. Why was it so difficult to believe he might truly be hers?

"This is not pretend?" she whispered, mindful of the lieutenant at the helm and his partner on the vanes, to say nothing of the aeronauts and the wounded men laid out on the deck. "This is real?"

He took her hand and pressed it against his heart. The wild beat pounded against her palm. "As real as the love I bear for you," he promised. "I know that statement lent—about doing me the honor of marrying me—is one that is used by many men. But I am very conscious of the honor. I would be marrying a woman admired on two continents, a woman capable of flying nearly to the stars. A woman who has captured my heart. Please, Celeste. I will only be the man I wish to be if you are at my side."

He had not always said the right words in her presence, but these—these were perfect. Everything inside her begged her to agree.

But she could be logical, too.

"What of teaching aeronauts in Cornwall?" she challenged. "I do not want to be parted from you."

"Nor would you be," he said. "Where you go, I will go. I can invent anywhere, but only when you are near."

She kissed him then. Really, what else was there to say? Together, they truly would reach the stars, just as her father had once envisioned.

The lieutenant looked back just as the kiss ended. "I beg your pardon, Captain, but I just realized something."

She struggled to bring her whole being back to earth—or at least, back to the bounds of *Royal Falcon*. "And what is that, Lieutenant?"

His teeth flashed in a grin. "Why, Captain, 'tis Christmas Day."

"Happy Christmas," croaked a soldier lying on the deck on a pallet.

"We have a lot to be thankful for," another managed, "now that the war is over."

Emory took Celeste's bare hand—she had managed to lose her gloves—and kissed it.

"We do," he said. "It is the happiest of Christmases indeed."

CHAPTER 21

The New Year had been rung in by the time they all
reached Cornwall again. But that didn't explain the
fireworks over Truro Harbor as the Royal Carriage rolled into
town just after sundown. Word had been sent ahead that Miss
Loveday Penhale, Lord St Ives, Miss Celeste Blanchard who
had been known as Aventure, and Sir Emory Thorndyke were
coming home in *Lark Deux*, escorting by air a very special
guest.

The Prince had come to Cornwall at last.

The Lord Mayor of Truro, the aldermen, Lord St Aubyn,
and the head of every other major house in the area were on
hand to greet His Royal Highness with an elaborate dinner at
the Red Lion Hotel, followed by an elegant ball at the
Assembly Rooms in the High Cross. It wasn't until the next
day, when the Prince flew to Hale House and Gwynn Place
with Loveday and Arthur that Celeste and Emory could visit
the Thorndyke home.

It was time to pay the piper, as the English said, and tell
Emory's family about their engagement.

A neat, three-story affair of good local stone, the Thorndyke house had multi-paned windows overlooking the front garden. She had seen it only once before, when they had returned from France the first time. Then, Emory's father had barely managed a nod of respect, which was more than she had expected. Would he be any more receptive now that she was to become his daughter-in-law?

Emory's second sister, Thomasina, had flung the door open before they could knock. She hugged Emory, then, to Celeste's surprise, threw her arms around her as well.

"I always wanted another sister," she said, her eyes sparkling. "Now I won't be the only one in the middle."

"You know?" Celeste asked, glancing at Emory in confusion.

"Of course," she said with a ready smile. "Madame Racine wrote us from London ages ago to say that she was very pleased by your engagement. Did she come back with you as well?"

The answer to that was only one of the stories they told and retold during the course of that memorable evening. Emory's father seemed so pleased to have his son back in Cornwall that he welcomed Celeste warmly. He and Emory's sisters had their own stories to offer. It seemed that Henrietta had found her calling in running Wheal Thorne and was only too happy to hear that Emory intended to continue inventing things rather than resume his former place. He was delighted to renounce that place to her.

"There's something to be said for a woman who knows her own mind," his father said with a satisfied nod and a wink to Celeste.

"Or *mine*," Henrietta said with an unprecedented wink to her brother.

Inspired by their sister, Thomasina and Georgiana were also considering how they might scandalize their neighbors by spending their lives in a larger world than that of kitchen and nursery.

More news awaited them at Hale House, where Emory returned Celeste later that afternoon.

"The Delaguards have been pardoned," Arthur reported from his place on the sofa in the Hale House withdrawing room. The cushion next to him was empty, as Loveday was showing the Prince her workroom. "I understand they have decided to set up a run—a legal run, I might add—between France and England, once all the negotiations have been concluded. It would not surprise me if the Misses Aventure intended to settle in England as well."

So, she might have Amélie, Josie, and the Delaguard brothers close enough to visit on occasion. Celeste couldn't help smiling at that.

"And the Prince?" She glanced out the window toward the terrace, where His Royal Highness was just returning with Loveday, Mr and Mrs Penhale and their younger daughters following like dutiful, if slightly bemused, chicks. Beyond them, on the lawn, *Lark Deux* tugged at her moorings, as though being fitted out and flightworthy once again were not enough. She wanted to fly. "Is His Highness ready to start anew?"

"I believe Celeste would like to put a proposal to him," Emory said, smiling into her eyes.

Celeste nodded, insides trembling at the thought. To teach

at the school for the Royal Aeronautic Corps. If only the Prince would agree!

As if he knew what she intended, Arthur sent her a smile, too, his eyes twinkling. "He is planning to inspire the Prince's Own, including Mr Barnes, to new heights. But I'm not sure what he'll think of any proposal just at the moment. It appears he has something special in mind for us. I'll leave him to tell you about it."

THE PRINCE REGENT seated himself in the armchair by the fire, instantly transforming it into a throne. Loveday knew that from this moment, her father would not allow anyone to sit there, even though it was his favorite chair. Mama had not yet recovered from the news that her eldest daughter, the tinkering hobbledehoy, was going to be a viscountess. She would have been over the moon about Loveday's engagement to Arthur Trevelyan, ordinary gentleman, but this? It was more than dear Mama could take in just yet.

Nor had Gwen quite apprehended that she was going to have to curtsey to her and call her *my lady*. Loveday was looking forward to the moment when she did.

The family settled themselves, and tea was brought in. Poor Morwen was in such a state at the prospect of bringing tea to the Prince Regent that Mrs Kerrow was obliged to help her carry in the trays. The Prince accepted his cup from Mama with a smile, and complimented Mrs Kerrow upon her biscuits. That lady retired to the doorway, beaming with the knowledge that her prowess as a cook was assured in perpetuity.

"I thank you for your kind hospitality," the Prince said with a nod to Loveday's parents. "Tea is just the thing on a cold day."

"Do have some fruitcake, sir," Loveday said, passing him the plate. "We made it before I came away to London to join the Prince's Own. It will be just at its peak now."

To Mama's and Mrs Kerrow's delight, he took two pieces.

"Captain Penhale, I wish to make some proposals to you and Captain Blanchard this afternoon, before I return to my hosts in Truro," he said to Loveday. "My word, this cake is exactly as you have described it. Dear Mrs Penhale," he said, turning to Mama, "I should be most obliged for the recipe."

"You shall have it at once, sir," Mama gasped and hurried out with Mrs Kerrow, quite forgetting to curtsey or back away from his presence.

This would make Mama's reputation as a hostess from Penzance to Torquay. The fact that the Prince was visiting Hale House in the company of Viscount St Ives had elevated Loveday's sisters' standing, too. No matter what the Prince's proposals were, today had already done more for the family than nearly anything could.

The Prince turned to them once more.

"I wish to convey my heartiest good wishes upon your engagements," he said to Arthur and Emory with a smile. "St Ives, you have acted on my suggestion with gratifying speed."

"Thank you, sir." Arthur took Loveday's hand. "I am one to follow orders—especially when I heartily concur with them."

He exchanged a glance with Loveday that made her warm all over.

"It is my dearest hope that the three of you in the Prince's Own will return to London to continue your work," their royal guest went on. "While I know that you have other matters to consider now, perhaps you might still turn your minds to some of the wonders we saw aboard the air ships from Flanders and the Karlsruhe Confederacy." Loveday opened her mouth to speak, but he forestalled her. "Yes, I know the Confederacy ships were based on the designs created by the two of you. But seeing what the engineers did with them was quite the learning experience, was it not?"

"Indeed it was, sir," Celeste said. "We are particularly interested in their movement toward a horizontal envelope. Already we have been talking of it."

"And about the possibility of a longer gondola that fits more closely against the corset," Loveday added, "perhaps even as part of that superstructure."

"What an interesting idea." Loveday could practically see the cogs and gears in the Prince's mind engage with this concept. "I say, would a prototype be a possibility? By the summer, perhaps? For I know you have some theories about the uses of such vessels in peacetime." He sat back and spread his hands. "You see how much I need my Cornish engineers."

"I foresee a change to the curricula at our universities, sir," Emory said with a glance at Celeste. "And even on St Michael's Mount, at the training school for the Royal Aeronautic Corps. Experienced aeronauts as flight instructors are rather thin on the ground as yet, but with a regular air corps they will increase."

"Indeed they are. What wouldn't I give for—" The Prince sat up and put his empty teacup on the low table. "I say, Captain Blanchard, you are the most experienced aeronaut of all of us. You were an instructor at l'Ecole des Aéronautes in Paris, were you not?"

"I was, sir." Celeste looked as though she hardly dared breathe.

"Well, wouldn't you be the perfect candidate for such a post? Bless me, why haven't I thought of this before? I was so intent on convincing you to come back to London with me that I completely overlooked the value you would provide to the Corps right here."

"I should be honored, sir," Celeste managed before shooting a grin to Emory.

"Then it is settled. I shall write to St Aubyn at once and tell him you are to be Flight Officer, and take over administration and training of the aeronauts as soon as it can be arranged. He is doing his best with his naval officers, but not a man Jack of them has actually been in the air. If it were not for Miss Edwards and Miss Stratham they would be completely at sea." He chuckled. "I say, that was rather good. Naval men. At sea."

"Thank you, sir," Celeste said when the laughter had died down. "It is my dearest wish to serve you and England here in Cornwall. When would you like me to begin?"

"Well, that brings me to my next proposal," he said, looking pleased. "You recall that envoy of Boney's saying something about a meeting in some neutral place to begin peace talks."

"General von Zeppelin favors Vienna," Arthur recalled.

"He does. Loves his coffee, that gentleman. Well, this event, this Congress, I suppose you might call it, is indeed going to take place there. A great delegation is to attend on my behalf —Lady Castlereagh was first in line to ensure I understood how necessary it was that she accompany her husband—and I should like the four of you to be members as well. You know how I value your thoughts and observations." He inclined his head to Arthur. "It goes without saying that the Walsingham Office must have a presence, even if it is disguised by a title and a beautiful fiancée."

Loveday blushed scarlet. Her mother, who had come in just in time to hear this proposal, seated herself with dignity, the fruitcake recipe quivering in her hands.

"Why, sir, I hope you have considered the reputation of my daughter in all these august plans and delegations. Engaged or not, it is quite impossible that she should attend without—"

Oh, Mama, do not say it!

"—a chaperone."

Loveday could have died of embarrassment on the spot.

"Why—why—" The Prince was at a loss to have such a rock appear in the sea of his generosity.

"Your Royal Highness, my dear Mrs Penhale," Emory said, "there is no difficulty at all. Since we have no reason to wait, Celeste has agreed to marry me as soon as the banns can be called at St Mary's. Captain Penhale and his lordship may attend the Congress of Vienna at His Royal Highness's pleasure, for who better to chaperone than his own Flight Officer, Lady Celeste Thorndyke?"

And amid the cries of pleasure and congratulations and general hubbub, Loveday slipped her hand into that of Arthur.

"It is a great occasion, to be sure, this Congress of Vienna," she said softly. "But I am glad I may venture there with you, and with the friends who have been so true."

"I am as well." He gazed into her eyes, and for a moment, there were only two of them in that room filled with celebration. "It is not the first adventure I have shared with you, and I am certain it will not be the last."

"Let us hope not," she said with a smile, and with a quick glance over her shoulder, leaned in for a kiss.

A stolen kiss. A blessed moment. And a sweet promise that, no matter what came next, from now on they would be sharing life's adventures together.

THE END

AFTERWORD

Thanks so much for reading the third book in our Regent's Devices series. If you missed the previous two books, we invite you to begin with *The Emperor's Aeronaut.*

To make sure you know when our next releases come out, sign up for Shelley Adina's mailing list and begin the adventure with "The Abduction of Lord Will." Sign up for Regina Scott's mailing list and learn what happened in France while Celeste was first in England.

And now, we invite you to turn the page for an excerpt each from another novel by Shelley and Regina. You may see a familiar name or two there!

Fair winds!

—Shelley and Regina

The Bride Wore Constant White
Mysterious Devices Book One
by Shelley Adina

Chapter One

July 1895
Bath, England

It is a truth universally acknowledged that a young woman of average looks, some talent, and no fortune must be in want of a husband, the latter to be foisted upon her at the earliest opportunity lest she become an embarrassment to her family. This had been depressingly borne in upon Miss Margrethe Amelia Linden, known to her family and her limited number of intimate friends as Daisy, well before the occasion of her twenty-first birthday.

"Certainly you cannot go to a ball, escorted or not," said her Aunt Jane. "You are not out of mourning for your dear mother. It would not be suitable. I am surprised that you have even brought it up, Daisy."

Daisy took a breath in order to defend herself, but her aunt forestalled her with a raised salad fork.

"No, I will invite a very few to lunch—including one or two suitable young men. Now that you have come into my sister's little bit of money, you will be slightly more attractive to a discerning person than, perhaps, you might have been before. Mr. Fetherstonehaugh, now. He still cherishes hopes of you, despite your appalling treatment of him. I insist on your considering him seriously. His father owns a manufactory of steambuses in Yorkshire, and he is the only boy in a family of five."

"I do not wish to be attractive to any of the gentlemen of our acquaintance, Aunt." *Particularly not to him.* "They lack gumption. To say nothing of chins."

This had earned her an expression meant to be crushing, but which only succeeded in making Aunt Jane look as though her lunch had not agreed with her.

"Your uncle and I wish to see you safely settled, dear," she said with admirable restraint.

Aunt Jane prided herself on her restraint under provocation. She had become rather more proud of it in the nearly two years since her sister had brought her two daughters to live under her roof, and then passed on to her heavenly reward herself. When one's sister's husband was known to have gone missing in foreign parts, one was also subject to impertinent remarks. Therefore, her restraint had reached heroic proportions.

"When you have been married fifty years, like our beloved Queen, you will know that a chin or lack thereof is hardly a consideration in a good husband—while a successful manufactory certainly is."

Daisy was not sure if Aunt Jane had meant to insult the prince, who from all accounts was still quite an attractive man. It was true that she could no more imagine Her Majesty without her beloved Albert than the sun without a moon. They had a scandalous number of children—nine!—and still the newspapers had reported that they had danced until dawn at Lord and Lady Dunsmuir's ball in London earlier in the week. Her Majesty was said to be prodigiously fond of dancing—between that and childbirth, she must be quite the athlete.

Daisy had never danced until dawn in her life, and doing so seemed as unlikely as having children.

Especially now.

For as of ten days ago, she was no longer a genteel spinster of Margaret's Buildings, Bath, but a woman of twenty-one years and independent means, having procured not only a letter of credit from her bank, but a ticket from Bath to London, and subsequently, passage aboard the packet to Paris, where she had boarded the transatlantic airship *Persephone* bound for New York.

"My goodness, you're so brave," breathed Emma Makepeace, her breakfast companion in the grand airship's dining saloon this morning, the third of their crossing. She had been listening with rapt attention, her spoonful of coddled egg halting in its fatal journey. "But at what point did you realize you were not alone?"

Daisy glanced at her younger sister, Frederica, who wisely did not lift her own attention from her plate, but continued to shovel in poached eggs, potatoes, and sliced ham glazed in orange sauce as though this were her last meal.

"As we were sailing over the Channel. At that point, my sister deemed it safe to reveal herself, since there would be no danger of my sending her back to our aunt and uncle." She gave a sigh. "We are committed to this adventure together, I am afraid."

"I certainly am," Freddie ventured. "I used all my savings for the tickets, including what I could beg from Maggie Polgarth."

"Who is that?" Miss Makepeace asked, resuming her own breakfast with a delicate appetite. "One of your school friends?"

Freddie nodded. "Maggie and her cousin Elizabeth Seacombe are the wards of Lady Claire Malvern, of Carrick House in Belgravia."

"Oh, I have met Lady Claire. Isn't she lovely? What an unexpected pleasure it is to meet people acquainted with her."

While Daisy recovered from her own surprise at a reliable third party knowing people she had half believed to be imaginary, Freddie went on.

"With Lady Claire's encouragement, both Maggie and Lizzie own shares in the railroads *and* the Zeppelin Airship Works, though they are only eighteen—my own age. But that is beside the point." Another glance at Daisy, who had been caught by the deep golden color of the marmalade in her spoon.

If she were to paint a still life at this very moment, she would use lemon yellow, with a bit of burnt umber, and some scarlet lake—just a little—for the bits of orange peel embedded deep within.

"The point?" Miss Makepeace inquired, and Daisy came back to herself under their joint regard. It was up to her to redirect the course of the conversation.

"The point is that, having had some number of astonishing adventures—I have my doubts about the veracity of some of them—Miss Polgarth was all too forthcoming in her encouragement of my sister's desertion of her responsibilities to school and family."

"You deserted yours, too," Freddie pointed out. "Poor Mr. Fetherstonehaugh. He is not likely to recover his heart very soon."

"Oh dear." Miss Makepeace was one of those fortunate individuals who would never have to settle for the chinless and suitable of this world. For she was a young woman of considerable looks and some means, despite the absence of anyone resembling a chaperone or a lady's maid. Perhaps that individual kept herself to her cabin. Her clothes were not showy, but so beautiful they made Daisy ache inside—the pleats perfection, the colors becoming, the lace handmade. Clearly her time in Paris before boarding *Persephone* had been well spent in purchasing these delights.

Miss Makepeace had been blessed with hair the shade of melted caramel and what people called an "English skin." Daisy, being as English as anyone, had one too by default, but hers didn't have the perfect shades of a rose petal. Nor did her own blue eyes possess that deep tint verging on violet. At least Daisy's hair could be depended on—reddish-brown in some lights and with enough wave in it to make it easy to put up— unlike poor Freddie, who had inherited Mama's lawless dark curls. No one would be clamoring at the door to paint Daisy, but Miss Makepeace—oh, she was a horse of a different color.

She absolutely must persuade her to sit for a portrait in watercolors.

But talk of poor Mr. Fetherstonehaugh had brought the ghost of a smile to their companion's face, so Daisy thought it prudent not to abandon the subject of gentlemen just yet, despite its uncomfortable nature. They had been in the air for three days, and after the second day, had found one another convivial enough company that they had begun looking for each other at meals, and spending the afternoons together embroidering or (in Daisy's case) sketching. The lavish interiors of *Persephone* fairly begged to be painted in her travel journal. In all that time Daisy had not seen Miss Makepeace smile. Not a real one. But now, one had nearly trembled into life, and she would use Mr. Fetherstonehaugh ruthlessly if it meant coaxing it into full bloom.

"Have you ever been to Bath, Miss Makepeace?" she asked, spreading marmalade on the toast.

"Only once, when I was a girl," she said. "Papa's business keeps him in London and New York nearly exclusively, and after Mama passed away, I did not have a companion with whom to go to such places. I remember it being very beautiful," she said wistfully. "And at the bottom of the Royal Crescent is a gravel walk. I wondered if it could be the very one where Captain Wentworth and Anne Elliot walked after all was made plain between them."

Frederica, being of a literal turn of mind, blinked at her. "They were not real, Miss Makepeace."

The English skin colored a little. "I know. But it was a pretty fancy, for the time it took me to walk down the hill to the gate."

"Poor Mr. Fetherstonehaugh," Daisy said on a sigh. "He

attempted to quote Jane Austen to me while we were dancing in the parlor of one of my aunt's acquaintance three weeks ago."

"That sounds most promising in a man," Miss Makepeace said.

"But it was the first sentences of *Pride and Prejudice*, Miss Makepeace." She leaned in. "And they were said in reference *to himself*."

To her delight, the smile she had been angling for blossomed into life. "Dear me. Miss Austen would be appalled."

"My sentiments exactly. And when he turned up on my aunt's doorstep the next morning proposing himself as the companion of my future life, I took my example from Elizabeth Bennet on the occasion of *her* first proposal. I fear the allusion was lost on him, however." She frowned. "He called me a heartless flirt."

Miss Makepeace covered her mouth with her napkin and Daisy could swear it was to muffle a giggle. "You are no such thing," she said when she could speak again. "I should say it was a near escape."

"Our aunt would not agree," Freddie put in. "She and my uncle have very strong feelings about indigent relations and their burden upon the pocketbook."

"Granted, it is not their fault their pocketbook is slender," Daisy conceded. "But that is no reason to push us on every gentleman who stops to smell the roses nodding over the wall."

"How do you come to be aboard *Persephone*?" Freddie asked their companion shyly.

She was not yet out, so had not had many opportunities to go about in company. Add to this a nearly paralyzing shyness

—for reasons both sisters kept secret, and despite the misleading behavior of her hair—and it still astonished Daisy that she had had the gumption to follow her all the way to London with nothing but her second-best hat and a valise containing three changes of clothes, her diary, and a canvas driving coat against bad weather.

Now it was Miss Makepeace who leaned in, the lace covering her fine bosom barely missing the marmalade on her own toast. "Can you keep a secret?"

"Oh, yes," Freddie said eagerly.

Which was quite true. Among other things, she had concealed from everyone—except perhaps that deplorable Maggie Polgarth—her plans to run away and accompany Daisy on her mission.

"I am what is known as a mail-order bride." Miss Makepeace sat back to enjoy the effect of this confidence on her companions.

"A what?" Freddie said after a moment, when no clarification seemed to be forthcoming.

"There is no such thing," Daisy said a little flatly. Well, it was better than sitting and gaping like a flounder.

"There I must contradict you." Miss Makepeace aligned her knife and fork in the middle of her plate, and the waiter, seeing this signal, whisked it away. "In the guise of a literary club, I have been meeting these last six months in London with a group of young ladies determined to make their own fortunes. An agency assisted us in finding the best matches of ability and temperament in places as far-flung as the Canadas and the Louisiana Territory."

"There are agencies for this sort of thing?" Daisy managed under the shock of this fresh information. It was lucky that

Aunt Jane was as ignorant of these facts as Daisy herself had been until this moment, or heaven knew where Daisy might have been shipped off to by now.

And what was a young woman like Miss Makepeace, with every blessing of breeding and beauty, doing applying as a mail-order bride? It defied understanding.

Miss Makepeace nodded. "I have been writing to Mr. Bjorn Hansen, of Georgetown, for some months, and am convinced that he will make me a good husband." She touched the exceedingly modest diamond upon the fourth finger of her left hand. "He sent this in his last letter, and I sent my acceptance by return airship."

"My goodness," Freddie breathed. "I have never met a mail-order bride. I thought they only existed in the flickers—you know, like *Posted to Paradise*." She and Daisy had stood in the queue outside the nickelodeon on Milsom Street for half an hour to see that one, much to their aunt's disgust. But it had been so romantic!

"We are quite real, I assure you." Two dimples dented Miss Makepeace's cheeks. "My suit and veil are in my trunk. I will meet Mr. Hansen in person for the first time when I alight in Georgetown, and we will be married two days later in the First Presbyterian Church on Taos Street. It is all arranged."

"Where is Georgetown, exactly?" Daisy asked.

Not that it mattered—she and Frederica were bound for Santa Fe, on a quest that could not be postponed. Their father, Dr. Rudolph Linden, had been missing for nearly two years. Influenza had taken their mother last winter—hastened, Daisy was certain, by the anxiety and depression she had suffered after his mysterious disappearance. Now that she had reached her majority, Daisy was determined to take up the search where her mother had left off. And this time, if love and determination meant anything, she and Freddie would find him.

"It is in the northern reaches of the Texican Territories, in the mountains," Miss Makepeace explained in answer to her question. "From Denver, it is merely an hour west by train. It is said to be one of the loveliest towns in the territory—and certainly one of the richest. Silver, you know. It is surrounded by mines on every side, and has a bustling economy, I am told."

A young man who had been passing on the way to his table now hesitated next to theirs. "I do beg your pardon. Forgive me for intruding, but are you speaking of Georgetown?"

If Aunt Jane had been sitting opposite, Daisy had no doubt there would have been either the cut direct—or an invitation to breakfast if she thought the young man might be good husband material. But they were en route for a continent where one might stop and strike up a conversation without having to be formally introduced by a mutual acquaintance—or to give one's family antecedents back four generations.

"We are, sir. Do you know it?"

His square, honest face broke into a smile, and Daisy noted with interest the quality of the velvet lapels on his coat, and the fashionable leaf-brown color of his trousers—not the dull brown of earth, but the warmer tones of the forest in autumn.

"I am bound there as well. Please allow me to introduce myself. My name is Hugh Meriwether-Astor, originally from Philadelphia. I have recently bought a share in the Pelican mine."

"And are you going out to inspect your investment, or have you been there before?" Miss Makepeace asked.

"This is my first visit. I'm afraid I have an ulterior motive —that of escaping the bad temper of certain members of my family, who are not quite so conservative in their business dealings. I should like to get my hands dirty, and do a little excavating myself if I can, before I go back to law school. And you?"

As the eldest, and practically a married woman, Miss Makepeace made the introductions. Daisy noted that she did not vouchsafe any personal details of their voyage, she supposed because she had no personal observations of her future home to offer him. They parted with promises of seeing one another at the card tables after dinner, and the young man continued to his table by the viewing port.

"What a nice person," Frederica ventured. "He does not seem much older than you, Daisy, and yet he owns part of a mine. His family must be rather well off."

"If my facts are in order, he is closely connected to the Meriwether-Astor Manufacturing Works in Philadelphia," Miss Makepeace said in a low tone. Heaven forbid the young man should know they were discussing him. "Surely even in Bath you will have read in the papers about his cousin, Gloria Meriwether-Astor, who owns the company."

"It's a difficult name to miss," Daisy said. "Wasn't she the one who singlehandedly stopped a war in the Wild West and returned home in triumph with none other than a railroad baron's long-lost heir for a husband?"

Honestly, while it might have been quite true, it did sound like one of the sensational plots beloved of the flickers.

"I am sure it wasn't singlehandedly," Miss Makepeace said. "But I will say that the union of two such industrial fortunes made headlines in the Fifteen Colonies, and London and

Zurich as well. It was all any of my father's cronies talked of at dinner for weeks."

"My friend Maggie knows her," Freddie said most unexpectedly. "Gloria, I mean. Mrs. Stanford Fremont."

"Nonsense," Daisy said. Honestly, she was becoming very tired of these references. "Another of that girl's absurd fabrications."

"It isn't!" Freddie drew back, affronted, and refused to speak for the rest of their meal.

There were some misfortunes for which one could only be thankful.

For more, visit https://shelleyadina.com/books/the-bride-wore-constant-white/

**Never Vie for a Viscount
Fortune's Brides Book Four
by R.E. (Regina) Scott**

Chapter One

London, England, late April, 1812

A townhouse had never looked so daunting.

Lydia Villers stood on the pavement gazing up at the four-story white row house situated on fashionable Clarendon Square. Her muslin dress had seemed light and airy when she'd donned it that morning, her pink velvet spencer hardly needed for the warm spring day. Now she felt perspiration trickling down her back.

"It is the best situation for your goals," Meredith Thorn reminded her.

Lydia glanced at her companion. Oh, for an ounce of that confidence! Meredith, owner of the Fortune Employment Agency, always looked in complete control of herself. Perhaps it was the sleek black hair, so unlike Lydia's pale ringlets. Or the depth of her lavender eyes, the color so much more compelling than Lydia's misty green.

Or maybe it was the grey cat in her arms, gazing serenely at Lydia as if she didn't doubt Lydia could win over anyone who stood against her.

Lydia drew in a breath. Her family and friends had consistently commented on her sunny smile, her optimism and enthusiasm. She should not allow her regrets over one man to dim her light.

"You're right," she told Meredith. "Let's go."

Meredith nodded in satisfaction. Her cat, Fortune, stood tall in her arms, tail waving like a cavalry flag as they moved forward.

A man answered their knock on the green-lacquered door, and Lydia could only marvel at his size in his sturdy brown coat and breeches. She was used to strapping footmen in white powdered wigs. His hair was brown and thick and short-cropped. He took the card Meredith held out in one massive ungloved fist.

"We'd like to call on Miss Worthington, if you please," Meredith said. "We've come about a position."

His gaze, brown like his hair and clothing, traveled over Meredith and Lydia and lit on Fortune in Meredith's arms. A smile tilted up, making him suddenly approachable. "Come in and wait. I'll ask Miss Worthington if she wants to see you."

Rather direct for a footman as well. As he ambled off, Meredith and Lydia stepped into the entry hall. It was not the most remarkable place, for all the work in this house had the chance to change her life. The painting of a ship in full sail still graced one of the light-blue walls as it had when she'd last visited a year ago. Like it, she felt the wind pushing her to new horizons. The gilt-framed mirror and half-moon table still stood opposite, the reflection in the oval glass showing her a bit paler than usual, her eyes luminous. The only thing to give her pause was the gentleman's tall hat and ebony walking stick on the polished wood surface. She swallowed.

She would not be working for him. Not directly. She had to remember that. If she never saw Frederick, Viscount Worthington, again, it would be too soon.

The manservant returned and tipped his head to the corridor on the right of the stairs. "This way, if you please."

She knew the layout of the house. He was no doubt taking them to the withdrawing room at the back. It had been a pleasant space, done in shades of rose and blue, with a settee in front of the wood-wrapped hearth and a few chairs scattered about. The Worthingtons entertained rarely. Far too busy with more important matters.

Charlotte Worthington was sitting at the walnut secretary along one silk-draped wall when they entered. Setting down her quill, she smiled at them. Lydia had always admired her. Like Meredith, she was cool, confident. She tended to speak her mind, even if she knew how to coat vinegar with honey. Only her auburn hair, coiled in a bun at the back of her head with tendrils escaping along her sculpted cheeks, was at odds with her polished demeanor.

"That will be all, Beast," she said.

Beast? The manservant didn't show any sign of resenting the rough name. He nodded and withdrew, leaving the door open behind him. Charlotte rose and swept toward them, grey lustring gown glinting in the sunlight coming through one velvet-draped window. Fortune leaned forward as if ready to welcome her.

"Miss Thorn," she acknowledged. "And Miss Villers. What an unexpected pleasure."

Another time, in another situation, it might have been a pleasure to see Charlotte again. She'd been polite, even friendly, the one other time they had met since Lydia had returned from her sojourn in Essex. Why? Charlotte's brother could have made no good report of Lydia. He'd been the one to sever all acquaintance, as if she'd developed some dread disease.

She shook off the thought and dipped a curtsey. "Miss Worthington. Thank you for receiving us."

"Of course. You are always welcome in this house."

She was? Straightening, she gazed at Charlotte in wonder, but those deep grey eyes did not suggest a lie. Still, Lydia could not embrace that truth.

"Please, join me," Charlotte said, going to sit on the settee. "Would your pet like a cushion?"

Meredith drew a hand along Fortune's back. "Fortune prefers to stay with me. But I appreciate the offer." She took the closest chair and nodded Lydia into another nearby. "I won't keep you long. I understand you're looking to add a member to your team."

Charlotte glanced between the two of them as if she wasn't sure who was being offered. "I had just begun making inquiries. Do you know of someone?"

Meredith glanced at Lydia.

"Yes," Lydia said, pausing to take a deep breath. "Me."

Charlotte's russet brows rose. "I wasn't aware you were interested in scientific pursuits, Miss Villers."

Few knew. She'd always loved learning about discoveries. When she was little, she used to sit on her father's knee in his study as he read aloud from *Philosophical Transactions*, the journal of the Royal Society. After he'd died, she'd made sure the subscription continued, devouring the latest advances in science, medicine, and industry. She thrilled to read how luminaries like Sir Humphrey Davy, Sir Nicholas Rotherford, and William Herschel were pushing back the boundaries of chemistry, peering into the recesses of space. She'd applauded the work of the Royal Institution, making such advances practical. She'd begged her brother to take her to one of the public lectures, but he'd been appalled by the very suggestion.

"Never speak of this unseemly fascination outside the house," Beau had ordered, glaring down his long nose at her. "They'll think you a bluestocking."

A bluestocking. A far too educated woman. The term conjured up spinsters gathered over tea, clucking like hens, dreams of husband and family supplanted by secondhand accounts of scientific advances. That wasn't her. She was destined to marry well. Beau had promised her parents before they'd died that he'd make sure of it.

And so she'd tried. She'd danced and flirted, sung at too many musicales, endured dozens of drives through the park. At Beau's insistence, she'd shoved herself at every titled gentleman on the *ton*. Several had shown interest. She knew how to dress and bat her lashes and smile winsomely, after all. She could play Society's game, appear more interested in the color of waistcoats than discussions of politics and natural philosophy. But no matter how much she flattered a gentleman's consequence, none had felt compelled to offer.

Even the one she'd prayed would offer.

Now she squared her shoulders. "I am very interested in scientific pursuits, Miss Worthington. I've spent the last six weeks working closely with Augusta Orwell as she developed a formulation to heal skin conditions. I understand the properties of various substances—animal, plant, and mineral. I am fluent in the actions of various change agents like heat, light, water, and air."

"Miss Orwell would be delighted to provide a reference," Meredith put in.

Charlotte leaned back, gaze uncompromising. "We work

long hours. There's little time for Society."

Lydia smiled. "Excellent. I no longer need to spend time in Society."

"So you are off the marriage mart?" Charlotte challenged.

That was the one question she was thoroughly confident in answering. "Absolutely. I plan to devote myself to the furtherance of knowledge."

"Hogwash."

The male voice behind her sent a shiver through her. Her breath left with her confidence. Her body swiveled of its own volition to face the man in the doorway. Hair as smoldering as his sister's, cut long enough to brush the collar of his coat. Eyes as grey but brighter, suggesting a spark of starlight within. High cheekbones, firm chin. A lean physique shown to advantage in a simple navy coat and fawn trousers. Beau would have known the name for that fold in his cravat. The Mathematical? How suitable. Anyone looking at Lord Worthington would see a gentleman of the ton.

She knew better. She could not move, could not speak, as the viscount she'd once vied for strolled into the room.

Frederick, Viscount Worthington—Worth to his friends and family—stared at the vision of loveliness seated on the chair across from his sister. Those blond ringlets, the big green eyes, the curves outlined by her fashionable gown. Lydia Villers, in his home? He'd never thought to see it again.

But he couldn't believe the preposterous story any more than he'd believed she'd cared for him, not after he'd learned the truth about her.

"Worth," Charlotte said, an exasperated tone creeping into her voice. "I didn't realize you were home. This is Miss Thorn, of the Fortune Employment Agency."

The other woman, a regal raven-haired female in a lavender-colored gown, turned to meet his look. He inclined his head in greeting, and his gaze lit on the grey cat in her lap. A handsome creature. The blaze of white down its chest made it look as if it were wearing a cravat. He couldn't help his smile.

"Miss Thorn, a pleasure," he said. "And I'm delighted to meet your companion as well."

"Surely you remember Miss Villers," Charlotte chided.

"Of course I remember Miss Villers," Worth said, refusing to look at the woman who had broken his heart a year ago.

"I believe your brother is referring to my other companion," Miss Thorn said with a smile. "This is Fortune, my lord. Fortune, meet Viscount Worthington."

He bowed, straightening to find the cat regarding him with interest in her copper-colored eyes. Miss Thorn relaxed her hold, and her pet dropped to the carpet and padded up to him to twine herself around his boots.

"She likes you." Lydia sounded shocked.

No more shocked than he'd been to hear her proclaim a love for natural philosophy. But then, that was part of her charm—her unbridled enthusiasm for everything.

And everyone.

He'd let it sway him before, convinced himself what she felt was real, unique to him alone. He knew better now. He'd far sooner trust the cat. People were unpredictable. Nature—for all its eccentricities—followed knowable paths.

He squatted and put out his hand, allowing Fortune to sniff at his gloved fingers. She arched her back, inviting his touch, and Worth ran his hand gently along the fur. "I see that Fortune is a highly discriminating creature."

"She is," Miss Thorn agreed. "She approves of you almost as much as she approves of Miss Villers."

Perhaps not so discriminating after all. But then, deciphering the motives of the human heart was his downfall.

He straightened. "Nevertheless, I believe we are fully staffed at present."

Charlotte was frowning at him. "We need one more to achieve your timetable, and you know it. Miss Villers has been working with Augusta Orwell. She has experience."

"Alas, distilling concoctions for beauty preparations does not usually equate with experimental rigor," he said, trying to keep his voice and look kind.

Lydia swept to her feet and turned to face him fully, and he took a step back from the intensity blazing from her eyes.

"Our work," she said, moving toward him, "may look simple to a man of your letters, Lord Worthington, but we follow the scientific method laid down by Bacon. We observe that certain elements appear to affect healing. We hypothesize that a particular ingredient may be beneficial."

With each step in the process she described, she advanced, and Worth could only retreat.

"We devise experiments to test its efficacy both alone and in combination with other ingredients. We measure response, attempt to replicate the experiment, and see if we gain similar results. We document our findings. Our work may never appear in *Philosophical Transactions*, but the formula we recently developed has been evaluated by other apothecaries and found to have merit. It is being sold on the market to help others. Can you say the same of your work?"

His back was to the wall, literally and figuratively. His best application, the result of years of painstaking experimentation and documentation, had been stolen by a colleague who had claimed all credit. That's when he'd first learned the pain of betrayal, even if hers had hurt more.

"Perhaps my brother questions your dedication rather than your credentials," Charlotte said. Over Lydia's head, he could see that a smirk had replaced his sister's frown. She was enjoying this, the brat!

"Six weeks is a short time to be involved in scientific pursuits," she qualified when he shot a glare in her direction.

Lydia drew herself up, until her pert nose was pointing at his chin and he could see deep into her eyes. "Six weeks laboring from breakfast until long past dinner. I'm not afraid of hard work, when it has a purpose."

Miss Thorn rose and came to collect her pet, who had retreated with Worth to the back wall. Fortune gazed up at him as if she expected him to make the right decision. Would that he knew what that decision should be.

Charlotte was right—their timetable was tight. He had promised the Prince Regent to have something to demonstrate by the end of May. He was so close! Another pair of hands, another mind focused on the task, might make the difference between success and failure. And if he accomplished what he'd set out to do, he could at last feel he had lived up to his family legacy and redeemed himself for his past mistakes.

"Miss Villers has already made significant sacrifices to pursue a career," Miss Thorn said, pet back in her arms. "She has left her position in Society, defied her brother."

Interesting. Beauford Villers had been instrumental in

introducing Worth to Lydia. He had always thought the fellow would be over the moon had his sister and Worth married. Did Villers still insist that she wed?

"Most women of our class face persecution when stepping away from traditional roles," Charlotte acknowledged. She knew. After several Seasons on the *ton*, she had retired to their home and focused on helping him. The result had been unkind comments from Society's reigning belles, slights from former friends. Charlotte had ignored them all to remain at his side and help him achieve. There wasn't much he wouldn't do for his sister.

Except, perhaps, hire Lydia Villers.

"I don't care," Lydia said, chin in the air. "I was ill-suited to the traditional role. I don't miss it."

Now, that he could not believe. Everything about Lydia Villers—from the artful ringlets framing her pretty face to her frilly muslin gowns and normal exuberance—was designed to appeal to a gentleman seeking a bride. She had certainly appealed to him. He was more than a little chagrined to find she still did.

"So, what do you want?" he asked.

She beamed up at him, the sun coming out after a storm, lifting his spirits despite his reservations.

"I want to learn more—how things work, why they function as they do." Her voice rang with determination. "I want to expand the boundaries of knowledge, discover great things that help others." She flung out her arms as if she would embrace the world. "I want to cure disease, double the food supply, soar beyond the stars."

She dropped her hands. "Surely that's not too much to ask."

Not in the slightest. The same longings pushed him. Indeed, they had been a hallmark of his family. As a military commander, his great-grandfather had earned the family its title and prestige. As a magistrate, his grandfather had helped establish civil liberties others now took for granted. In Parliament, his father had championed minimum wages for the poor.

From an early age, he'd been praised by his parents and tutors for his keen mind. That mind, he'd soon discovered, demanded challenges. He wasn't suited to be a fighter, a judge, or a politician. Those spheres were too narrow. How much better to embrace the grand challenge of advancing knowledge to improve lives?

Now he experimented, evaluated evidence, and calculated the chances of success. Until Lydia's declaration, he would have put her chance of joining his team at less than twenty percent. How had she known the one thing that might sway him? Was he that obvious? Was this a trick? Was he looking at the situation all wrong?

He glanced to his sister, once more unsettled and unsure of his answer.

As always, Charlotte knew his mind better than he did. She rose, serene in her grey gown.

"Well said, Miss Villers," she declared. "I believe you will get on famously with the rest of the team. When can you start?"

For more, visit Regina's website at http://www.reginascott.com/ nevervieforaviscount.html.

The Engineer Wore Venetian Red

The Judge Wore Lamp Black

The Professor Wore Prussian Blue

REGENCY ROMANCE as Charlotte Henry

The Rogue to Ruin

The Rogue Not Taken

One for the Rogue

A Rogue by Any Other Name

OTHER REGENCY-SET BOOKS BY
REGINA SCOTT

Grace-by-the-Sea Series

The Matchmaker's Rogue

The Heiress's Convenient Husband

The Artist's Healer

The Governess's Earl

The Lady's Second-Chance Suitor

The Siren's Captain

Fortune's Brides Series

Never Doubt a Duke

Never Borrow a Baronet

Never Envy an Earl

Never Vie for a Viscount

Never Kneel to a Knight

Never Marry a Marquess

Always Kiss at Christmas

Never Pursue a Prince

Never Court a Count

Never Romance a Rogue

Uncommon Courtships Series

The Unflappable Miss Fairchild

The Incomparable Miss Compton

The Irredeemable Miss Renfield

The Unwilling Miss Watkin

An Uncommon Christmas

Lady Emily Capers

Secrets and Sensibilities

Art and Artifice

Ballrooms and Blackmail

Eloquence and Espionage

Love and Larceny

Marvelous Munroes Series

My True Love Gave to Me

The Rogue Next Door

The Marquis' Kiss

A Match for Mother

Spy Matchmaker Series

The Husband Mission

The June Bride Conspiracy

The Heiress Objective

ABOUT THE AUTHORS

Shelley Adina is the author of more than 50 novels published by Harlequin, Warner, Hachette, and Moonshell Books, Inc., her own independent press. She writes steampunk adventure and mystery as Shelley Adina; as Charlotte Henry, writes classic Regency romance; and as Adina Senft, is the *USA Today* bestselling author of Amish women's fiction.

She holds a PhD in Creative Writing from Lancaster University in the UK, won RWA's RITA Award® in 2005, and was a finalist in 2006. She appeared in the 2016 documentary film *Love Between the Covers*, is a popular speaker and convention panelist, and has been a guest on many podcasts, including Worldshapers and Realm of Books.

When she's not writing, Shelley is usually quilting, sewing historical costumes, or enjoying the garden with her flock of rescued chickens. For more, visit www.shelleyadina.com.

R.E. (Regina) Scott started writing novels in the third grade. Thankfully for literature as we know it, she didn't sell her first novel until she learned a bit more about writing. Since her first book was published, her stories have traveled the globe, with translations in many languages, including Dutch, German, Italian, and Portuguese. She now has had published more than sixty works of warm, witty historical romance.

Regina and her husband of more than 30 years reside in

the Puget Sound area of Washington State on the way to Mt Rainier. She has dressed as a Regency dandy, learned to fence, driven four-in-hand, and sailed on a tall ship, all in the name of research, of course.

Learn more about her at www.reginascott.com.